THE ILLUSIONS OF EVENTIDE

THE HOUSE OF CRIMSON & CLOVER VOLUME III

SARAH M. CRADIT

Cover Design by Sarah M. Cradit
Editing by Shaner Media Creations

First Edition
ISBN: 1494267020
ISBN-13: 978-1494267025

Publisher Contact:
sarah@sarahmcradit.com
www.sarahmcradit.com

FOREWORD

With the introduction of the Empyrean race, this series takes a more formal turn toward paranormal, even bordering on the edge of fantasy.

What I present to you in this story, and others, is merely the tip of the iceberg. I have family trees for the Sullivans and Deschanels spanning over three hundred unique characters, many of whom you, reader, have yet to meet. There are rich family histories waiting to be told. Because of this, you may see brief appearances from characters who add only hints to the current story. But I can assure you, Quillan Sullivan and Amelia Deschanel will both play very important roles in future books. I wanted to give you a chance to get to know them, just a little, before we dive into their lives further. And I promise, you'll get more about the Deschanel Magi Collective, and the Deschanel Curse, as well. Soon.

Some readers have requested family trees, and you can find these on my website: sarahmcradit.com.

If you're reading this, this version is a re-edit—and you might recognize this note from the last two books, if you read them in their re-edited versions, too. Much like when Stephen

King tackled his own re-edit of *The Gunslinger*, when you've been writing in a world for a long time, sometimes things change. Most of the edits are cosmetic. Some are small details that make later reconciliations in the series (and other series, like The Seven) smoother. If you've read the original version, and now this one, though, you'll hopefully notice no changes aside from readability. The story is the same. The characters, still the characters. The outcomes, and the tragic consequences, no different.

Finally, a note of historical importance. Aidrik's sword, Ulfberht, is based on a very real sword by the same name. It was produced in Scandinavia between 800-1000 A.D., and to this day, scientists are impressed, and often baffled, at the technology used in its creation. The facts presented in this novel about the sword are all pulled from real research, and if you're interested in learning more, I highly suggest the NOVA program on the topic. The only fictional addition by me is that it was crafted by an Empyrean named Blacksmith. Or is it fiction? The truth is, no one knows who really crafted it. To this day, it remains a mystery.

ALSO BY SARAH M. CRADIT

~

THE SAGA OF CRIMSON & CLOVER

The House of Crimson and Clover Series

The Storm and the Darkness

Shattered

The Illusions of Eventide

Bound

Midnight Dynasty

Asunder

Empire of Shadows

Myths of Midwinter

The Hinterland Veil

The Secrets Amongst the Cypress

Within the Garden of Twilight

House of Dusk, House of Dawn

~

Midnight Dynasty Series

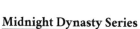

A Tempest of Discovery

A Storm of Revelations

The Seven Series

1970

1972

1973

1974

1975

1976

1980

~

Vampires of the Merovingi Series
The Island

~

Crimson & Clover Lagniappes (Bonus Stories)
Lagniappes are standalone stories that can be read in any order.
St. Charles at Dusk: The Story of Oz and Adrienne

Flourish: The Story of Anne Fontaine

Surrender: The Story of Oz and Ana

Shame: The Story of Jonathan St. Andrews

Fire & Ice: The Story of Remy & Fleur

Dark Blessing: The Landry Triplets

Pandora's Box: The Story of Jasper & Pandora

The Menagerie: Oriana's Den of Iniquities

A Band of Heather: The Story of Colleen and Noah

The Ephemeral: The Story of Autumn & Gabriel

Banshee: The Story of Giselle Deschanel

For more information, and exciting bonus material, visit www.

"The years that are gone seem like dreams—if one might go on sleeping and dreaming—but to wake up and find—oh! well! Perhaps it is better to wake up after all, even to suffer, rather than to remain a dupe to illusions all one's life."

Kate Chopin

1- NICOLAS

*L*iving no longer held much interest for Nicolas Deschanel.

This realization came amidst a rare instance of clarity for him. He couldn't pinpoint the exact moment when it initially crossed his mind, or when it moved from a whim to a done deal. Like most things in his life, it didn't occur to him slowly. The idea didn't evolve so much as appear, although looking back, every moment leading him here essentially shouted the same forgone conclusion.

He was only numbly aware of his plan as he gassed up the Porsche, packing a small leather bag, carefully nesting inside the box housing his father's handgun. Even the drive to Deschanel Island on New Year's Day was free of interesting revelations. If he were the insightful type, Nicolas might have started putting the puzzle pieces together sooner. He'd have seen the sojourn to his family's small Gulf island wasn't just another spur-of-the-moment getaway. He'd have understood this was more than Deschanel spontaneity.

There were plenty of assholes who expected something like

this from him years ago, after the accident that killed off most of his family.

He grew up with four half-sisters, each products of his father's inability to stop rutting with his son's French nanny. Sisters his father loved far more than he ever loved his only son. This didn't bother Nicolas the way it should have. He grew up doing whatever he pleased, whenever he pleased, however he pleased, and there was no one who cared enough to stop him. Even his own mother, who he'd loved despite her faults, was too self-absorbed in misery of her own creation to tend to his emotional needs.

What should have been an exclamation point in his life was, in reality, more of a footnote. His entire family—except his youngest sister, Adrienne—died in a car accident deep in bayou country. At the ever-so-tender age of twenty-one, Nicolas had faced unfathomable tragedy. Most of the family biddies were on edge, waiting for him to do something characteristically selfish like drink himself into oblivion and walk down the Mississippi River levee naked.

He was too stubborn to give the Deschanel Sewing Circle the satisfaction of being right. Besides, he'd already done his share of drinking naked on the levee. He could think of far more creative ways to go off the deep end.

It was easier to let them believe he didn't care. He'd loved his father, even if he'd been an insufferable prick. He'd loved his conniving mother, even if it was her fault Charles excluded Nicolas. And he'd loved his half-sisters too, though he suspected they never knew it.

His illusion was very convincing. He should've been on suicide watch then, the subject of everyone's thoughts and prayers. The kitchen at *Ophélie* should've been swimming with shitty casseroles. No one ever saw Nicolas mourn. They mistook his lack of tears for apathy. The ones who did come by, like Aunt Colleen, Uncle Augustus, even Aunt Elizabeth, he drove away with convincing claims of apathy.

But Nicolas did grieve. He grieved for what he *could* have had, but never did. And now, never would.

But this wasn't why he went to Deschanel Island to die. It had nothing to do with some repressed grief or inexorable loneliness stemming from a crappy upbringing or his family's accident. That was almost a decade ago. He'd experienced very little heartache in his life since, and despite his often dysfunctional rearing, he'd never been lonely. Until about a month ago, he was happy.

Nicolas knew what people thought of him. That his partying, womanizing, and travels, passing from one experience to another, were just replacements for the lack of sincere affection in his life. He let people believe that because it sounded a lot less fucked up than just admitting he preferred his lifestyle to normalcy. He loved excess. He loved money. He loved women.

Of course, it was *love*, and his screwed up definition of it, which inevitably brought him to where he was now.

His family had owned the small island off the Gulf Coast of Louisiana for many years. Since before he was born, but how long exactly he really didn't know, or care. What he did know was that it was small, private, and he'd taken steps to ensure he'd be the only living soul there.

There were five houses altogether on Deschanel Island, all owned by the Deschanel estate. Rentals, mainly, although there'd be no tenants at all now, as Nicolas had been very clear with his agent he wanted the island to himself until the end of January. He didn't know how long it would take him to sort his shit out, but he definitely didn't want company.

Of course, he didn't consciously acknowledge his intentions when he made these plans.

Neither Oz nor Ana had been surprised at his decision to go away for a while. Guilt, most likely.

"You do realize there'll be no women, and no booze, correct?" Oz had said. Nicolas resented him for thinking they'd come to the point where jokes were okay again. *Newsflash, asshole: I still hate you.*

Ana had been less flippant about it, instead sending him a brief email with the line: *Oz told me what's going on. This isn't like you.* No, she hadn't earned the right to have an opinion about his life again, either. That email, like all the others she'd written to Nicolas since he'd left her to her new life in Maine, went unanswered and promptly deleted.

Why he continued to humor Oz, but not Ana, was somewhat of a mystery, even to him. He only knew he felt the need to punish her more, because her actions broke his heart the most.

But they could *both* go straight to hell, as far as Nicolas was concerned. If it weren't for them, he wouldn't be sitting in his parents' beach house with his father's .357 on his lap.

The only two people Nicolas had ever cared about—the only two people in the world who he knew cared about him in return—were now the only two people in the world he wanted nothing to do with. But, like a chump, he continued letting things go on in their vaguely passive manner. Continued his surface-level discussions with Oz, and resisted the urge to reply to Ana's tentative emails with an award-winning rant. Continued pretending, superficially, he was over what they'd done.

Storm clouds formed over the crystal blue water. It was too late in the season for hurricanes, but a winter storm in the Gulf could be nasty, too. He supposed he could wait until tomorrow to do the deed. It wasn't like he was on a damn schedule.

Nicolas ran his fingers over the cold steel of his father's gun. He actually had to look online to figure out how to shoot the cursed thing. Oz knew about guns. Hell, he'd handled one like a pro not so long ago, back when everyone's world started to fall apart.

Why did Oz have to unburden his conscience on him? If ignorance was bliss, Nicolas had lived an entire life of utopia. He was perfectly happy not knowing a goddamn bit about anything. He liked that his only concern in the world was whether to spend Christmas in Switzerland, or France. He didn't care what his apathy said about him, because he usually didn't give a damn what others did with their lives, either.

Knowing about Oz and Ana changed everything. Now that he knew, the rug had been pulled out from underneath his hazy, fantastical world, and he was left standing on a foundation of crumbling sand.

HE SENT A TEXT MESSAGE TO OZ THE FIRST NIGHT. HE KNEW HE shouldn't, but it was an old habit, and old habits had always been hard for him to break. *You said to tell you when I made it to the island. Here you go, asshole.*

Oz responded almost immediately. *Thanks for your endearing note. Enjoy your self-induced solitude, Thoreau.*

Nicolas grinned, then kicked himself for it. This is how they'd talked to each other for years, for as long as they'd been friends. Hell, all their lives. Nicolas had loved Oz like his own brother. They *were* brothers, if you considered he'd married Nicolas' half-sister Adrienne. Oz had been martyring himself on Adrienne's behalf for years, and they were finally together, and happy. At least, Nicolas thought he was happy. All happiness came at a price, and Oz had paid for his, the way everyone does to have the things they want most in life. Adrienne had paid, too.

Nicolas knew Oz didn't deserve a text, didn't deserve the

peace of mind. He didn't even get credit anymore for his care of Adrienne, after what he'd done to her. If Nicolas hadn't loved his sister, he might've told her all about what her husband had been up to with her cousin. But he did love her, so he didn't.

Nicolas didn't know how to see Oz through this new, darker lens. What he'd done was fucking terrible. Nicolas' heart, that cold, dark organ renting space in his chest, had been torn asunder by it. But somewhere deep down, he also knew Oz was the best man he'd ever known. Those perspectives were warring in his head, constantly. Reasoning shit out was not something he enjoyed under any conditions.

A conversation he had, years ago with Ana, suddenly popped into his head. About a year after his family's accident, she'd claimed he could control his reaction to any situation, with practice.

That's some bullshit, he'd said.

Is it?

If it were true, you wouldn't be such a raving basket-case, he'd countered.

If it weren't true, you'd have never survived the demise of your family, she said, bluntly, right to the point as always.

Explain.

You don't actually believe it didn't bother you?

No, Ana, I really didn't give a fuck, he'd said, though they both knew that was patently untrue.

No. You quite clearly decided not to give a fuck, and therefore, a fuck was not given.

Of course, Nicolas resented her insinuation he was being stingy with his fucks, and he told her so. They'd debated it for another hour or so, before she'd conceded—knowing she was right— and he'd won—knowing this particular victory was hollow.

But sitting there, watching the Gulf tides, feeling the brisk, cool air tug at his jacket, Nicolas knew she'd been wrong all along. If he could control how he felt about this situation, he'd have forgiven her and Oz both, and all would be well. He'd be off to Greece for the winter, beautiful but unmemorable women on each arm, not a care in the world.

Blissfully ignorant.

2- MERCY

*M*ercy froze when she saw the lights come on in the large house at the end of the island. Impossible. Her Inner Voice wouldn't have led her here if there was a chance of encountering anyone.

She required isolation for events to take their proper course. To be alone, where she could speak to Our Father in delicate prayer, and contemplate her final days of confinement upon Earth. While she wouldn't miss this existence, she also wouldn't affront Our Father by being remiss in showing her appreciation of all He had given her.

Mercy waited. And watched. As daylight slowly waned, and the lights in the house remained lit, she accepted it was time to formulate a course correction. While it was possible to remain undetected by the house's inhabitant, she couldn't risk the potential danger. A careless slip now would cast a long lifetime of planning to the wind.

Expect the ideal, but prepare for the catastrophic, Aidrik used to say. He meant it, too. She doubted he ever experienced a moment's rest in his long life. Even in his sleep, his mind held his weapon drawn, ready for anything. There were many things about their relationship that had caused Mercy angst, but she couldn't complain of ever having worried about her safety when he was at her side.

Her mind churned over her options. What she would say if she came in contact with the home's inhabitant. Once she stepped out of the shadows, she risked detection. It was impossible to predict their reaction, so she needed to do as Aidrik would have advised, and prepare for the catastrophic; assume this individual would wish her harm. Once in proximity, their thoughts and intentions would be bare to Mercy, and she could make a stronger assessment. Until then, she had no choice but to operate under the assumption she was in danger.

Mercy paused, reflecting. Of course, there was always the possibility that encountering this individual was part of her final test, before meeting Our Father. Just in case, she'd ensure this Child of Man came to no harm, unless she determined him or her a risk to her own life.

Figuring out ways to distract a Child of Man was nothing new. There was no reason this should be any different. This was a pause, not a setback.

Her mind went to work weighing options, between entreaties to Him for grace.

3- NICOLAS

*N*icolas' instructions to the agent had been very explicit.

That in mind, his first thought was he *must* be seeing things. He was the only one with authorization to board the ferry, and had confirmed all the rentals had checked out before his arrival.

But no, there she was. A woman. On his beach, at eventide.

Confusion gave way to being more than a little pissed off. Nicolas set the gun on the railing and went to handle the situation.

He marched through the sand, calling out to her as soon as he was in shouting range. The woman was about a quarter mile down the beach, not far from one of the smaller rentals on the island, huddled along the shoreline.

She didn't acknowledge him. She instead sat calmly, knees drawn to her chest, gazing off into the water. As his shouts went unanswered, Nicolas came raging down the beach, angry, violated, and ready to tear apart whatever excuses she'd have for being there illegally.

"Is there a reason you're ignoring me?" Nicolas called once he was a few feet from her.

Still, she didn't look up. As he drew even closer, his anger shifted to a vague but growing concern.

"Lady?" he asked, moving slower now, no longer charging around like an angry bull. A lump caught in his throat as he wondered, for one terrible moment, if she was dead, and had washed up this way.

He knelt cautiously before her, and the relief was immediate. *Alive.* Her chest moved up and down in slow, rhythmic motions, though her expression remained vacant, jagged lines of tears rolling down her face the only evidence of activity within. Her mouth hung slightly open, breathing shallow breaths as her shaking hands struggled to keep purchase on her wet knees.

"Hey," Nicolas tried again. "Lady," he repeated, when she didn't look up. He snapped his fingers. Still nothing. He wasn't sure if she was catatonic, or just rude. Maybe deaf? This was definitely not his area of expertise, and it was the absolute last thing he wanted to be dealing with.

A small sob from her startled him out of his confusion. Reluctantly, Nicolas eased down beside her in the sand.

Her chest heaved as she cried silent tears. She hadn't acknowledged him yet, but her gaze pulled more to the right now, a sign *something* had changed. That seemed like progress.

Nicolas folded one hand atop hers. She gasped and drew her body upright, snapping her mouth closed. Now, she did look at him, fresh tears pooling.

He lost his own breath for a moment as he took her in. She was beautiful. And vulnerable. And very likely fucking insane. Briefly, he wondered if she'd dog-paddled from a mental hospital on the mainland.

The unanswered questions piled up fast.

"Lady," he tried again, this time gentler. She seemed harmless. Of questionable sanity, but harmless. He grabbed her hand more firmly this time. "It's okay," he encouraged.

Her mouth tried to form words, but nothing coherent

emerged, only a jumbled mess of sounds. The trembling escalated, and he worried she might be on the verge of a seizure.

"All right, all right," he quickly soothed. "It's okay, just relax. You're fine." But he didn't really know if she was fine. He had no idea what was going on. He wasn't sure he wanted to.

She continued staring at Nicolas, lower lip trembling in the cold, but she'd given up trying to communicate. Her lips were hued in blue, and he noticed then that her eyes were color of charcoal embers. Her hair, though... it was the most unnatural, and yet most interesting, color he'd had ever seen, a silver flame, like rods of bright sterling chrome mixed with orange and red flecks of fire. On the overcast dark day she flickered, shining like a torch.

Her hair especially made her age difficult to determine. Not that it mattered. She could be twenty or eighty, she was still on his beach, and he had shit to do.

Nicolas finally accepted leaving her there wasn't a viable option. "We need to get you inside. Into something warm." How long had she been sitting there? Was she hypothermic? It was the Gulf, but it was also winter, and her bluish lips indicated she'd been suffering for some time.

The woman said nothing, but obligingly rose, legs wobbling. As she straightened, he was startled at how *tall* she was, at least half a head taller than Nicolas, her long, lean limbs muscled and strong. Closer to twenties, he deduced, with pale skin and bright eyes, reminding him of a wild Norse goddess. A Viking warrior.

She looked around in dazed surprise, as if taking in her surroundings for the first time. Nicolas had a feeling there would be one hell of a story here, if she were able to ever speak. More important, though, was getting her help, and off the island.

The walk back to the beach house was slow-going. She hobbled at his side, accepting the support but never looking at him, her eyes instead fixed on the incoming tide. He couldn't guess what she thought was out there. The Gulf was unusually quiet that morning. He didn't even hear the herons singing.

"Did you come from out there?" Nicolas asked. He felt like an idiot as soon as the words left his mouth.

When they reached the house, he eased her down on the couch and went to find towels. He expected more frustration in the form of resistance, but she surprised him by taking the towels and drying herself off, saving him the trouble and awkwardness.

"I'm going to get you a change of clothes." Was she even listening to him? "Okay then," he said, after a pause, and went to his room. He had no idea what to give her. Nothing of his would come close to fitting properly.

She couldn't stay in her wet clothes, either.

Nicolas started to process the implications of her washing up on his shore. He assumed she came from the water, like some fucking tragic mermaid, but who the hell knew for sure?

Sighing, he grabbed a pair of his sweats and returned to the living room.

Once she'd changed, Nicolas threw her wet clothing and the soaked towels in the wash. The washing machine was a bewildering assortment of settings. He studied the options with a blank, but purposeful glare. His staff back home would enjoy this, no doubt, and he was glad they weren't there to witness it. In a burst of optimism, he pressed a button labeled "Start." The machine churned responsively before filling with water.

Now all he needed was a drink.

When he returned to the living room, she hadn't moved at all, still in the same dazed state from earlier, staring out the bay window and off into the Gulf. He resisted the strong urge to shake her until some kind of explanation spilled out.

"So, since I don't know your name, I'm just going to call you Lady for now. Unless you wanna tell me your name?" No response. *Of course not.* "Right. So, Lady. I'm at a bit of a loss here. I don't know who you are, how you got here, or even how to help you. I need you to work with me."

She sighed, but it was difficult to tell if it was in response to his words or something entirely unrelated. His frustration bristled anew at her continued rebuff of his efforts, on the same scale of annoyance he experienced when people left him around their kids too long.

Lacking ideas, and needing *something* useful to contribute to the weirdness of the evening, he fixed her dinner.

4- NICOLAS

*W*hen she didn't move for the next hour, fixed to that same spot by the window, Nicolas accepted she wasn't going anywhere. She still refused to talk, although she'd eaten the food he put in front of her. But when he asked her to follow him to the guest room, she responded by laying down on the couch. He brought her a blanket, but she didn't seem to notice.

Nicolas was at a loss. Damsels in distress were Oz's thing. As soon as a woman started pouring out her troubles, that was Nicolas' cue to close out the tab.

Oz would know what to do. Ana too probably. But they weren't here. It was only Prince Nicolas, in all his selfish, spoiled glory.

The longer the strange woman maintained her silence… the more time that passed with no visits from the Coast Guard… the greater the sensation something was really, horribly wrong. All he had were questions, and no answers, so he focused on what he did know.

Years of womanizing had honed his powers of observation to a science.

She had no ring on her finger, and no ring line, either. She looked to be generally in good health, aside from the oddity of her present circumstances. Her nails were dirty, but her hands looked soft and well-manicured. It was evident she took care of herself, and until very recently. But something, somewhere, somehow had changed, and now she was here, catatonic on his couch, a woman with a hole in her life. A hole that might, inside, contain any number of terrors.

Against his better judgment, Nicolas found himself reviving an old habit.

The light from his phone screen blinded him in the darkness.

Oz- let's be clear. Still not friends.

Oz replied right away. *Thanks for the reminder.*

Anyway, not looking for your hero complex to get in the way but I found a woman. Washed up on the shore or something. I don't know. She's not talking. Imagine that, a beautiful woman who doesn't talk. Jealous?

You're kidding, right? Call the police, NOW. Don't wait. This isn't your problem but it will become your problem if you don't act. This is crazy, even for you. Yes, Adrienne agrees.

They were getting somewhere, even if he had to wade through admonishments on the way.

I knew that's what you'd say, because you're as predictable as the fucking tides. I'm not calling the police until I know what her deal is. Of all people I thought you might be the one to tell me to stay mounted on my white steed and see her through this.

Nicolas gritted his teeth and added, *if I wanted Adrienne's opinion, I'd have asked her.*

His phone rang almost immediately, but he didn't answer. *If I wanted to talk to you, I'd have fucking called, asshole.* Another twenty minutes passed before Oz's next text came in.

Nicolas. You have no idea why she's there. No idea how she got there, who might be after her. Maybe she's escaped a crazy ex, or maybe she's playing a long con on you. You could fill a book with what you don't know, and the problems those things might cause you. Legal problems, for one, like an abduction charge for keeping an incapacitated woman without notifying the authorities. Even my white steed thinks this is a bad idea.

A few seconds later:

CALL THE POLICE!

Nicolas decided Oz was more than likely right, but his gut told him involving the authorities was a bad idea, at least until she was coherent, so he didn't.

He retrieved the .357 from the porch, slipping it back into the drawer for now. *You brought me here, jackass. When are we gonna dance?*

"Soon," Nicolas whispered with a long, heavy exhale. "Once I figure out what the fuck to do with the mermaid."

NICOLAS DIDN'T SLEEP THAT NIGHT. HIS MIND VACILLATED between all the scenarios and outcomes available to his imagination, not quite stopping short of conspiracy theories. When he exhausted himself overthinking, his cowardice whispered in his ear, reminding him why he'd come here.

When the sun crested over the horizon, he gave up on sleep.

He wasn't surprised to see the woman hadn't left. He switched on the television, turning it to the local news. If nothing else, maybe they'd learn something.

She ate the food he made, and when he brought her the clothes he'd washed the night before, she accepted them and changed back when he gave her privacy. Nicolas discovered talking to her felt less weird as the day wore on, and he decided that wasn't necessarily a good sign.

Their dysfunctional game of house went on for the rest of

the day. Oz blew up his phone with texts, all varying degrees of caution and reprimand, and Nicolas ignored them all. He threatened to come out, but this was an empty warning, and they both knew it. When he then suggested they ask Ana what *she* though, implying she'd be another voice of reason, Nicolas turned his phone off.

Much as it pained him, Oz was right again. He had to do something.

"LADY?" NICOLAS SAT DOWN NEXT TO THE STRANGE WOMAN WITH the silver and orange hair. "Look, I've respected the fact you don't want to talk, but because you *won't* talk I have no idea what happened to you. I don't know if you were attacked. I don't know if you're sick and need help. I don't know anything at all about you, other than the fact you're still breathing after eating my shitty cooking. You should know I'm going to be calling the police in a few minutes to see about getting you proper help."

The woman turned and looked down at Nicolas, meeting his gaze with icy cool. "Nicolas, please don't," she said, with a delivery that was disturbingly monotone, like something without a soul.

Shivers traveled down his spine. "So, you *can* talk," he observed, lamely.

She nodded.

"All right, well... are you okay?"

Her eyes glazed over, and it seemed she might slip back into the land of catatonia, but she finally offered, "I... don't really know. Maybe. Where are we?"

"Deschanel Island," Nicolas answered. Nicolas couldn't help adding, "a *private* island."

Her brows knit together in consternation. "Deschanel Island. Where is that, exactly?"

Was she serious? "South of Abbeville. Vermillion Parish," he said.

"United States?"

Oh boy. When she asked where they were, Nicolas thought her range was more narrow than "world."

This will be a long night.

"Where are you from?"

She glanced upward, thinking. Probably deciding whether or not to tell him the truth. "New York," she said, finally.

"You're a long way from New York. Do you know how you got out here?"

She shook her head.

"Were you on vacation somewhere nearby? Maybe a New Year's party that went sideways?"

"No," she said, shaking her head again.

"What's the last thing you remember?"

"Going to bed in New York," she said, and then Nicolas knew for sure it was going to be a long night. He sighed, thinking of his metal escape in the desk drawer.

"You have no idea what happened to you? No idea how you might've come to be on the beach?"

"No, I really don't remember anything," she said, but this time there was a glint in her eye, one which told Nicolas she was lying. It sent his bullshit meter off the charts.

"Okay. Do you at least know your name?"

"Clementyn," she responded. "But I go by Mercy."

That sounded more like a Southern name. "All right then. Mercy. That's a start. And you remember you're from New York, so at least we know where we can send you," Nicolas said.

"Send me?" Her grey eyes widened; the color was a startling contrast to her silver red hair. Wolf-like. Calculating.

"Well, obviously you can't stay here," he said with a short laugh. From the look on Mercy's face, that hadn't been so obvious to her. "I mean, you don't even know me. We really need to get you some help."

"I can't go back to New York," she asserted, looking down at her folded hands.

"Why the hell not?"

"I just can't."

Nicolas didn't meant to groan audibly, but here she was, finally talking, and saying nothing at all. "Clementyn. Mercy. Whatever your name is. Look, here's the deal. I don't know you and you don't know me. I'm willing to help you, but my version of helping does not include letting you sit here for the next however long, staring out the window like a depressed puppy. You can either give me the information I need to get you off this island safely, or I can call the police and let them sort it out. Understand?"

Mercy paused only briefly before saying, "You can't call the police because they'll be expecting it. He's already been in close contact with them."

"He? What?" Nicolas started, but she ignored him and kept talking.

"—And if the police come out here, they'll notify him, and he'll know I am not dead. Then all this would've been for nothing." Her face was impassive.

Realization struck with immediate clarity. This bitch had faked her death. Naturally, he had to confirm this brilliant deduction with his next question. "Did you fake your own death?"

"Yes," she admitted, after a deep breath.

"So," Nicolas concluded, "you pulled a Julia Roberts in *Sleeping With the Enemy*. You *do* know how you got here. You know damn well you're in Louisiana, and you definitely could've opened your mouth yesterday and told me all of this instead of letting me sit around talking to you and feeding you like Norman Bates and his dead mother."

"I have no idea what you're talking about."

"You toyed with me. Used me."

"I didn't intentionally do either. Yes, could have opened my mouth earlier, but I really didn't know what to say. I didn't know if I should come clean with you and hope you'd understand or just keep pretending to be lost and hope you'd let me stay. I didn't think this far ahead." There were tears in her eyes and she had both hands on top of her head, nervously tugging at her silvery hair. "I thought this island would be private. I did my research. Almost no one ever stays here."

"Well, your research sucked, because, one, people do stay here sometimes and two, it's *my* island and I plan to stay here a while. Alone."

Mercy's eyes widened.

"Besides, what did you expect to do even if it *was* empty, stay here illegally?" Her silence at this was intolerable. That's *exactly* what she'd intended. "You want my help? Spill. All of it."

Mercy sighed and folded her long fingers together in her lap. "My name is Clementyn Marie Christensen. I was born on August 12th, twenty-six years ago in Syracuse, New York. I was an only child, probably considered privileged by most standards. My mother paid for me to first attend New York University, and then graduate studies at Yale Law. It was in law school I met my husband, Andrew Christensen. I learned he liked hiking and movies. A few months after we said our vows, I also learned he liked to hit women. I decided then there'd be no children. I never told him about the birth control, or he would have probably killed me. A year ago he broke my jaw. Six months ago, one of my arms. Leaving him wasn't an option because he'd find me and then it would be a lot more than my jaw and arm. I'm not a weak woman, and not the type to sit back and take any kind of abuse, let alone from someone supposed to love me. The abuse was escalating, so it came time for me to make a decision. Either I kill myself, kill him, or lead him to believe I was dead so he'd leave me alone. I love my life too much to take it, and I value my freedom too much to take his. So that left only one option."

Nicolas recognized a rehearsed speech when he heard one, but he let her continue, curious how far she'd dig herself into this pile of bullshit.

"The vacation was my idea. He was thrilled, taking it as a sign of my interest in marital relations again. I chose the Gulf because of the improbability of any kind of body recovery from drowning. I also knew he was smart enough to research that once the search started, and so would be more likely to accept I'd drowned. When I got here, I intended to stay in one of the empty houses for a couple of nights until I could recover and go on to the next part of my plan." She paused, drawing in a deep, exasperated breath. "Does that work for you, or would you like me to tell you about my time in Girl Scouts, or what I wore to prom?"

"No need to get testy with me, lady. I'm not the one who faked my own death and planned to squat on someone's private island."

"If I'm testy it's because you have no idea how hard I worked to arrange this. And the bag I left here with everything I needed —a new ID, passport, hair dye, clothing, everything—is missing."

"You were on the island *before* you pretended to drown?"

"Only briefly. I couldn't drown with a bag of stuff, so I decided to leave everything I needed in one of the sheds. My plan was to come back, retrieve the bag, pick a lock on one of the empty homes, and do everything I needed over a day or two. Dye and cut my hair, get at least one night's rest, get some food in me, and then prepare for my new life. I knew one day would buy me enough time, but two might be careless, since they'd begin the search immediately."

"So… you washed up onshore, went to find your bag, and it was gone?"

"I left it in the shed of the next house over. I remember it because the shed is this funny green color. I put it behind an old shelf. But when I went to retrieve it, it was gone."

"What do you think happened, then?"

"I think he came and took it," Mercy revealed, more calmly than he'd expect.

"How would he have known?" Nicolas asked, growing annoyed with himself for getting so involved in this ridiculous story. And it *was* a story, he was certain. He had other things, better things, to do. One thing in particular.

Mercy laughed without amusement. "Oh, I don't know. Andy has always had ways of knowing things that astound me. But clearly, he found out."

"But if he found out you were here, why hasn't he done anything about it?"

"I think he believes my plan backfired. He thinks I actually died."

Nicolas frowned. "But then, why take the bag?"

"For the same reason I'd take the bag if I were in his shoes. At some point, the police will show up on this island, as I'm sure they've already started to do on the neighboring ones. I'm honestly shocked they haven't been here yet. And when they do, since most of the houses are unoccupied, they'll ask your permission to search them, seeing if maybe I survived and found shelter. Since you have no reason to say no to them, you'd let them in, of course, and they'd find the bag. And then he'd have to answer as to why his wife would leave a bag on an island and then accidentally drown."

This was officially the craziest shit Nicolas had ever heard, and he'd fielded a lot of whacko stories after Adrienne reappeared and people came out of the woodwork trying to claim a portion of the family fortune.

"Mercy, this puts me in a really uncomfortable position," he ventured.

"Excuse me? You?" She laughed, coldly. The exaggerated disbelief in her voice didn't add to her credibility.

"Don't confuse your issues with mine," I said. "You don't deserve what happened to you. I'm willing to help you. But I'm not getting involved beyond getting you safely to someone who can *actually* help you."

Mercy was speechless, her expression somewhere between dumbfounded and incensed. *She must think I'm the biggest motherfucker on the planet.*

"Look," Nicolas continued, "I can give you as much money as you need, I can make arrangements for you. I can do a lot of things. But the thing I *can't* do, is let you stay here."

Mercy's face was a mingled buffet of shock and anger, but when she tried to form her rebuttal, Nicolas stopped her. "No, hear me out. Let's say your ex figures out you're here. Let's even say he knows you're here already. It's quite possible, if what you say about your damn bag is true. So then let's say he decides to come for you. It wouldn't take him long at all to search the empty houses on the island, and then find himself at the one that's occupied."

Mercy's expression was guarded, but it wasn't hard to guess what she was thinking, likely torn between his nearly inarguable logic, while simultaneously realizing she must have the world's worst luck to land in the lap of the one guy in the world who didn't want to rescue her.

She lifted herself up off the couch and towered over Nicolas. There was a heat to her, as if she was radiating. If Nicolas didn't know better, he'd have said she was glowing.

"I do *not* need rescuing. I do not *want* rescuing. I handled this all on my own, without the help of anyone. I'm not a woman who gets into situations like this, but I *am* a woman who gets herself out of them. I didn't intend for you, or anyone, to be here, Nicolas. If you'd listened to what I was saying, instead of jumping to your own anti-chivalrous conclusions, then you might have understood all I was asking is that you don't turn me in. I don't need your... protection, such as it were. I just need you to keep your damn mouth shut until I can get out of here. Will that be all right with you?"

Her rant caught Nicolas off guard. Tears he'd expected, maybe please, or further fabrications. He'd pissed off plenty of women over the years, but this was different. Mercy wasn't scorned, and she was no victim, despite what she'd allegedly gone through to get here.

Her warrior fists were balled, as she fought to control her trembling. Glowing again.

"Message received," he murmured, and showed in his body language he was backing down. "Keeping my mouth shut is something I can do, believe it or not."

"Good," Mercy said, "thank you." Her fists loosened some, but the heat only slightly eased. "I didn't mean to disrupt you in whatever it is you're doing out here. I never wanted to bring anyone into this, let alone a complete stranger. I'm sorry for that. I won't ask for anything except to give me enough time to get off the island. I'd prefer if you never say anything to anyone who comes asking, but I won't ask for that, I'll only ask for your silence long enough to give me a head start."

Nicolas was starting to feel like an asshole. "Look, I'll help you search for your bag. Tomorrow." He gestured toward the storm brewing outside, dense sideways sheets of rain. "When the weather clears."

"No. I'm fine." She made for the coat he'd left drying on a dining chair. "I've wasted quite a bit of time already. I'm going to go look myself."

Nicolas started for his jacket as well. "I guess now works—"

"No," she put her hand out. "I appreciate it, but you've already done quite enough."

Nicolas hadn't really done anything at all, but he still had half a mind to disagree with her, because that's what she was looking for. She was manipulating him, but, why, he didn't yet know. "All right. If you have no luck, I'll make some calls and see what we can get for you," I agreed.

Mercy nodded and walked out the door. If he'd had followed her, would things have turned out differently?

Isn't the answer to that question *always* yes?

DARKNESS CAME, AND MERCY HADN'T RETURNED. THE RAIN continued, but harder, and even for winter the chill outside was shocking. He turned all the exterior lights on for a better view down the beach, and he hadn't seen so much as a shadow.

Something stilled him from going after her. He wanted her to be safe, but equally wanted to distance himself from her and whatever weird shit she'd gotten herself into. There was a hardness about Mercy he found appealing, and even liked. But she'd caused him enough trouble already, and he didn't feel much except contempt for her presence.

Sure, he'd come here to die, but what he hadn't come here to do was be disrupted, and certainly not judged. Oz thought it was hilarious that Nicolas wanted to be alone, but he *loved* being alone. Being alone came with the gift of picking and choosing the shit he wanted to deal with. Of never having to unpack someone else's baggage.

His concern for Mercy shifted to concern for himself. What if her husband *had* found her? Would he show up here next? There was the gun in the drawer, but if Mercy couldn't handle the guy, it wasn't likely he'd fare any better. She was hard, like granite. There was something calculating about her, and not at all warm.

Nicolas rarely thought twice about decisions, never dwelt on their ramifications. While most of his choices were rather self-serving, it was this code that allowed him to feel little to no regret on the events of his life thus far.

He said a silent prayer, to a God he didn't believe in, that Mercy had found what she was looking for.

5- MERCY

*N*icolas was startlingly unlike most Children of Men. She'd never struggled to attract aid from them before, and his standoffish attempt to distance himself from her problems meant she'd fallen out of character once, if not twice, to adjust to this. Thankfully, he was also a bit too attached to his comfortable life to be any threat to her plan. Since Father Emyr had not clearly revealed this Child's role in her Ascension, Mercy left him content in his illusion of control.

In actuality, Nicolas' complete lack of empathy worked well for her. He would form no attachment, and neither would he wonder about her after she was gone. All at once, though, it became clear why the Eldre Senetat had outlawed Empyreans mating with Men. *Selfish and destructive,* she recalled Eldre Saxon saying, many years past.

She *had* expected to find the island vacant. That part was true. The rest—other than her name, a truth that flowed before she could switch it to a lie—she'd fabricated. It wasn't the first time when dealing with a Child of Man, because truth wasn't an option. Quick, creative thinking was a trait Mercy had learned for survival.

Mercy hadn't intended for things to go so far. The silence wasn't part of the act, but a needed focus. What would the arrogant Child of Man have said had she told him she was preparing for her Grand Ascension? His naïveté, his money-cures-all dismissiveness, would have crumbled in the face of a truth far larger than either of them.

But while Mercy found Nicolas exasperatingly narrow-minded, it was not her wish, nor Our Father's, that Nicolas be harmed.

Nicolas wasn't her concern anymore, however. She wouldn't be returning to his house, a fact they'd both appreciate, she was sure, in their own ways.

Mercy was tired. Bone tired, a soul deep exhaustion only someone like her could ever appreciate. After three thousand years of wandering, and waiting, the agonizing weariness was all she knew.

Over two millennia had passed since she felt the first "itch." She'd been searching for the signs since maturity, even though the Scholars and fellow Empyrean peers had counseled patience. *It takes nearly a thousand years before your mane will be woven with its first silver strand. And that is only the beginning, Child. Then your Years of Wisdom commence.*

History backed up their words, but there *were* stories of Empyreans who'd Ascended earlier. She clung to those tales, in desperate hope. What had made them worthy? What had they done to earn their welcome into the arms of Our Father, Emyr, before others? She'd focused on finding the answer, devoting her life to His name.

All her days were colored with signs. Everywhere, proof she was on the right path. Much like the Christians of Man and their stigmata, Mercy felt Emyr's presence burning through her silken hair, would see his face in the trunks of trees, the petals of flowers, and even the swirls of dust lining the many streets she roamed. Aidrik the Wise would tell her the mind saw what it most wished to see. That their desires and reality were not always as intertwined as they'd would like to believe. But Aidrik had never believed as Mercy did. Sometimes she wondered if he'd ever believed at all.

She'd ignored him, setting the stage for her Ascension each time the itch grew too great to ignore. But the Mark never glowed. The phoenix on her breast, over her heart, never roared to life; never rose from the ashes to bring her home to Our Father. But this time was different. More than her childlike hope, this time there'd been a distinct longing. A burning. Mercy was *burning* to Ascend, and her skin glowed in eager anticipation. She had earned it. It was her time, long overdue, and she deserved this. She was ready. *I am, and always have been, your willing disciple.*

Despite the unexpected presence of Nicolas, he hadn't done anything to disrupt the process. Once it began, there really wasn't anything anyone—especially no mortal—could do to stop it.

But it was more than just the itch now. There was another feeling, one that wasn't uncommon among the older ones like Mercy. Depression, a Child of Man might call it, for they possessed no better word in their limited minds. Better described as a combination of fatigue and hopelessness, the kind only someone who'd lived thousands of years could understand or experience. She felt it so keenly that if her reward did not come soon, she was not sure she could go on any longer.

Anders had understood. They'd stayed up days on end sometimes, sharing feelings, experiences. Unlike Aidrik, he never asked anything of her. Anders shared her malcontent, the day he disappeared. She awoke to find the spot next to her empty, lacking even a trace of his warmth. She looked out the window that morning, knowing something was different, and saw a beautiful flaming bird, sitting on the fence. Staring at her.

Anders' departure was a painful lesson Mercy didn't care to repeat, so she lived alone by choice. There were barely a thousand left, and the Eldre Senetat was debating easing mating restrictions. In the broad family of Emyr's Children, few had seen as many years as she had. Fewer still whose silver strands outnumbered the red ones. She was alone, in all ways that mattered.

Mercy feared ending up like Old Aita, walking the earth in exile, with her forsaken white mane. To an Empyrean, there was no worse fate. Death would be preferable. The Scholars often used her story as a way of keeping the young Empyreans in line, and it was effective. *You don't want to end up like Old Aita... do you?* None knew what Aita had done to invite such vengeance from the Eldre Senetat, they only knew they didn't want to find out.

The Gulf waves crashed rhythmically on the shore, lulling her near to sleep. This was a beautiful place. Peaceful. She could see why Nicolas' family owned the island, although he didn't seem the type to crave solitude.

Of course, reading minds was only as accurate as the mind was clear. His mind was awash with contradictions, leaving Mercy mildly curious where his truth resided. Almost any other Man would have sheltered her, cared for her, promised her the world. Not this one. He was so concerned with his own agenda and comfort, he almost didn't care what happened to her.

Pushing Nicolas and his unconventional priorities aside, Mercy laid back and dreamt of Farjhem, her home...

6- NICOLAS

*N*icolas dreamed of Ana twice that night.

The first ran through his mind like a disconnected set of memories, and when he woke, the real memories
hit him like a sneaker wave.

It was Ana who'd reminded him about the island. Nicolas
had no real concept of his family's assets, never caring much for
details. He paid other people to understand investments,
aggressive growth funds, diversification, and an assortment of
other dry accounting terms. Money well spent.

Are you going to ever talk to me? Ana pleaded a few days
before, when she was finally able to trick him into answering
her call by blocking her number. *Nicolas, please. I'm worried.*

I'm hanging up.

Oz thinks you're going to turn it into a party island, she'd said
quietly, hopefully, an attempt at finding an open door through
humor. Humor was their thing; their place.

*What Oz does or does not think is completely irrelevant. Neither of
you are my warden.*

I don't like this, Ana had said. *This* intentionally carried a
thousand meanings.

Goodbye, Muffins. In a fleeting weak moment, Nicolas had used her old nickname, a silly moniker he'd given her years ago. He regretted its use immediately because it felt empty now. Dishonest. Akin to telling a woman you loved her simply to get in her pants.

He'd hung up feeling cruel rather than empowered. He hated himself for hurting her. He hated her for hurting him.

When Ana had told him in October she was running off to Maine, Nicolas assumed she was struggling with the late nights; the random men. He knew about all that, of course, because she'd told him—and he'd told *her* that she should stop punishing herself for doing essentially what he'd done his entire adult life. He suspected there was something else she wasn't telling him, but she was his Ana. She'd never lied to him before.

When several days went by without hearing from her, he panicked and booked a flight north, Oz in tow. His sidekick. His pal. His partner. The brother Nicolas wished he'd had. What ensued was a drama none of them could've anticipated, punctuated by a selfish unburdening of the truth behind Oz's motivation for going on the trip to begin with. If he'd told Nicolas beforehand, things might have ended a lot differently.

But if he'd never gone to Maine, Ana could've died in that old Victorian on the shore of Summer Island.

They'd arrived to discover Ana and her two neighbors, brothers Finn and Jon, held hostage by the odd caretaker. Their unexpected arrival upset the situation enough to turn the tide of the tense standoff. Shots were fired. The caretaker ended up dead, Ana and Finn hospitalized. Both should have died, but Ana was a *gifted* Deschanel; a healer. Until that point, she'd only been capable of healing herself, but miraculously, she was able to save Finn, too. The terrifying situation had ended as well as it could have, by all accounts.

Everything would have been fine if Oz had kept his goddamned mouth shut.

I know why Ana went to Maine.

We all do, Ozzy. She's fucked up, has daddy issues, and needed a break.

She came to Maine because... we had a thing.

A *thing*. Oz, the man Nicolas had grown up with, treated as his own brother. The man who'd married his sister. *Slept* with Ana. *His* Ana. And they'd kept this from him.

Yes, Ana was Nicolas' cousin. Yes, she was off limits. He had no opinion of the long line of men who'd come through her life, but sleeping with his best friend had obliterated an important dynamic between the three of them. Nicolas didn't care that they had a history, going back to high school. Hell, maybe they'd even fancied themselves in love once upon a time. He didn't give a damn what their reasons were for rekindling it, or why they'd done it. Nicolas would never, ever look at them the same again. He could never love them the carefree way he once had. And, without love, he had nothing else to give his life proper meaning.

The rational argument was that he shouldn't care so much. That maybe it wasn't okay to be in love with her.

But he did care, he *was* in love with her, and his heart was broken.

THE SECOND TIME HE DREAMED OF ANA, THE IMAGES WERE crystal clear. Precise. Unlike any dream he'd had ever had before.

Ana stood naked in the center of a bedroom, examining herself. Finnegan St. Andrews slept on the bed behind her. They'd just finished making love, and Finn was passed out, dead to the world. Ana was troubled.

Nicolas ould see the side of her face in the dresser mirror. The entire scene played out through her pain-filled eyes.

She ran her hands over her hips, and stomach, then crossed

her arms over her torso in a gesture of self-loathing. Something about the clinical, inventorial way she watched herself made Nicolas sad, and more than a little uncomfortable.

He felt the hollow sorrow in her soft heartbeat. It seemed like he should look away, but he couldn't; he *was* her.

Ana still tingled from their lovemaking. For someone so kind and gentle, Finn completely dominated her in the bedroom, taking her hips in his soft, worn hands and demanding more than she knew she had to give. She loved how the muscles in his tight bottom felt when she held on, encouraging him to thrust harder, while he moaned in ecstasy. In these moments, he was all hers. In these moments, she believed she could even be his.

Nicolas really didn't want to be seeing this, but was frozen, locked in. He didn't know how he got there, but there seemed no way of getting out.

Ana watched Finn, and her heart swam with affection. He was so unlike her. Young. Playful. He was a fisherman, a man of the sea. She loved how his strong muscles felt holding her, and the smell of his salty blonde hair. Like Ana, he'd never loved anyone before. He was the most beautiful thing she had ever seen. The kindest man she had ever known.

She was afraid she would destroy him.

Ana's thoughts wandered to the other room, where Finn's older brother, Jonathan, was asleep. Jon, the recluse. He was introspective, like Ana, but he was also cold, rude. They understood one another, including all the ugliness contained in their hearts.

She dwelt in agony over the intense moment she shared with Jon, before she and Finn made things official. How alive and electric Jon made her feel. But Ana knew he was too much like her for them to be happy. The darkness in her resonated in a dangerous way with Jon.

She'd tried so hard to put it behind her, yet Jon insisted on finding passive, but hurtful, ways of reminding her. A punishing refusal to let go.

So the darkness between them grew, and carried over, tarnishing

Ana's love for Finn. For this secret of her and Jon's tryst had burned deep inside of her, until in one horrible moment Finn learned the truth. Though their blossoming relationship wasn't yet in flight when she'd slept with Jon, she'd known it would nonetheless break Finn's heart. She was right, but what she hadn't counted on was his understanding, and his love. His insistence on being with her, and his inexplicable belief he was meant to be with her. Beyond forgiveness, which was more than she dared to hope for, Finn supported her against his brother.

The world had been flipped upside down. Finn was not speaking with his brother, and the icy chasm in the house was unbearable. Desperate to convince Ana of his unconditional devotion, Finn proposed. When Ana protested they had been together mere weeks, Finn countered he'd known the moment he first kissed her she was the one. It wasn't so strange; his own parents had known on their second date.

Ana's final thought was of Nicolas. She recalled their tradition of long talks that stretched into morning, or the pranks they played on unsuspecting tourists in Jackson Square. She remembered his braiding her hair in secret, catching crawfish in the creek behind *Ophélie*. All lost with a single bad decision.

Then, just like that, it was over. Nicolas was back in his own body, his own thoughts and senses returned to him. He rolled forward, bracing his hands on either side of his knees as a nauseating dizziness overtook him. He clapped a hand against his mouth, as his dinner surged forward, threatening to erupt. The room was weaving circles, and for a moment he thought he was Ana again. Then himself. Then Ana. He was in the cold bedroom in Maine, standing over the ancient bureau, and then he was Nicolas, digging his fingers deeper into the bed sheets. He spun back and forth, watching both images as if looking through one of those children's picture viewfinders. He tried to scream, but the sensation stole his breath away.

Eventually, it passed.

He shouldn't have seen any of this. The insight was shocking for a bigger reason. He knew, absolutely knew, what he'd seen was real, not simply a dream.

Unlike other Deschanels, Nicolas had no special gifts. He couldn't even read minds. But he was damn near positive what he'd experienced was a genuine psychic connection with Ana, the first time in his life anything like that had ever happened to him.

It was too much to process, along with everything else. Nicolas closed his eyes and slid his hand down under the comforter, directing his thoughts to the hot girls who worked his favorite bar on Frenchman Street. There were other ways to get much-needed sleep, and he was only slightly ashamed that, after spending a few minutes in Ana's head, seeing her lithe naked body in the mirror, he was already semi-hard.

Minutes later, Nicolas drifted into restful sleep.

THE SUN WOKE NICOLAS, FAR EARLIER THAN HE WAS USED TO. HE looked at the clock. It was just after seven in the morning, which was really the middle of the night as far as he was concerned.

He still didn't know what to make of last night's vision, but, as with the Mercy situation, there was little use in fixating on things beyond his control.

Still, Nicolas couldn't help wondering if Mercy was okay. He hoped she'd found her bag and was on her way, the rest of her plan unfolding just as she'd intended. But then, that would mean her story wasn't a load of bullshit, and there was way too much weirdness about Mercy Christensen and her recital of facts for him not to have doubts.

Outside, the heavy rains created a shroud between his windows and the Gulf. The cypress trees bowed and flexed in the wind, creating gaps in the canopy they formed over the house. The staccato beats from the intermittent rain on his skylights was almost soothing.

Thinking again of the .357 in the drawer, he resolved he'd do it after breakfast. It wasn't civilized to go out on an empty stomach.

7- MERCY

The rain continued through the night and into morning. Mercy remained in bed, not bothering with light or heat.

Empyreans, born of fire, had internal temperatures warmer than any other species on Earth. She was not cold. Was, in fact, feverish with anticipation. When emotions were most acute, the heat emitted a soft, pulsing orange glow. She had to be careful not to do that in front of Men. There were already those who had grown too curious for their own good over the years.

Her hand came to a rest atop the phoenix on her chest. At their age of maturity, Empyreans were given this infusion before being sent out into the world. A tattoo, Men would have called it, though it was not colored by ink, but instilled with magic. The Mark of Emyr was a piece of Him, embedded into all of them. If Mercy listened carefully, sometimes she could even hear the small hisses and trills of hers, imagining it was Him calling, soothing.

They were allowed to choose the selection of their Mark, and Mercy had chosen hers to be placed over her heart, on her left breast. Her love for Emyr was pure and strong, and there was nowhere she could place it that would be truer to that love than over the part of her which belonged to Him first and most. She envisioned the moment of her Ascension, the glow from the Mark matching the burning in her heart, and together they would combine into a symphony of love as she moved toward His arms.

Mercy was no longer picking up much of Nicolas' thoughts. He'd been sleeping since she left, and she never bothered listening in on dreams. While Men liked to place special meaning on them, she knew dreams were nothing but the mind's way of taking inventory behind the scenes.

But as Nicolas woke, one thought in particular jumped into hers, one that gave her an, albeit momentary, pause. She diverted a small amount of precious focus and saw him in her mind's eye.

Looking down at a Weapon of Man. A gun. *Courage. I came here to opt out, not to over-think shit.*

She released him, processing. His solitude was even more selfish than she initially thought. He meant to take his life. To release his soul from his vessel and travel... where? Mercy did not know where Men went after their body died. Most Men she had known held varying opinions on the matter. But if he valued his life so little, he didn't deserve it anyway.

She cringed as her Mark shifted, lifting his head with a small, tousling shake. The silver feathers rippled across her chest, flashing red. *You can't let him do this. You need him. Your congress with him was not coincidence.*

You need to leave the island, together.

"It cannot be,"Mercy whispered. But she knew. Her Inner Voice was always right. Her blind desire, not her Voice, sent her false signs over the years, and she'd learned to listen.

She'd erroneously assumed the island was the end of her

journey, Nicolas merely an unforeseen obstacle. That her Mark would take flight here, ending her wandering, her seeking.

The rippling phoenix on her chest told otherwise. Mercy's meeting with Nicolas Deschanel was no chance, and unfortunately, far from over.

MERCY HAD NEVER ENJOYED MANIPULATING CHILDREN OF MEN. There were other Empyreans who derived immense pleasure from the practice, to the point of losing themselves in it. Some even kept humans as pets. It was said Duchess Oriana, the beautiful, wayward daughter of Grand Emperor Aeron, had an entire menagerie of them. She supposedly spent her leisurely days delighting in their diversions.

This behavior was distasteful to Our Father, whose love taught them to respect all living things. It was a bastardization of the advantages he had bestowed. An affront to his love.

Yet, the manipulations always worked, without fail. Even with the difficult ones, like Nicolas. Her powers of persuasion were finely honed over the years, and if she asked him to swim into the Gulf and never look back, he would do it. He was not as simple to control as other Men, no. But her influence was the only reason he hadn't called the police. She was skilled enough he simply believed his desire to not get involved was his own intuition or selfishness. A gut feeling.

In the end, he would do exactly what Mercy needed him to. She didn't have to like the process to accept it as necessary. She had waited far too long for this to risk anything going wrong. Being abandoned to the fate of Old Aita was incomprehensible. Better to die, disappearing entirely.

"Our Father of Light, Our Father of Fire. I am but a vessel of Your Love. I seek Your absolution for that which I must do, as a means to an end. I am Yours in the Flames." Mercy whispered the incantation over and over, feeling His love and warmth building within her, slowly, until it felt on the verge of bursting forth into a whirlwind of ember flames.

Emyr, dismiss from Your mind this temporary divergence. I am Yours in the Flames.

8- AIDRIK

*W*atching. Aidrik had done little else for nearly a thousand years.

Forged with volcanic fire, and quenched in glacier's ice, Empyrean patience was made in the same manner as their swords: strong, resilient, unbreaking. When one's life was measured in millennia, as opposed to the mere decades of Man, it would have to be.

Mercy no longer detected him. The scar on his temple acted as both a badge of courage, and insurance of such. Once realizing the Mark's profane power, he'd sliced it off, fully believing it would hasten his death. It did, in a way. To all he had known, to his people, Aidrik *was* dead. Freedom and death often live in tandem.

Clementyn, she had been named, after a Scholar of Latin who journeyed to the villages surrounding Farjhem. Mercy was Aidrik's name for her; one she still favored. Back then, he had believed her to be his salvation. In his middle epoch, he even supposed her grace and joy could reconcile his angst.

He knew differently now. She was a catalyst, not a remedy. Salvation was earned by moving beyond prescribed limitations.

43

No longer allowing a narrow predestined path to direct your steps.

As a Youth he envisioned his Grand Ascension, as all fledglings did. He'd idealized the dream of moving into the arms of Emyr, Our Father. Love supplanted that ideology. Love, he learned too soon, too late, led to loss. Loss, once over the shock, bloomed into an icy paralyzing slide of desperation. Desperation pointed, quite logically for some, to a predetermined path, which had no return, the Grand Ascension no longer a reward earned, but a separation from pain. Unaccepting, he'd enlarged his reality, forcing desperation and illusion aside, allowing enlightenment to shine like the sun reflecting off clean ice.

Believing Aidrik had Ascended, Mercy mourned his loss, unaware of his defection of their ways. He remained her guardian long after. Resigned, he watched behaviors he'd previously counseled against grow cancerous. Protector, yes. Her keeper, he was not. Mercy's mind, and future, were hers alone. In recent centuries, as he regarded her pernicious doings, he came to terms with this.

The luxury of silent observation, and emotional distance, ended when her Mark activated. Knowing this day was imminent kept Aidrik vigilant even while he indulged in errant speculation as to why she'd gone unnoticed for so long. Outside the Eldre Senetat, there were few alive older than Mercy, save Aidrik. Once Empyreans approached an age rivaling those of the Eldres, the Mark activated and their "Grand Ascension" would commence. Mercy had long been due. Overdue. The Senetat's inaction flew in the face of all Aidrik knew about them. Their swift and sudden action to remedy an apparent oversight now, was alarming.

Under the cover of moonlight, he could remove his hood. His hair, originally waves of red and yellow reminiscent of boiling lava, had long since transitioned to a silver shimmer with only undertones of its molten beginnings. As with Man, silver was the mark of distinction for the Farværdig. Venerability. Wisdom. It also marked him as defiant, much like the now absent Mark. If shorn, the nearly luminescent strands would only grow back. Dyes and hues would not adhere to the dense follicles. His death hoax would be discovered should even one Empyrean see him, and his distinctive mane.

Having died already, death did not scare Aidrik. Dying before he could help Mercy did.

Inhaling, he took in the damp mossy fragrance. His lip curled involuntarily. This musty swampland was cadaverous.

Crisp glacier blanketed fjords. Scalding hot iron and carbon yielding to Blacksmith's hammer. Yeast and honey rising from loaves baking in stone ovens. Four thousand years roaming the earth had not diminished his memory of Farjhem's scent. Recollections all painfully underscoring the knowledge he would never be home again. For the Farværdig, or Empyreans as they had called themselves for many millennia, home was a dynamic concept. Home was wherever their feet landed.

Ulfberht effortlessly decapitated the nutria. It fell into the moss, twitching though already dead. Unappetizing, but the mammal meat braised over an open fire would be more tender than most of what roamed these unholy bogs. He wiped the blade briefly on his robe, noting the persistent clarity of the **+vlfberh+t** inscription along its length. Not so much a label, but as if the metal spoke its own name. While a few Children of Men had spent great gold earning the right to carry this weapon, it was created for Empyrean hands. More than simply a sword, Ulfberht was power.

Aidrik wondered, briefly, what power might be capable of saving Mercy.

9- NICOLAS

Nothing's changed, Nicky boy, the handgun called to him. *You're still miserable.*

Yeah, yeah. But he was also distracted as hell, wondering what fate had befallen Mercy, and he'd never been very good at multi-tasking.

AROUND SIX THE BEACH LIGHTS CAME ON, AS SENSORS DETECTED the fading light of sunset. They illuminated the sand from the shoreline area to a few feet into the water. Nicolas glanced out the window and something foreign caught his eye, slowly undulating in and out with the waves. It hadn't been there earlier, and it wasn't small enough to be driftwood. It seemed bigger than any animal roaming the island, too. It was—"

Jesus Christ. No.

Nicolas sprinted out of the house, forgetting shoes, forgetting a jacket. He slowed when he hit the beach, but his momentum didn't give as he cast aside his prior annoyance with her and focused only on willing his body to move faster.

By the time he reached her, his lungs were on fire. Her long body was folded nearly in half, hair swimming out around her head in jagged, fiery waves. Nicolas was terrified to flip her around, fearing her dead, knowing she was dead, but then was doing it anyway. Her head flopped back, hitting the wet sand with a *thwap* as it bounced off the packed sand. Her eyes were closed, and her mouth, unlike the last time he'd found her on the shore, was a grotesque shade of purple.

Nicolas straddled her, tilting her head back to begin the sloppiest CPR in the history of mankind. He'd taken a course once, in junior high, but spent the entire time making sexy poses with the mannequin. Glimpses of that day came back to him, and he paired this with the knowledge he'd gleaned from movies and television.

Every few breaths, he beat on her chest, and each time, streams of frothy water spewed from her mouth. He kept up the breathing, compressions, over and over and over. Everything he'd felt before, about her being an unwanted nuisance, about wishing she'd never come, disappeared. She was victim of something he'd been too self-absorbed to save her from, and the burgeoning realization he could have prevented this rose with him him, a horrible blackness.

This is my fault.

His heart finally caught up to his mind, as he began to understand his efforts were in vain. She'd likely been gone a while. He released her head and let it fall softly on the sands, and climbed off, helpless, feeling. nothing but the cold, piercing blade of his own selfishness.

He curled up next to her, the waves tickling his feet as the tide rolled in. Mercy would never feel this again. He closed his eyes, his breaths shallow, sad, scared. It was one thing for his selfishness to cause harm to himself, but to cost someone their life? Was his life so important? He didn't value it anyway, as he'd come here to end it.

He wanted to lay with her, and let the water sweep him out to sea, his life as forfeit as he'd treated hers.

10- MERCY

*M*ercy was surprised to realize she felt terrible.

She'd known the sight of her lying near death would stir something in him, but in all her searching of his thoughts, she'd not anticipated in him this engulfing sense of failure. She'd predicted guilt, not passion. Not grief.

It was time to end the charade and wake up, putting him out of his misery. She did not wish to see him prostrate with sorrow at her hands.

She opened her eyes, gasping, coughing the seawater out of her lungs. Though she couldn't die from lowering her body temperature, or the simulated drowning, the expulsion of seawater was painful. She felt him stiffen and then shoot bolt upright from beside her, toppling over backward. When he sat forward again, she had full view of his face. Shock. Relief. Happiness.

"Mercy," he whispered, reaching out to touch her face, trying desperately to gauge the reality of what he was seeing. She suppressed a smile at his joy. Perhaps this Child of Man did have some redeeming qualities.

"I'm... alive?" she feigned. She didn't enjoy acting. It was tedious, inefficient, and beneath her. She ached to get on with it, but had to remind herself one misstep could nullify centuries of planning. *I am Yours in the Flames.*

"Thank *God!*" Nicolas exclaimed, reaching for her in jagged, desperate motions, first touching her face, then pulling away. She sensed his innate discomfort with intimacy.

"Why did you save me?" The question rose unplanned to Mercy's mind and lips simultaneously. Not part of the act.

He laughed out loud in chirpy, nervous excitement. When he spoke, his accent was thick and heavy, unlike the smooth, lyrical intonations back at the house. "What kind of question is that? How could I not?"

"You didn't seem terribly concerned about it earlier," Mercy noted, unable to bite back some of her distaste. She had to be careful. She needed his sympathy, not his anger.

Nicolas looked properly contrite. "I'm not used to being in situations where I have to make tough decisions." *Or decisions at all,* she could almost hear him thinking. He suddenly perked up. "Jesus. We really need to get you to a hospital."

No need for that. "No! You can't call the hospital. He'll be expecting that."

"But..." Definitely not a planner, this one. He had no idea what to do. "You need medical attention, Mercy. Immediately. What would you have me do?"

"Don't," she started to say but was silenced by very real shivers. It was excruciating to be this cold, as a Daughter of Emyr. Nicolas placed both of his hands on her arms, in an awkward attempt to warm her. "Sorry, I mean, don't you have a way to get us off this island? A way that doesn't involve people knowing?"

"Yeah, but... I really think you need to see a doctor *now.*"

"As long as I stay awake, I'll be fine," she soothed, making things up. It worked in her favor that he was rather clueless. "If I had brain damage, we'd know already, right? I'm talking to you, aren't I?" It was much like coaxing a child. A sweet, albeit hand-some, child who only wants to please but isn't sure how.

Nicolas thought about it for a moment. It was apparent he was waiting for the right decision to come to him. The confidence in her voice, and a not-so-subtle persuasive nudge, finally overrode his concerns. "Okay. Okay. God help us, I hope you're right," he said breathlessly, kneeling to help her stand. She slipped her arm around his neck, weakly, but with enough effort to not draw the matter out too long.

"Thank you," Mercy said, as she struggled to rise, making it apparent her legs were wobbly from the experience. She'd have to remind herself she was supposed to be recovering. If she suddenly broke into a sprint, there'd be some explaining to do.

They struggled back to the house, Mercy giving him a little more trouble than she needed to, not wanting there to be any doubt about what he'd seen. When they reached the house, Nicolas went to get her a change of clothes, likely the same ones she had borrowed before, and into a warm bath. He looked troubled as he asked if she'd be all right in the bath alone while he made the arrangements, plainly not wanting to stay but also not wanting to find her drowned a second time.

"The warm water will help keep me alert," Mercy assured. "Don't worry, I'll call for help if I need it."

The relief on his face was palpable as he went to arrange for their departure.

The warm water felt heavenly on Mercy's skin after being jostled in the cold ocean for the couple of hours it took him to notice. She could slow, and even stop, her metabolism and heart rate when needed, in order to withstand a lot more than Men could, but it wasn't easy and the impact lingered. She was exhausted, but was also the imbecile who'd told him staying awake was key to her being okay, so she had no choice but to remain alert. She only hoped it wasn't too far, and that the accommodations included a warm and comfortable bed.

About thirty minutes later, Nicolas came in to check on her. She was resting her eyes, not sleeping, but at the sound of his footsteps she opened them so as not to scare him. He told her the arrangements had been made, and a helicopter would be arriving within the hour to take them to an open field near New Orleans. From there, they'd drive.

"New Orleans?" Excellent, that was only a few hours away.

He shrugged. "It's where I live. Well, near New Orleans, anyway. Vacherie. My family has a big plantation outside of the city, very private, and we won't be bothered. When I say my family, I really mean just me. I live there by myself."

"Where is your family?" Mercy asked.

He looked uncomfortable as he answered. "Mostly dead. I have a couple half-sisters. Aunts, uncles, cousins. Whatever."

What he didn't say, but thought, was, *everyone expects me to have a child, but that's never gonna happen. Adrienne wants nothing to do with the estate. Someone has to be the heir.*

The location—the seclusion, no family, no one to disturb us —was perfect. Her Inner Voice confirmed this. "I look forward to seeing your home. Thank you for your help, Nicolas."

"I just wanna make sure you're okay. Then I'll help you get back on your feet, and off to wherever it is you wanted to spend your next life."

"I appreciate that," Mercy replied with her best effort at sincerity, followed by a gentle nudge once more. Nicolas obligingly left to allow her some final privacy.

"Our Father of Light, Our Father of Fire," she whispered, once she knew Nicolas was far away.

11 - NICOLAS

*T*he helicopter was late to arrive, which made Mercy anxious, him nervous, in light of all that had happened.

Mercy's eyes fluttered, threatening to close, as she sat in the seat across from him. This kept his heart in a panic, but she'd catch herself when she noticed him growing startled.

She hadn't said the words, but he knew what he'd seen in the waves. She had no bruising, no other signs of struggle. This wasn't the work of her horrible husband, whom Nicolas now believed was real, her story true. Nothing about any of it made sense, but he'd stopped doubting, at least, that she was in trouble.

Nicolas had never known anyone who'd taken their own life. He recalled, fleetingly, a girl from high school who'd done it, but he didn't actually *know* her. His only memory of her was this final one, and the assemblies and memorials which followed.

Seeing Mercy, rolling in the surf amidst her desperation, had finally opened his own eyes to the reality of what he'd planned to do. He could relate to her helplessness, that imperfect idea that nothing could change, could get better. If they had nothing else in common, this bound them in terrible understanding.

But the image of her lying there, painfully still, wouldn't leave his mind. His unquenchable angst and utter uselessness as he understood she was beyond saving. He couldn't help imagining Ana finding him like that. Or Oz. There was no crime they could, or had, committed against him deserving of that agony.

The experience shifted things between Nicolas and Mercy, in a way he had yet to define. He didn't know what he felt for her. It wasn't quite fondness, but something bordering between responsibility and compassion. He'd refused to help her when she needed him, but now he had a second chance to do the right thing. And he would.

"I also arranged for someone to meet us at my home," Nicolas ventured. "There's, uh, something I need to tell you."

Mercy immediately tensed, as if sensing a trap. It wasn't a trap, but it would sound like one, though she didn't have the luxury of being selective at this point."

"I come from a very interesting family," he began, with guarded hesitation. Mercy still wore the look of a startled cat, and he didn't suppose what he was about to say next would help much. "We can, well, do things most people can't."

"I don't understand," Mercy said slowly. He sensed her trust in him was fast waning.

"Ah, fuck it." Nicolas sighed. *Why not?* "My Aunt Colleen is a healer, okay? Meaning, she can put her hands on you and *bam*, you'll be good as new."

A slow grin spread across Mercy's face. Her hands relaxed. "Oh, is that all?"

"I'm serious," Nicolas insisted. *Fucking hell, she thinks I'm screwing with her.* "I mean, she's a doctor, a legitimate doctor, but she's also a healer." He was rambling, like a raving lunatic. He should have just said, *yes, my Aunt Colleen is a doctor.*

He opted to leave it at that. If he told her about the Deschanel Magi Collective, she might jump out of the helicopter. Aunt Colleen and the other healers were the least interesting members of *that* group.

"Oh, I believe you," Mercy returned in a soft, but mocking voice. His expression was no doubt mutinous because she quickly added, "I do! I've seen some pretty weird things in my life, too, Nicolas. A healer barely even makes the list."

Interesting. A lawyer's wife from New York had seen *pretty weird things*. Right. Well, there were few things weirder than what went down at a Deschanel family picnic.

"Anyway," Nicolas continued, still a little miffed at her flippant tone, "once Colleen gives you a clean bill of health, she'll go on her merry way and we can figure out what happens next."

"Yes... what happens next," Mercy said, her voice drifting off and away from the conversation. He wondered what she was thinking, and then realized he probably didn't want to know.

With women, you never did.

THE PILOT ESTIMATED NINETY MINUTES TO VACHERIE. NICOLAS intended to keep watch over Mercy, but couldn't force himself to stay awake. He'd been running on pure adrenaline, and the crash was imminent.

As he started to drift off, he was flooded with the catapulting sensation of someone lifting him upside down and spinning him in fast circles. Just as he was certain he'd throw up, the spinning abruptly stopped.

But he was no longer on the helicopter.

He was seeing through Ana's eyes again.

Ana helped Jonathan take down the Christmas tree, in their living room. She was up on the ladder, carefully plucking decorations from the top. When she handed him the star, he ripped it from her hands and heaved it into the box, shattering it, before he stormed from the room.

Ana turned away, biting back tears. The living situation—having both brothers under one roof—was unbearable. The tension was rising to levels that would inevitably result in something far more valuable than a Christmas star being shattered. The ticking time bomb of their household had already gone off once. Now that the secret was out, it felt more like a minefield.

Finn startled her by easing up behind and slipping his arms around her. The smile rising to her lips was natural, and sincere. She melted into him, forgetting about Jon, and her problems, momentarily. His lips were warm and comforting, and then warmth quickly turned to fear as she realized how easily she could lose this. Fear progressed to sadness, because she could no longer pretend walking away wasn't an option.

She had to leave. For him. For Jon.

Flipping, turning again. Then, swiftly, Nicolas was in the kitchen. He pivoted, confused, and as he gazed toward the living room, toward where Finn was caressing Ana. And then, he understood. He was Jon now, seeing through his eyes.

Jon moved toward the sink, gripping the ceramic tub so hard his fingers were a painful shade of white. He gripped even harder to stop the trembling, but his breaths were coming quicker and more ragged by the moment.

Though it was torture, Jon couldn't stop his eyes from wandering back to the living room. Ana was buried in Finn's arms, his hands running the length of her back... her ass. She tilted her head and Finn kissed her. This wasn't the lustful indiscretions littering Finn's history. Finn was in love with her.

Jon needed to get out of the house. To leave. To move away and never return. It wasn't possible to live in the same house with her when she looked at Finn with such love in her eyes. Jon's own love of Ana had festered into hatred, and knowing this was a childish and irrational reaction didn't make it any less real.

. . .

"Nicolas!" Mercy shook him, yelling over the loud din of the blades. "We're here!"

Nicolas squinted, clearing the sleep away, but it hadn't been much of a nap anyway. Unexplained visions had a way of of nullifying restfulness.

As with the last episode, the wave of nausea was so overwhelming he had to bury his head between his knees. Panting, he closed his eyes, channeling his focus into regaining his bearings. *Nicolas. I'm Nicolas. Not Ana. Not Jon. Focus.*

"Motion sickness?" Mercy asked.

"Something like that," he muttered against his knee.

The chopper blades and the hiss of the engine were nearly deafening as they exited, and it was a relief to climb into the silence of the long, black town car.

Ahh, the bayou. The smell of the Mighty Miss.

They'd be home soon.

As the car eased on to River Road, the sinking feeling in Nicolas' stomach returned. The last time anyone in his family left for Deschanel Island, they hadn't returned. When he'd set out on New Year's Day, he hadn't expected to, either.

He weighed updating Oz on the latest development. When Nicolas' sister, Adrienne, came back from the dead, with no memory of who she was, Oz secretly harbored her so she could gain her bearings. This situation wasn't the same, but there were enough similarities. Oz liked to preach about doing the right thing, but his moral compass was tuned somewhere between being a "unrelenting rule follower," and "savior of tragic women."

Oz would be both a bad, and a good choice, if Nicolas could set aside the betrayal. Good, because he would want to do whatever he could to help Mercy. Despite what he'd said in his emails, he wouldn't have called the cops, either, just as he hadn't called the cops when Adrienne showed up, wide-eyed and desperate.

But Oz was also a man who went to dark places, where personal sacrifice was inevitable. Nicolas was well aware of the price Oz had paid, mentally, emotionally, for helping Adrienne. The Oz he knew now was a little bit less than the Oz he'd known before Adrienne. His big heart would eventually be the end of him.

Nicolas shouldn't care about that, when Oz hadn't given much thought to Nicolas' broken heart. But he could only process one thing at a time, and currently that one thing was Mercy, and how to best help her.

Aunt Colleen would be waiting at *Ophélie*. Though Nicolas was about as invested in his family as he was in their real estate dealings, he loved his aunt. She was smart, and reasonable. She'd stepped up to run the family when her two older siblings, Nicolas' father and Uncle Augustus, both failed to, in their own ways. He could almost overlook the fact she actually believed in the supposed Deschanel Curse.

Nicolas texted Oz instead of calling, because he wasn't sure exactly what he wanted to say, and how much to say in front of Mercy. Unlike their texts from the island, he didn't bother with long explanations. Mercy was already suspicious of him.

Need 2 talk. Important. U avail in an hour?

Within a minute, Oz responded. Good old reliable Oz. *We should be done with dinner by then. Is it urgent?*

Kinda. Not life or death but need u. Can u be at O in an hour?

Make it 90 minutes. We're reading bedtime stories to the kids.

Alright, Mr. Family Man.

Oz added a couple minutes later: *Will try to be there sooner if possible.*

"What are you doing on there?" Mercy nodded at his phone.

"On my phone?"

"Yeah." She frowned. "Your phone."

"I was texting a friend."

"Texting," Mercy repeated, and though she said no more, she seemed to give this word serious contemplation, whispering it once more as she closed her eyes.

12- MERCY

*N*icolas hadn't told her he'd engaged the help of his friend, but he didn't need to. She read it in his thoughts. And really, this worked out better, because she needed to stall him long enough for the Grand Ascension to complete. Her Inner Voice assured her *Ophélie* was the key; that this plantation of his was exactly where she needed to be. The only thing that could go wrong now would be Nicolas rushing her away before the process completed.

Nicolas' plantation was exactly what she needed. Secluded. Large. Easy to hide, to find privacy when the moment finally arrived. If all went well, in a few days he'd simply think she'd run away. She might even leave a note, thanking him, telling him not to worry. Yes, that would be best. Better if he had closure.

On their way to *Ophélie*, he kept looking at her as if on the verge of asking some great question. Instead, he settled on pleasantries. Did she want a drink? Did she need help staying awake? It was almost endearing, though if she remained with him long enough, that sentiment would fade away. She only needed him to stay this way long enough.

A few days. A week. Hopefully less. But soon.

His confession about his aunt was mildly endearing. She'd considered feigning shock, but her creative energies were all focused on something more important, so instead, she put his mind at ease.

Healers. It was true Mercy had seen far more interesting and bizarre phenomena in her long lifeline, but she'd never met more than a handful of Men with legitimate abilities. Interestingly, Nicolas didn't seem to possess any of his own, and she'd never have suspected it anyway, so her thoughts would've been laid bare, unprotected. Fortunate for her that he'd missed whatever gifts were bestowed on his relatives.

His aunt, on the other hand. She might see something peculiar, such as the lack of tissue death, or other missing symptoms. Mercy hoped she was like other magical healers, sensing general ailments rather than specifics. The fact that she was a medical doctor complicated things, because, in Mercy's experiences, the smarter ones could always tell something was a little bit *off* with Empyreans.

But Mercy, unlike Colleen, was expecting this. She could prepare for this, with a little nudge. And then Mercy could settle in for her long sleep. One long enough that Nicolas would no doubt worry, once again.

THE LIMO SLOWED AS THEY TURNED INTO A LONG DRIVEWAY AND approached Nicolas' home. Home, though, didn't do the place proper justice. It was one of the largest plantations Mercy had seen, with beautiful Ionic columns running from ground to roof, and a balcony wrapping the entire house. On either side of the driveway were large, ornate gardens, interspersed with live oaks and banana trees. All of this was blocked from road view by a thicket of thicker trees and shrubs.

Nicolas caught her gaze and smiled, the first genuine smile

he'd offered her. "This is *Ophélie*," he said, with a great deal more pride than she'd have expected.

"You grew up here?"

"Born and raised," he said. "It's been in my family since before the Civil War. I don't have a clue about the details, sorry. My friend knows more than I do." Nicolas laughed. "That dude knows more about my family, and this house, than most Deschanels."

Another version of Mercy wished she could ask this friend about the house. It was that same Mercy who'd once toured museums, studied ancient ruins, taking in culture like it was water. She didn't really know that individual anymore, though. None of it mattered; it was all of such little consequence compared to what awaited.

"Do you do tours?"

"Oh, no," Nicolas said answered. "But, we do maintain proper preservation, and the historical society comes out and does their shit every year, so we do our part." He paused and then added, "We used to allow tours on Halloween, as part of the haunted plantation circuit. But, there's really nothing haunted about *Ophélie*, so I stopped it after the family died."

Mercy had a hard time believing no ghost had ever haunted the old, beautiful mansion.

There was another vehicle at the end of the driveway. A large, black car, nearly camouflaged in the dark shroud of night. It came in and out of view against the backdrop of flickering gaslights on the long porch.

Nicolas confirmed this was his aunt.

Colleen Deschanel was a very handsome woman, in her middle age. She had chestnut brown hair pulled back in a loose, but exquisitely neat, bun, and came across as quite formidable in her tan linen suit and four-inch heels. Mercy's early attempts to read her mind were blocked. This wasn't surprising. She struck Mercy as the kind of woman who was always prepared for anything, including the rogue telepathic reading. If wisdom was a scent, she was fragrant with it.

Another woman stood off to the side, near a large oak tree. Younger. Nicolas' age. She wore a thin sweater and jeans, and her long, almost white hair fell to the small of her back. Same almond-shaped, blue eyes as Colleen, same full mouth.

Ahh, yes. Mother and daughter.

Colleen offered a firm handshake. Nicolas then turned and introduced her to the flax-haired waif, Amelia.

Unlike her mother, who exuded overflowing confidence, there was something almost menacing about Amelia. Was she a healer too? Why was she here? Mercy couldn't read her mind, either.

"Will this take long?" Mercy asked Aunt Colleen sweetly.

The woman smiled, but something in her eyes twinkled. A hint of something else. Distrust? "Why no, I don't believe so," she replied as she looped her arm through Mercy's. She smelled of lavender and verbena. A real Southern belle.

"How are things? Uncle Noah?" Nicolas asked, making unnecessary small talk.

"Splendid," Colleen replied. "I don't suppose you've spoken with Ana in the past few days?"

He shook his head. "Why?"

She pressed her lips together, studying her nephew. "We couldn't pry you two apart, and now you're ignoring her."

"Clearly, I've had some things on my mind," he said with a flippant nod Mercy's direction.

"Yes, well, men *are* historically wretched at multitasking," Colleen agreed with a nod. "But please consider getting over yourself and reaching out. She's been having a time of it lately, and when I saw her a few days ago—"

"A few days ago? She's here?"

Colleen laughed with a small shake of her head. "Of course not. I visited her in Maine."

"Why'd you visit her in Maine?" Nicolas looked as if a meteor had been dropped into the earth several feet away and he couldn't decide whether to investigate or run for his life.

"Can I not visit my niece?" Colleen challenged his question with a slightly raised eyebrow.

"WELL, MY HANDIWORK ISN'T NEEDED HERE. I'VE FOUND absolutely nothing requiring my assistance."

No surprise there. Mercy thanked Colleen for taking the time to come out on such short notice, and for being so gracious.

"Any friend of Nic's is a friend of ours," Colleen said, mimicking the same saccharine falsity Mercy had offered her in the driveway. Her Uptown drawl only drew the effect tighter.

"I donate enough to the hospital," Nicolas quipped.

Colleen chucked good-naturedly with a small wave of the hand, but it was clear from her body language she knew something was amiss. Mercy studied her as best she could without drawing attention. Her affection for her nephew was genuine.

It was Mercy she was wary of.

With a start, it occurred to Mercy the woman may have tried to read her mind and found it blocked. Blocking required training, and more, knowledge of the need to employ such a defense in the first place. No wonder she was suspicious.

As they started their goodbyes, Amelia asked to speak with Nicolas alone. He gave his cousin a side-long, nervous glance and then followed her to the side of the house, leaving Colleen and Mercy alone.

Colleen's smile faded. She tapped her heel against the gravel, glancing at her watch.

"How did you meet my nephew?" she asked finally. Mercy stifled a laugh. That wasn't the question she really wanted to ask.

"I was renting one of the houses on Deschanel Island," she lied cheerily. This was more than an act; it was a carefully constructed game of chess. Her move.

"Mmm," Colleen said, as she considered her next query carefully. "I thought he suspended rentals for the winter." Her smile was thin and forced, but there was that glint again in her eye.

"He must have changed his mind," Mercy replied, smiling through gritted teeth.

"Indeed," Colleen remarked, still studying her. *She knows something is off. The question is, what will she do about it?*

A few minutes later, Amelia and Nicolas stormed back. Amelia was flustered, and Nicolas looked angry.

"Thank you. We're done," he said, his tone unnecessarily abrupt as he turned toward the house.

"Please do call us if you need anything else at all," Colleen encouraged, giving Mercy one final assessment. Satisfied—or not—she pivoted on her heels and glided back toward her Mercedes. Amelia leveled her eyes on Mercy as well before following her mother.

Mercy was dying to know what they'd talked about that put him in such a foul mood. It shouldn't be hard to find out.

Nicolas watched as their car faded down the driveway in a cloud of dust and moonlight. His expression was troubled. As usual, his thoughts were a swampland, and Mercy struggled to glean anything specific.

"Nicolas?"

"Huh?" He wasn't there, with her. He was elsewhere, possibly still engaged in conversation with his strange cousin. "Oh, sorry. You must be exhausted."

"I am. Where can I get some rest for a bit?"

Nicolas led her up the stairs, to a large bedroom suite. He mumbled something about it belonging to his parents, once, but she missed most of what he said, because she realized this was *perfect*. Spacious. Quiet. She would have no problems recharging here.

"Thank you again." She rewarded him with a smile.

13- NICOLAS

$\mathcal{N}$icolas was relieved to have some time to himself.
Amelia had hit a nerve. No, *hit* wasn't strong
enough. She'd trounced on it with all the care and delicacy of a
raging elephant. Empaths. Thank god there weren't that many
of them in the family.

Something isn't right about her, Amelia charged, when she
pulled him aside.

*You're probably picking up on the fact that she's fucking trauma-
tized,* Nicolas snapped, glancing over his cousin's shoulder to
make sure Colleen wasn't giving Mercy a hard time.

Amelia caught his gaze squarely. Her powder blue eyes had
always been a little intense, and he felt it then. *It's more than that,
Nic. What do you know about her?*

Not a whole hell of a lot, he admitted, then quickly added, *But I
know she has a reason to be guarded.*

It's not fear, or even excessive caution, I'm sensing, Amelia
pressed.

Then, what is it your little spidey senses are picking up, Amelia?

She dropped her voice even lower. Her eyes widened.
Nothing, she whispered. *Nothing at all.*

Nicolas had had more than his share of dramatic revelations so he shook his head and walked away, pissed off, but not at her, exactly.

But as Mercy slept upstairs in his parents' old room, Nicolas more carefully considered his brief conversation with Amelia. Level, sensible Amelia. Amelia the empath. Amelia, whose intuition was stronger than nearly any other Deschanel.

Nothing. Nothing at all.

He drained the cognac and poured another.

"She's not what I expected," Oz revealed after Nicolas gave him a quick peek into his parents' bedroom.

"In what way?"

"She's stunning."

"And?"

"And, I can't imagine you being such an asshole to someone this hot," Oz finished.

"You seem to have forgotten my hot piece of ass rule has caveats about baggage and tears."

Oz laughed, though there was concern in his face. Had been since he met Nicolas at the door. "Baggage or no, I'm shocked she didn't turn you into a hero." He studied him. "Well, I suppose, in the end, she did."

"That's more your wheelhouse, dude," Nicolas pointed out.

Nicolas told him everything that had transpired over the past days. When he was done, Oz said one word: *Wow.*

"Wow? That's all you have to say?"

"Was there something specific you were after, Nicolas?" Oz asked.

Nicolas. He never called him Nicolas, and when he did, he always used that condescending, annoying parent voice. "No, *Colin,*" Nicolas snipped, returning the favor, "but knowing your proclivity to offer opinions on matters involving damsels in distress, I expected you to have considerably more feedback."

"Okay, fine. I probably wouldn't have called the cops, either. I also can't really fault you for bringing her here. It's clearly a stupid move on many levels, but it's totally an Oz move, and I can appreciate that for what it is. What I can, however, fault you for is waiting so long to make a decision. She could've died, and if she had, you know you'd have some culpability in that."

Why do you think I'm helping her now? "So, what would you do? Now? If you were me?"

"Well, if it were me," Oz said in a way that meant, *I'm not you but since I'm here you're going to do what I say anyway,* "while she rests, I'd investigate her husband."

"Investigate her husband?" Nicolas repeated, dumbfounded. This hadn't even occurred to him.

"Yes, investigate him. Find out anything we can. Who he is, does he have a record, any public notices? Does he use social networking, or anything else that might give you some clue to his personality?" He paused, thinking. "I assume you know his name?"

"Yes," Nicolas hedged. "She gave me that much. But you didn't hear her tell her story, Oz. The whole thing sounds like bullshit, even if her fear doesn't. She was smart enough to fake her own death. Who can say how much of what she told me was even true? I mean, who the fuck names their kid Mercy?"

"You're probably right, but it's all we have. Even in a completely fabricated story there's bound to be some shred of truth." He must have detected the disgust in Nicolas' face, because he quickly added, "Not to be nosy, Nic, but to help her. We can't count on her for much right now, so information is the best tool available. You understand?"

He did. But he still didn't like it. "What happens if we find nothing? Then what?"

"Then we'll have to make do with what we have. But I'd sure

SARAH M. CRADIT

as hell like to know what this guy is actually capable of, because if he figured out where her little bag was hidden, don't you think he might've noticed she left the island on a helicopter? He's clearly resourceful, and I'd like to know more about who we're dealing with here."

"If he's even real."

"We have to assume he is, because it's all we have."

"And if we do find something?"

"If we don't think he's an immediate threat, we can take our time to help her plan and get her where she needs to go. If we think he's on our trail already, then we need to figure things out fast and sort the rest out later," Oz said.

"You're so adorable when you talk like this," Nicolas teased. It was easy to forget what he'd done, sometimes.

"Ah, go fuck yourself."

"I just might. It's been a while."

"Well, if you find the need to go procure yourself an escort, by all means do so, but do it fast. We have work to do," Oz said, only half-joking.

"Nah, I'll just call up your mom."

They could do this all night.

Nicolas had Condoleezza put on some coffee. When he returned to the study, Oz was busily ticking away on his laptop.

"I have one of the juniors starting the research, and he's going to report back to me hourly with everything he finds," Oz said. "You might remember my little cousin, Quillan? Patrick's son? He's recently graduated law school."

"Aww, you have your own little bitch now. Remember when you were the little bitch, Ozzy?"

"Yes, but unfortunately, you still are one," he retorted awkwardly.

"You can do better than that," Nicolas insisted.

70

"I know," he conceded, and Nicolas saw there was more than worry for him on Oz's face.

"Everything okay?" Nicolas asked, despite that he sort of enjoyed Oz's discomfort. He'd invited him here, but that didn't mean he'd forgiven him. He needed him, that's all.

Oz's expression darkened, and Nicolas could visibly see the debate raging within his mind about whether to say anything, or not. Finally, he spoke.

"I wasn't going to tell you, but I may as well. Adrienne got pregnant again, but she lost the baby a couple nights ago." The devastation on his face appeared as soon as the words left his lips.

Empathy kicked Nicolas squarely in the chest. "Wow. God, I'm sorry," he said and laid a hand on his forearm. He *was* sorry. This was bigger than the shit with Ana. "You should've called."

"What could you have done? It's just something we have to deal with." Oz dismissed his pity with a frustrated wave of his hand. Nicolas knew they'd been trying for a third child. After Christian was born, Adrienne had developed some medical condition Nicolas didn't understand, and they'd told her she could never have children again. She tried anyway. The whole family tried swaying her into allowing Colleen, or one of the other healers, to help her, but when Adrienne got her memory back, the craziness of who they were had stayed buried. Fearfully, she refused to have anything to do with it.

"I shouldn't have brought you into this mess," Nicolas apologized. "I had no idea, Ozzy. Go home."

Oz shook his head, falling back in his chair. "Maybe I'm terrible for saying this, but I was almost praying for a distraction. Being in that house…" He held his breath and then blew it out in one terrible gust. "Anne is with her, and I think maybe that's better right now. I'm not good for Adrienne when I'm… like this."

Nicolas winced, understanding. When you mixed a brooding Oz with a brooding Adrienne, the result was often toxic.

"I understand. But if at some point you feel you need to go, don't be a martyr, just go. Okay?"

"Okay," he agreed.

They sat in silence until the message came in from Quillan.

"Well?"

Oz tapped the screen of his laptop. "I had him search Mercy first, since we know what she looks like and can confirm her identity easier. We find her, finding the husband becomes an easier task," Oz explained. Nicolas waved his hand in impatience, urging him to get to the point. "So, I had him search for every female Christensen in New York with a first name similar to Clementyn or Mercy. I asked him to pull every one between the ages of twenty and forty, and to try every possible spelling of the first and last names. I then directed him to send us pictures of all of the women who met that description."

"And?"

"He emailed me three hundred and twenty pictures for us to look through."

"He can't do this shit for us?"

"No, Nicolas, he doesn't know what she looks like," Oz scolded, as if speaking to a child who'd been told something for the hundredth time. "And anyway, he put them into a slideshow, so it shouldn't take us long at all to flip through them."

"Fuck's sake," Nicolas sighed, but moved his chair so he could see the screen. Oz was right, it didn't take long at all. But none of them were her.

"I don't understand," Nicolas said. "Why isn't she here?"

Oz twisted his lips together. "She may have a driver's license in another state. She might still use her maiden name, which we don't have. More than likely, as you said, she lied to you," he speculated.

"Could we maybe try some marriage records? Search for

Andrew Christensen? She said she went to both New York University and Yale."

Oz stared at him. "You could've mentioned the colleges before." He went to message Quillan back.

"Whatever," Nicolas said, still proud at his contribution.

"Do you happen to know how long she lived in New York? Is she from there, moved there recently? The farther back we go, the harder it will be to make sense of the results."

Nicolas shook his head.

"It's fine," he said. "We'll go with this for now."

Several minutes later, Quillan came back with full results. "Twelve marriages match the criteria. Potentially."

Once again, they came up empty-handed. "I don't get it."

"Let me try a couple other things," Oz suggested, tempering their disappointment by putting Quillan back to work. But when Quillan returned, neither option produced any results.

"Nic." Oz folded his hands. "She's lying to you about *something*. Maybe we could go talk to her, go ask—"

"No," Nicolas said, firm. "She'll think I'm a dick if I tell her we spent the past few hours researching her. She didn't want me to know for a reason. I need to respect that."

"First of all," Oz said smartly, "you *are* a dick. And second of all, she lost the right, to at least some extent, to such privacy when she wrapped you up into this mess of hers. If she really wants your help, we need a little information."

"We can help her without it, Oz. And that's final."

"Then I have a feeling we're in for a world of trouble," he said, with a slow shake of the head.

"If it comes to that, I'll make sure you're far enough away not to catch any shit to the face."

"I'm not sure you can make that guarantee," Oz said, "but we're in this now and we have to see it through, for better or worse."

14- MERCY

*M*ercy slept. Her vessel required it. She was only vaguely aware of the men downstairs worrying over her, but she couldn't ignore her Inner Voice. Not satisfied to whisper suggestions any longer, it was nearly screaming them in her head. *Rest! Wait! Soon!* Well, she was no stranger to *rest*, and *waiting* was a cruel, but familiar, mistress. But *soon...* that was a promise her Voice had yet to keep.

In the beginning, she dreamed of the rolling green hills and valleys of the fjords. Farjhem was nestled between two glaciers in the far north of Norway, but the Empyreans saw all of the Nordic lands as their playground. Where Men sought to cram as many activities as possible into their limited lives, Empyreans were not bound by mortality. Lying in the tall grass, daydreaming and singing, were far more common activities than traveling the world or jumping from hobby to hobby. There were even some who spent hundreds of years in one spot, never moving. Full of joy, hope, idealism, and the innocence only the young can truly possess.

Not Mercy. Even as a Youth, she was always moving, always seeking that next thrill, or adventure. From the moment the words "Grand Ascension" fell from the Scholars' lips, she sought to make herself worthy. While in awe of the elder Empyreans with their chromatic locks and cool gazes, she had no desire to be one of them. No desire to age, or to line the tree trunk of her life with unique experiences. She meditated daily, prayed daily, to be deemed worthy of an early transformation.

All around her, she absorbed everyday things as signs her time was approaching. That she had passed the tests. Aidrik the Wise made his pleas for her to slow down and enjoy the process. At first, she found his concern endearing, but over time fondness grew into resentment. She would no longer surround herself with those like him, who sought to clip her wings when her destiny was to soar.

One of the first signs came when she was very young. It was not long after the Romans—once so enlightened, filled with wisdom to share with the world—crucified that kind and benevolent Christ child. She was in Rome when Peter came to build the foundations for his great church. But it would be many years before the Children of Men heeded Peter's words.

She sat near the banks of the Tiber, watching as they built the mausoleum of Hadrian, later known as *Castel Sant'Angelo.* The dusty orange haze of the filthy city rose with the sun, and the scents of sewage, sweat, and poverty filled her nostrils. Several feet away, a crow landed on the rotting corpse of a dog, long dead. Instead of pecking at the carcass though, the bird dropped dead right on the hind end. As she looked away, her eyes caught a bright flash of fiery light, building, expanding.

Refocusing, Mercy saw there was only a black and silver dust where the crow had fallen, but above, a large, flaming avian so brilliant in color and stature her eyes burned. The Phoenix. The sign of her people, of Our Father Emyr, and of the Ascension. She wanted to shield her eyes, but it seemed an affront to this vision, this *gift* which had been bestowed upon her. She knew, beyond doubt, she had been chosen. Her time was near.

That was 136 Ano Domini. Nearly two thousand years had come and gone since, and she still walked among Men. If Aidrik could see her now, she wondered if he would console or counsel her. But of course, Aidrik was long gone. Ascended many years past. Though they had not parted well, one of her few regrets was not seeing him once more before he moved on to the arms of Our Father, Emyr.

Voices crept into her rest. Nicolas and his friend, the kind Oz. Nothing coherent, just random strings of concern and errant attempts at chivalry. The men and their fretting seemed so small and insignificant to Mercy. Yet, she could not pull her mind fully away from their attempts at kindness. She took an odd, unexpected comfort in their presence. Clearly, this was one of the side effects of slipping away.... this *softness*.

Emyr must have a sense of humor to place her with these Children of Men in her final days.

Rest. Wait. Soon.

15 - NICOLAS

*N*ight turned to morning. He tried to leave Mercy to her rest, because it seemed that's what she wanted, but she hadn't eaten dinner, and now also refused breakfast.

She'd asked for his help, but Nicolas didn't feel like he was helping her at all.

"Talk to her," Oz suggested, again. After sending Quillan on another pointless scavenger hunt, he'd spent the rest of the morning off and on the phone with Adrienne.

"And say what? How are you enjoying balmy Louisiana? Or perhaps I can ask her what kind of music she listens to, or who she voted for in the last election."

Oz frowned. "It was your decision to bring her here—"

"Wrong," Nicolas corrected, "I never asked for any of this."

"My point being," he continued, with emphasis, "this is your home. She's a guest and you suck at playing host. Even if we don't have the facts, we know she's been through at least *one* trauma, with her near-drowning. Waiting for her to come to you is a little unfair."

When Nicolas started to object, Oz added, "Neither one of us expects Quillan to come back with anything useful. Spending time with her might lead to some truth, which will speed up this situation considerably. If nothing else, we can start working on where she wants to go next."

Nicolas hated Oz logic.

He wandered upstairs and paused outside of the room. Hesitantly, he rapped his knuckles on the door.

"I'm awake," Mercy said, from the other side.

She was laying atop the covers, still dressed in the clothes he'd given her on the island. Her face was pale, drained of energy, but otherwise she looked fine.

"I apologize for not being more social," she said, though she didn't sound sorry at all.

"It's more important you rest up and feel better," Nicolas replied, because it seemed like the right thing to say. What he really wanted to do was suggest she come downstairs and pick a flight.

Mercy smiled knowingly. She really had a way of making him wonder if she was inside his head whenever he thought something inappropriate or unchivalrous. "You're kind to worry so much."

Nicolas shrugged.

"You really live here by yourself?" Mercy asked, breaking the awkward silence. She slid to a sitting position and moved to one side of the bed, giving Nicolas invitation to sit next to her.

"Yeah. For the past few years, anyway." He thought, then, of his family. He'd told Mercy *Ophélie* wasn't haunted, but the truth was, sometimes he still felt their presence. Giselle's coquettish giggles. Nathalie's light, dignified steps. Lucienne's soft whispering. His father's booming voice, and his mother's measured words.

Mercy nodded, slowly. "The house rings with the personalities of all its past inhabitants. It's been in your family a long time."

"Yeah," Nicolas said. "There's a ton of history here, which, as

I said, Oz knows more about than me. Some nonsense about a family curse, too."

"A curse?" She raised one curious eyebrow. "That sounds interesting."

"Or like bullshit," he countered. "Deschanels like to place great importance on ourselves. We can't simply have problems, like normal people. No, it has to be some ancient fucking malediction."

"Us? So there are more of you? Other than Colleen and Amelia, of course."

He laughed. He'd forgotten for a moment she wasn't from here. "New Orleans is full of Deschanels. My father had six siblings, and all but one bred like rabbits. And that's to say nothing of all the other offshoot relatives."

"Your cousin, Ana, is the daughter of one of those siblings?" Mercy asked.

Nicolas frowned, slightly, almost positive he'd never mentioned Ana in Mercy's presence. "My father's brother, Augustus. Ana is his only child."

A guilty look crossed Mercy's face, and he was immediately curious again. Perhaps he'd called Ana's name when he was locked in her vision earlier.

Then he remembered, with relief. The conversation with Aunt Colleen, in the driveway.

"And your Aunt Colleen. She's also your father's sibling?" Mercy pressed.

"She is."

"Does he have others?"

Her curiosity confused Nicolas. "Yeah, I mean, there's four of them. There was five, but one died before I was born."

Mercy looked away, thoughtful. "I can't imagine all those siblings. What an experience that must have been."

"How many brothers and sisters do you have?"

"None," she said quickly. There was a remote sadness in her tone, as if reflecting on something long ago.

"Well, you aren't missing much. More headache than they're worth, most of the time." Being an only child sounded awesome. He reminded himself he was there to ferret out information. Siblings were apparently a dead end.

"Still, must be nice to have others to relate to."

"What about your parents? Do they know about this situation with you and your husband?"

Mercy appeared surprised at the question. "No. They're both dead."

"I'm sorry." He resisted the urge to add that parents could be kind of a headache, too.

"It was long ago," Mercy went into her familiar soothing mode, offering a smile. Her smile transformed her entire face from that of a menacing warrior, to the young, kind woman she likely was. "And anyway, I never trouble myself with sad thoughts for long."

My kind of woman! "I'll drink to that," he cheered heartily, and she gave him a funny glance.

"Drink what?"

"Whiskey... cognac... whatever," he said. She still looked confused. "It's an expression. I'm agreeing with you."

Her eyes widened momentarily. "Ahh, I see."

Had she really never heard that before? Nicolas knew it wasn't just a Southern thing. He'd made that same social toast all over the world.

"I know you're not feeling a hundred percent yet, but we should talk about how and when we're going to get you to safety."

Mercy's face was expressionless, but he didn't miss the tight clench of her fists against the bed. "I need some time," she said. Her voice trembled. "Maybe a few days, if that's okay."

"Of course it is," he said quickly, but wished he had the balls to say what he should have: *No, it's not okay. We need to get you out of here before old boy comes knocking on the door.*

"I'm confident he won't find me here," she added, addressing his last thought. Her apparent mind reading was becoming so commonplace he almost forgot to note it.

"I wish I shared your confidence," he replied. Pushing her was insensitive, but waiting was risky.

What would Oz do? All men should ask themselves this question when their backs were against the wall, Nicolas thought. But he already knew the answer before asking the question. He would support her, and do all he could to help. He wouldn't rush her.

Nicolas sighed. "I'll have Oz's office hire some security for the perimeter. So if your husband does show up before we have a chance to send you off, you'll be safe."

Mercy's smile lit up her whole face. Despite not sharing her joy, the smile was so contagious he returned it. "You're my hero," she effused.

Nicolas Deschanel, a goddamn hero.

There was a first time for everything.

WHEN NICOLAS REJOINED OZ DOWNSTAIRS, HE WAS ON THE phone with the firm.

"I know, and I appreciate it. But try harder," Oz said. Moments later: "Fine. I'll be here."

"Bossing your bitch around?" Nicolas asked, taking a seat in his father's high back chair across from him.

Oz ignored the teasing. "As expected, he's still coming up with nothing. Any luck in your conversation?"

"None at all," I replied. "Parents dead. No siblings. Seems confused about basic colloquialisms. Possibly reading my mind."

Oz released a long, tired breath. It was a helpless, uncomfortable sound. "I don't know where to go from here, except to

SARAH M. CRADIT

start making plans for her departure. Maybe a woman's shelter in the area?"

"That's all on the back-burner for a bit," Nicolas said, waving his hand. "Call your bitch back and tell him we need a security detail out on River Road, and around the property perimeter."

"You're serious?"

"Yes, I'm serious, why wouldn't I be?"

Oz leaned forward and his face fell into his hands. "For how long?" he asked, without looking up.

"As long as she needs it."

"You know I can't stay forever, right?" This time he did look up. His eyes were bloodshot. "Adrienne needs me."

"Once the security is in place, go home."

"So be it," he replied, picking up the phone once more.

To protect Mercy's privacy, Nicolas dismissed all the staff, except Richard and Condoleezza. The duo, brother and sister, had been with the Deschanels since before he was born, and were in their seventies now. They were born and raised on the property, and had attended the births of all Deschanels born on the estate in the last fifty or sixty years. Rumor was their grandmother was a mistress of Charles Deschanel II, who would have been Nicolas' great-grandfather. In light of the crazy Deschanel gifts, it made sense. Condoleezza knew about every little thing that went on in the house, always showing up at just the right moment. And Richard was known to close doors from across the house, when his old bones were not up to the trek.

He trusted them both implicitly, and knew, whatever happened, they would remain unfazed and loyal as always.

Security was in place by the evening, but Oz didn't leave.

82

He was still there after Nicolas checked in on Mercy for the night, and when he awoke the next morning.

"Are you just being extra helpful, or avoiding your wife?" Nicolas finally asked.

"Both," he replied. There was something else behind his words, though he couldn't grasp it. "Mostly helpful."

"Go home," Nicolas urged. "If more research is needed, you can do it from New Orleans. There's nothing I can do until she decides to leave, anyway."

"On that topic," he replied, ignoring his request, "maybe keep trying to talk to her?"

Nicolas rolled his eyes, but obediently started toward the stairs. "Yeah, yeah, yeah."

16- AIDRIK

*A*idrik observed the convergence at the large, ivory manor. Never did it cease to amaze him how Men chose to live. More currency led to larger abodes, richer furnishings. For what? Life ended the same way no matter how much space you had to stretch your limbs.

The Empyreans amassed wealth for far different reasons. Security. Survival. It mattered not how powerful a race was if they were the minority upon the earth. Their prosperity was a matter of practicality. Though he had long since shrugged off most teachings of the Senetat, in some things they were still of equal mind.

That Mercy still walked upon the earth baffled Aidrik. The ambiguity of her continued existence was alarming. Once triggered, a Mark was swift to justice. A once comforting talisman became a vessel of horror. It was usually a matter of hours, not days.

He no longer operated under the illusion he could save her. He could not. Her salvation would have been an easy matter had she not been a zealot. Emancipation for Mercy was not as simple as severing a cosmetic mark. Aidrik had removed his own, with less precision than it deserved, the small, jagged scar at his temple a lasting testament to that anger. Yet, he had always known she would refuse the same freedom.

And now, it was activated. Her cells, already dying. Her fate, thus sealed.

He could give her comfort in pending death. A reprieve from the devastating truth of the Mark's malicious purpose, instead swathing Mercy in the knowledge she was loved. Knowing her as he did, it was love she wanted most.

He sheathed Ulfberht. That it had been out, poised for action, was a shock, but only in that it had not been necessary after all. Often instinct alone was his call to action. Since tracking her recently, his instincts had become muddled. There was no immediate threat beyond the infernal magic now sucking life from her very breast.

Days passed since Mercy and her protector entered the manse. Since the other Man had come. What they were doing, Aidrik could not guess. He was not close enough to peruse their thoughts. Yet, curiosity plagued him as he wondered if Mercy was even aware of why she had chosen Nicolas Deschanel to begin with?

Likely, she believed it to be some sort of divine sign from Emyr, perhaps even attributing it to her ridiculous Inner Voice, which was, in fact, *Aidrik's* voice, guiding her. Humorous that she had not discerned the "voice" started in correlation with his "death."

He had been sending her messages for many years now. Guiding her away from danger. Eventually, toward Nicolas.

A belief in coincidence was nearly equal in peril to disregarding instinct. Perhaps Mercy saw her joining with the Deschanel Man as coincidence. But she was wrong. It mattered. Understanding why was still beyond her grasp. Not, though, for long. Aidrik would tell her what she need know most, if time did not remove that opportunity. Not everything, but only that which her heart craved. His parting gift, another damned illusion.

He was drawn to the Deschanels through fate, watching them for over four centuries. It was a secret he could tell no one. A desecration of Empyrean Law.

Had his protection of the Deschanels extended to Mercy, when he led her to Nicolas? It was a possibility.

He gnawed on the last of the nutria. Foul, but filling.

Soon, he would present himself. Knocking upon a wooden threshold was a bizarre custom of Man, but he'd would observe it, to maintain some degree of order.

Time enough. Once Mercy saw his face, hell would unleash.

17- MERCY

*N*icolas' cold assessment of family stuck with Mercy through that evening and into the following day. She'd grown to maturity without siblings or parents, and though she didn't require support, she couldn't see herself so easily discarding it. Nicolas had an entire family at his fingertips and chose to be alone.

Then again, Mercy's latest bout of solitude had lasted more than a century. Maybe the customs of Men had changed since last she walked among them. Perhaps this was now the way of things.

Empyreans were unlike Men in many ways, but the lack of nuclear family was one of the more distinct differences. Due to the toll birthing an Empyrean took on a mother's body, Empyreans could only bear a single child. An attempt at a second resulted in almost certain death, and even those who lived eventually wasted away. To protect their women from themselves, the Eldre Senetat passed an inviolate law.

They needn't have bothered. Most Empyrean women would not endure the process twice for anything in the world.

The other difference in their parenting regime would have been even more shocking to Men, had it ever been revealed. A scientist's dream. For, unlike Men, who came from one father and one mother, Empyreans could have many fathers. Once a female experienced conception, any mates she connected with during the course of her pregnancy resulted in a fusion of their DNA to the growing embryo, called Sveising. The more Sveising fusions, the stronger the Empyrean. Their abilities more acute, more powerful. Their lives, longer. The process resulted in such a clear advantage the Senetat eventually adhered regulations to it, requiring Empyreans to formally apply for Sveising. Going forth without approval was punishable by death, and approval was rarely granted.

This discouraged many Empyreans, and so it became mainly a practice of the royal family and their closest allies. All Empyrean children born to the crown were a result of a carefully orchestrated group consummation, with only the strongest Empyreans chosen to contribute to the child's lineage.

Mercy had three fathers. Her mother was of close relation to the Emperor Aeron, and her petition for Sveising was granted with little resistance. All three of Mercy's fathers were gone now. Two, long since Ascended. The last one, her First Father, executed by the Senetat, alongside her mother.

The parental duties of an Empyrean were limited to shepherding a child into the world, and then leaving them with the venerable Scholars to determine the proper course of their time on Earth. Empyrean children, thus, were never given time to bond with their mothers and fathers; were not taught the importance of familial bonds, because such notions were nonexistent. To an Empyrean, *all* fellow Empyreans were family. No distinction for nuclear family existed.

The time with the Scholars was the closest any came to the idea of a familial coexistence. Empyrean children remained with the Scholars for a hundred years, until the age of spiritual maturity. Their graduation was punctuated by the application of Emyr's Mark and the permissive release to leave Farjhem and run free in the wider world.

Most parents accepted this arrangement. Scholars having been a tradition for several millennia, this was all parents knew. But there were others—like Mercy's—who could not accept the predetermined boundaries. Parents who refused, and insisted upon challenging authority, like heathens.

They'd visit Mercy at the temple gates, to engage her in discourse about what she was learning. This by itself, though uncommon, was not against the rules, but it did raise suspicions. Their visits were closely scrutinized, their behaviors monitored. Before long, they were suspected of impiety, and it was only a matter of time before the accusation of heresy would follow.

That they refused to leave Mercy, leave Farjhem, was an affront to the Senetat and their judicious leadership. Farjhem, though their sanctuary, was not meant for long-term habitation by most Empyreans. Only the royal family, and young Empyreans under Scholarly tutelage, remained for long periods. It was not unusual for a parent to linger for a year or two after the release of their child, to help ease the transition, but much longer than that and the behavior became suspicious and undesirable to the Senetat, the wisest among all Empyreans. Regrettably, Mercy's parents showed no signs of leaving.

It was Mercy who inevitably, and unwittingly, issued their death warrant.

Scholar Saxon, her theology instructor, was especially fond of using Old Aita as a means of making his point. It was also his go-to counterpoint for any question or objection to the lessons he taught. *What do you mean* why? *Do you want to end up like Old Aita?*

Despite Mercy's feverish love for Emyr, even she sometimes

found his use of threats tedious. Faith was strengthened by questions, not weakened.

After a particularly treasonous meeting with her parents, she was emboldened to share what she'd learned from them.

Is it not true Old Aita is in fact very powerful?

Saxon's eyes narrowed. *Powerful? If you would call the wandering of an outcast powerful, though I would argue we have very differing ideas on the meaning!*

The class laughed. All except Mercy. *But... what if Aita* chose *to wander? What if she is doing exactly as she desires?*

Saxon looked around the room, encouraging more cajoling support. This was a being who required an audience to perform, and fed off their energy. *Why, in the name of Our Father, would anyone choose this path for themselves? And where did you even read such a ridiculous thing?* More laughter.

Do we not have free will? Are we not allowed to choose our own path? My father and mother say—

Mercy realized her error as soon as the words left her mouth. From the darkening of Saxon's expression, to the downcast looks of my peers, her folly was revealed. What she had said was blasphemy, and the only thing that saved her from the fate of her parents was her youth. She could not be blamed for their attempts to leave treasonous impressions upon her. She was still young, still absorbing the dogmatic interaction of the Scholars, and her parents' meddling was further emphasis as to why they were not allowed to take an active role in a child's upbringing.

She'd thought—hoped—the Senetat would send her parents to Farskilt, deep in the bowels of Farjhem, in the base of the volcano. Those caught blaspheming the word of Our Father were often assigned there for spiritual rehabilitation. The success rate was a hundred percent. Once sent to Farskilt, an Empyrean never again emerged. Instead, they were cured, and given the gift of Ascension.

But her parents were thought beyond rehabilitation, and

instead, sentenced to death, and an eternity of confusion and hatred. They would not meet the loving arms of Our Father. Not ever.

Mercy watched, with mingled curiosity, horror, and a certain degree of reverence, as their Marks were removed. They bravely faced one another, on the dais, in the middle of the town square. Scholar Saxon was given the honors, as it was tradition the accusing party mete the sentence. He did so with a sadistic relish, seizing the magical blade and slicing slowly and deliberately into their flesh, taking his time with it. As with his classes, he thrived on the energy of his audience. Each cheer made him go slower, and his gaze regularly flickered to what he saw as his adoring fans.

Mercy promised herself she would meet the eyes of her parents before death took hold. She was not given the opportunity to say goodbye, but in hindsight this was a blessing. She had already begun hardening her heart to their subversive ways, and to hold them one last time might have crumbled her resolve.

But her parents refused to meet the eyes of any member of the crowd, choosing instead to focus on each other. As the pain overtook them, and the rotting blackness spread over their bodies, they saw only one another. Their words comforted each other, though no one could hear their whispers over the roar of Saxon's bloodthirsty audience.

Some later whispered of their bravery. Yes, it did take bravery to face your own death. But Mercy knew bravery was not what drove them to be traitors of Emyr, but cowardice, and a startling lack of faith.

Their crime and death was a turning point for her. She stood at a pivotal crossroads, forced to make the biggest choice she would ever make.

Believe in a traitor's teachings, or believe in Emyr. She chose Emyr, and never, ever looked back.

Perhaps Nicolas was not so strange after all, in his defiant dismissal of family. Perhaps Men and Empyrean were not so different, in the end. The bonds of family were merely shackles of confinement, strangling one from their intended destiny.

Maybe Nicolas and I have more in common than I thought.

18- NICOLAS

*T*he third day passed as uneventfully as the preceding two.

Nicolas spent the day upstairs with Mercy, making small talk. She asked him more questions about family, what it was like growing up with a gaggle of sisters. Asked about *Ophélie*, and his friendships with Oz, and Ana. Thankfully, she didn't press further about Ana.

I don't suppose you've spoken with Ana in the past few days?

His attempts to volley similar questions to Mercy led to misdirection and more stilted answers. He wasn't exactly dying to hear her life story, but he did find it suspiciously odd how reluctant she was to share anything.

What she had shared, he now knew, wasn't true. Definitely some of it, perhaps all of it. What of her estranged husband? Was he real? Was any of it?

Nicolas had been right to be suspicious, but being right didn't change that there *was* something wrong with the woman. Her need to hide there confirmed that, if nothing else.

"What kinds of activities do you engage in for entertainment?" Mercy asked, as they lay side-by-side, staring at the detail in the plaster molds of the tray ceiling.

"Travel," Nicolas said. His eyes were trained on a particularly plump cherub laughing at two skinnier angels. He'd never noticed it before. Old school Deschanels sure had a weird sense of humor. "I try to stay away from Louisiana as much as possible."

"What about when you *are* here," she clarified.

"Same things as anyone, I suppose," he answered distractedly. He imagined the chubby had come to murder the skinny pair. He pictured his father's .357 in his fat little fingers. *Piggy from* Lord of the Flies *will have his revenge.*

Beside him, Mercy chuckled.

"Nothing," she said, before he could ask what was so funny. "Specifically, I mean. What specifically do you do for fun?"

Nicolas sighed inwardly. He was tired of her questions, which he suspected were either stalling tactics or more ways to divert the conversation away from herself. "Partying. Drinking. Movies. Shit, I don't know. Stuff."

"Movies," she said, thoughtfully. Her eyes were on his chubby angel now, too. "You mean, like picture shows?"

"If by picture shows you mean movies," he replied testily.

Mercy tilted her head sideways, lost in memory. "I used to sneak into picture shows in the morning, and then stay and watch them over and over through the night," she said wistfully. "I suppose you think that's odd."

"No, not at all," Nicolas lied. At least now he knew *something* about her. She liked movies. It wasn't much, but it was a start.

"I haven't done that in years," Mercy sighed, still caught up in her memories. "Maybe I'll do it again one day." Her eyes prickled with tears.

"Do you... wanna watch some movies?" She was obviously hinting at exactly that, and if it stopped the waterworks, he was all in.

"I shouldn't go anywhere," she said cautiously.

"No, I meant here. We have a pretty big collection."

Mercy's charcoal eyes widened. "You have picture shows *here?*"

"Uh, yeah?"

She sat straight up and her chromatic hair followed like rippling crimson wave. It was mesmerizing. "I would love to watch movies," she said, her expression serious and alert.

Nicolas studied her, trying to figure out the huge chasm between her intelligence and her experiences. First, she'd marveled at his cell phone, then his expressions, and now this.

He rattled off the names of some of the newer releases in his collection, but she only looked more and more confused. "Do you have anything older?" she asked.

It took a few rounds before she realized that by "older" she meant the shit his grandparents watched when they were kids.

He didn't have much in the way of old movies, so instead turned on the satellite and found a classic movie channel. *Gone with the Wind* was on. Not his cup of tea, but Mercy lit up and smiled, so he put down the remote and settled in next to her.

Her reactions were surreal. Before long, he was watching *her* more than the movie. She erupted in gut-busting laughs when Rhett walked in on Scarlett professing her love to Ashley, gripping his arm when Ashley and Scarlett were caught in a scandalous embrace. She sobbed devastating tears when Bonnie fell off her horse, and released clucks of disappointment when Scarlett begged Rhett to take her back and, frankly, Rhett did not give a damn.

Nicolas couldn't help getting caught up in her reactions. Cussing at Scarlett, shaking his head at Ashley, cheering Rhett. Who was this person? He was glad Oz wasn't there to witness to his shocking breach of character. He'd never live that shit down.

For over four hours, he lay by Mercy's side, forgetting why she was there.

"I can't believe I've never seen that show," Mercy said, dabbing at her eyes.

Nicolas laughed and moved toward the bathroom. "Would you like a kerchief? From the privy? For your picture show?"

She laughed and tossed a pillow at him. Something about the gesture, from her, made him tingly inside.

"And what is with Scarlett?" Mercy asked, sniffing.

"What's with her?" Nicolas handed her the tissue.

"Are all women like that?"

There she went, being weird again. "You would know better than me," Nicolas replied, in his best approximation of Rhett's voice. "But yeah, I've known a few Scarletts in my time."

"What an insufferable cow," she replied thoughtfully. She seemed personally offended, as if all women somehow shared equal responsibility in the matter.

"Amen to that," Nicolas agreed. He glanced at the clock. Dinner time. Oz would be wondering what they'd been doing half the day while he was working downstairs.

"It's fine. I need some rest anyway," she reassured him.

Reading his mind was apparently as easy as looking at his face. "I'll send Condoleezza up with a tray," he offered. Then, in an almost hopeful afterthought, added, "Unless you want to join us in the dining room?"

She smiled, still sniffling from the movie. "No, but I wouldn't mind watching more movies with you after dinner."

Nicolas wasn't at all amused by the fluttering feeling in his stomach at the thought of spending a few more hours tucked at her side.

AFTER DINNER, THEY WATCHED *REBECCA*, FOLLOWED BY *JANE EYRE* and *Citizen Kane*. She especially loved *Jane Eyre*, remarking she could relate to Mr. Rochester's stubbornness.

"You don't say," Nicolas said.

As she drifted off to sleep, he observed again the sensation of her glowing. A trick of light, he assumed. Her posture unguarded, he was also treated to a glimpse of something on her breast. A scar maybe? A tattoo?

He fell asleep beside her, dreaming of Thornfield Hall and insufferable Southern belles.

"*I*t's been five days," Oz was saying, again, like goddamn broken record.

"Yes, I'm aware, and I'm *also* aware of the fact you're a giant pain in my ass right now," Nicolas responded.

"Oh, well I wouldn't want to be a pain in your ass, so I'll go."

"Stop being a fucking *girl*."

"I'm doing my best to look out for your thickheaded ass. This isn't normal, even under the circumstances. She hasn't left the bedroom, and she hasn't said a word about moving on. We need to call Colleen, or someone, who can make sense of this. I, for one, *am* worried."

"What makes you think I'm not?"

"Are you sad to give her up, is that it? You realize your little game of house is over once we have to start moving her on her way?" Oz asked.

"Oh fuck's sake, Ozzy, you know me better than that," Nicolas snapped. "I'll be happy when she's gone because it will mean shit can go back to normal. I'm not like you, I don't deal with this kind of nonsense all that well. I feel all fucked up and weird inside right now, and I don't like it one bit."

"Could that fucked up feeling... be love?" he teased.

Nicolas threw his glass and it shattered in a very satisfying manner on the marble mantle behind Oz, who looked genuinely shocked. "Have you lost your mind? Seriously, who actually does that in real life? Who throws a glass?"

Nicolas shrugged. He'd seen it in *Gone with the Wind*, and it looked like a pretty boss move. "Maybe you'll watch your mouth now."

"You'd think someone who called *me* for help would be a little less testy," Oz challenged, still looking at the broken glass.

"Just because I need your help doesn't mean I'll take your shit any more than normal. I didn't ask for this added stress to my life."

Oz shook his head. "You are some piece of work."

"A work of art."

"So, later tonight, you're gonna be mad at me," Oz abruptly changed the subject. He looked as if he'd been dredging up the courage for some time.

"I don't like the sound of this."

"I really need to go home," Oz explained. Yes. He did. Nicolas wasn't sure what had kept him here all this time. Even his pleas wouldn't have been enough, under normal circumstances. Oz's stubbornness to stay, up to this point, felt more like he was a puppet being controlled by a marionette. And that marionette was him. "Nights there, days here, it's too much, and Adrienne needs more than I've been giving her."

Nicolas had been selfish in letting him stay. He needed to be with Adrienne.

"I knew you shouldn't be alone," Oz continued, but warily. He dropped his eyes.

Ah, fuck. "Who did you call?" There was really only one person he could, or would, call. Nicolas didn't want that person involved. He wanted to see her face. Hear her voice.

"Ana," he confirmed in a timid voice. He mimed ducking as if expecting Nicolas to throw another glass.

"Oh, fuck's sake, Oz, *why?*"

"Maybe Finn, too," he replied, not answering the question.

"Well, then, it'll be a regular party at *Ophélie*! Do they know what's going on?"

"Not really. I just said there was a situation, and you were okay, but you really needed family right now. That's all I needed to say."

"You really are deplorable," Nicolas said, and meant it.

"That's a big word for you, Nicolas. I appreciate you pulling it out just for me."

"Not in the mood."

"You mean to tell me you're still mad at her?"

"Not just her," Nicolas snapped.

Oz paused for a moment, plainly choosing his words carefully. "Maybe it's time for you think about the unreasonableness of your anger, and consider it might not be proportionate to the crimes involved."

"Oh? So my anger at you cheating on my sister is unreasonable?"

"That isn't why you're angry," Oz accused, accurately. "I was hoping by bringing Ana here, you could mend things. You two have been close your whole lives, and—"

"I don't require your mediation services," Nicolas blasted back, moving toward the bar. Cognac. He needed it, and badly. "And if I wanted a shrink, I'd already be overpaying for one."

"Drinking might be a cheaper form of therapy, but it's not going to fix things," Oz scolded. "Maybe it's time to grow up and actually deal with your feelings. Ana doesn't deserve the punishment you've put upon her."

Oz had some nerve, thinking he could push guilt on him! "People in glass houses shouldn't throw stones, asshole."

"Nicolas," Oz's voice dripped with condescension, "that expression doesn't mean what you seem to think it means."

"Go fuck yourself," he snapped. When Oz just stood there, he added, "Now!"

"All right, well, I'm not in the mood for that exactly, but I'm sure I can find something else to do," Oz quipped as he left the room.

NICOLAS WAS BEING TURNED UPSIDE DOWN AGAIN, FLIPPED INSIDE out. He gripped the back of the armchair for leverage, but it was almost unnecessary. He was getting used to these visions now, though he had yet to figure out how to control them, or determine why they were even happening.

Ana looked down at a sleeping Finn, and her heart swelled with painful love. Real love. The first safe place I've ever known.

But love was more than the connection of two hearts. It was more than passion forged in the melding of bodies. Love was about doing the right thing, and putting the other person's needs ahead of your own. It was about repairing a hurt by cutting off the source of the wound.

Ana set the diamond ring on the nightstand. Finn's soft snoring ceased, and Ana froze, fearful he might wake. Instead, he smiled in his sleep, and turned over, returning to his dreams.

"I'm so sorry," Ana whispered. She reached a hand out to touch him one last time, but pulled it back. No point in making this harder than it already was. "I really do love you, Finnegan James."

Ana tiptoed into the hall, resisting the urge to turn back and take him in one last time. She knelt, picking up her duffle bag, and continued with light steps down the hall, past Jon's room.

Ana loathed confrontation, but the urge to launch a barrage of assaults against Jon was almost too tempting to pass up. You're wrong. You and I are nothing alike. You're cruel, and have no qualms about bringing others down into your despair. We are both pariahs, but I, at least, refuse to continue to hurt people I love.

But she wouldn't say that, or the thousand other things burning in the dark corners of her heart. Waking Jon meant waking Finn, and it would be easier to close both chapters at once. They'd both hate her, for different reasons. She couldn't care less what Jon thought of her, but Finn's inevitable confusion tore her heart in half. She'd have to find comfort in knowing he would be better off, in the end.

Angus padded toward her as she reached the front door. Finn told her once that Angus had never taken to anyone the way he took to Ana.

"Goodbye, little friend," Ana said, kneeling to allow Angus' relentless kisses. She scratched behind his ears, allowing herself one final, small distraction before walking away. "Take care of your master."

Ana left, looking back once more at the old Victorian as she trudged through the snowy driveway. The best, and the worst, memories of her life had happened here. And now, Nicolas needed her. She didn't know if he even knew she was coming, but she had to at least try to make things right. If she couldn't mend the situation here, perhaps she could at home.

Nicolas dry-heaved over the side of the chair, the wind knocked out of him. His stomach felt like a tidal wave was forming within, and once again he had the lingering sensation he was not himself, but Ana. He was in Maine, standing knee-deep in snow, but staring out the window at the oak trees of *Ophélie.*

He needed to lay down.

Nicolas curled up on the chaise, squeezing his eyes shut.

The visions were getting out of hand. He had to learn to control them, or eventually the two worlds would bleed together so thoroughly he wouldn't be able to discern reality from fiction. And fucking hell, they were exhausting.

This vision confirmed what he already knew: Ana was coming. But she'd been planning to leave even before Oz called, her state of mind continuing to grow increasingly more frayed as the visions went on. She was nearing a breaking point, just as he was.

Would she tell him about it when she arrived?

Did he really want to know?

NICOLAS WAS AWARE OF THE MESSY DYNAMIC BETWEEN ANA AND the St. Andrews brothers even before the visions, but he wasn't up to speed on the particulars. He should have known the whole story, but as soon as she'd recovered from the trauma in Maine, he'd severed his communication with her, too wounded by her betrayal with Oz.

But Ana was on her way now. Oz had given almost no notice to prepare for it.

"I really don't know how having more people here is going to make the situation any better," Nicolas whined, pointlessly. The sky outside was darkening, and that meant the hour approached. "Mercy is going to feel like she's being ambushed."

Oz flashed a humoring look. "Listen to you trying to be the voice of reason for once. As much as I think it's noble you want to get her 'permission,' I think you've forgotten she's the one who barged into *your* life. I'm happy to help make her feel comfortable and safe, but asking her approval is unnecessary. If she wants help, she does it our way."

"Fuck you for being right," Nicolas lashed.

"Look, I get it," Oz said, understanding what Nicolas didn't say out loud. "I understand you're afraid she might bolt, and run, and then make the situation worse. But we're safe at *Ophélie*. Even the perimeter is guarded, for her safety. If she didn't feel secure, would she be able to sleep as peacefully as she has? I doubt it. If she was worried about her ex finding her here, or whoever the hell is *actually* after her, she wouldn't be sleeping at all. In fact, she seems in no hurry at all to do *anything*."

"I know," Nicolas grudgingly agreed. He was already thinking about how they'd explain this to Ana. "What have you told Adrienne?"

"I told her the truth, in a way. I said you'd gotten yourself into some trouble with a girl."

"Oh Christ, she probably thinks we're here doing some sort of at-home abortion."

Oz laughed. "She knows me. Although, she probably wouldn't put it past *you*." Nicolas glared at him. "But you know I can't stay any longer. Unless your sleeping mermaid comes downstairs tonight, I have to go. My family needs me."

"Yeah, I know." Nicolas didn't like it, but understood. He'd been coming to terms with it even before Oz brought it up, thinking of his somewhat estranged friend as optional rather than required.

Nicolas asked Condoleezza to fix her famous jambalaya. She was excited to be able to serve the first big meal at *Ophélie* since his family had passed.

Might as well do it up, he thought. *If nothing else, we'll be awkward on a full stomach.*

20- MERCY

*T*he Mark burned hot against Mercy's breast. Occasionally, a tiny puff of smoke wafted up as the phoenix of Our Father huffed, breathing his impatience. *Well, I'm ready whenever you are!*

When the time came, she wouldn't forget to show her gratitude to either of the Men downstairs. She was beyond mortal concerns, but was not ungrateful, or blind to their role in helping her to her destination.

The day the Mark was embossed upon her chest lived in her soul as clear and fresh as a recent memory. Many of her peers ached to make the world their playground, talking of the places they'd go, the things they'd see and do. She'd never related to any of them over the hundred years they sat side-by-side. They were no better than Children of Men, with their selfish precociousness, and insatiable desires. Emyr was but an afterthought to many of them.

Mercy knew they ridiculed her chaste behavior. She wished it didn't bother her, but she'd found significant comfort in the belief she would Ascend long before any of them..

Empyreans often returned to Farjhem for the graduation

ceremonies. Though the ritual was focused on the young fledglings, it was also a chance for elder Empyreans to come together for a reunion, to congregate in a way that was unnatural under other circumstances. The Feast of Officium Maximus, or Great Commitment, was a time of merriment and celebration for the entire race. Because childbirth was regulated and approved by the Senetat, births were only sanctioned to occur once a century. Graduation celebrations, then, happened only once a century as well, and there was more than feasting going on.

The crowd watched as each stepped forward to take their Mark. Many chose inconspicuous locations like their back, shoulder, or upper arms, places which allowed them to worship privately, but still blend into the society of Men with relative ease. Others chose to boldly display theirs on their face, like Aidrik. For Mercy, it had never been about outward appearance. She wanted Our Father to be near that part of her which felt the most connected to him: her heart.

As the Scholars branded Mercy, she looked out into the crowd of robes and gowns and her eyes locked upon him: Aidrik. His beautiful face appeared carved out of the very glaciers of Farjhem. His lips, arched like the phoenix in flight, curved into an impassive expression, but his eyes were an ocean of intensity. He met her gaze, and the effect shocked her so roughly she nearly fell off the dais. There was no discernible change in his expression at her discomfiture, but the slight cock of his head to the right seemed to hold a valley of words unspoken.

Desire fluttered within her, a response both foreign and unwelcome. Unlike her peers, who had turned schooling into a game of dating and intrigue, Mercy had not made time for such trivial pursuits. There was not room in her heart for both Emyr and a mate. Or, so she thought.

Later, at the great feast, she was startled when Aidrik stood before her, casting a deep shadow. *Your devotion is admirable.*

Four words. That was all it took for Mercy to fall in love, and for her heart to be rent in half.

Even the Scholars had never paid her such compliment! They employed a curriculum of fear, teaching only of the horrific things that would happen if they were *not* faithful. None had taken the time to understand what she, innately, felt from the moment she'd witnessed her parents stand up to meet their execution. Faith was about love. Without it, they were nothing.

Aidrik the Wise spent most of the evening fading into the crowds, but at certain points would stand and lead their people in song, or dance. He was an enigmatic swirl of privacy and showmanship, and Mercy was desperately intrigued.

She had heard of him, of course. Everyone knew of Aidrik the Wise. One of Emyr's greatest disciples, and only a millennia old back then. He was known for many great feats, but the most valued of all was his ability to rouse great numbers to a common cause. A desirable trait to have in an ally of Emyr.

But if Mercy thought Aidrik was an enigma, she was not the only one. His presence at Farjhem ignited a slew of whispers, rumors, and suppositions. Where had he been? What had he been doing? And with whom? Had he evigbond yet? She wanted to smack the words right out of their mouths, but she didn't understand then why it bothered her so.

The jealousy escalated to a new level of toxicity when her peers heard she was leaving with him. Well, it had been news to her, too! In fact, she heard of Aidrik's plans to take her under his wing not from him, but from those spreading gossip. She was little more than a Child, and he clearly deemed it his duty as she had no one else to guide her.

She was in love, though she did not understand it then. In awe of his stoic ideals, she idolized how his resounding faith perfectly melded with logic. He alone brought reason out of chaos. Aidrik was engaging to the point of intoxication, and she was addicted from the moment she laid eyes on him.

In the five hundred years Mercy spent with Aidrik, he taught her about the world. Showed her how to listen and absorb everything around her, how to take some enjoyment from the gifts she'd been given. But those things also deeply offended her sensibilities. How could she enjoy anything without taking joy from her love of Emyr? And how could listening to anything of this world bring her closer to her spiritual connection with Our Father? It was Aidrik's patience and acceptance that kept Mercy with him all those years. But her own patience and acceptance of him eventually ran its course.

The beginning of the end started with an innocent discussion about the Empyrean evigbond. Unlike Men, for whom bonding consisted of forming a connection, joining in marriage or handfast, and producing a family, for Empyreans the process was innate. Biological. There was little choice in the matter, and once the evigbond was formed, only Ascension, or untimely death, could tear it asunder.

She knew that later, but could not grasp it then. She asked Aidrik why, though they had been lovers many years, they were not evigbond. But she asked in the petulant words of a spoiled child not getting their way. In return, she got her answer accordingly.

It doesn't work that way, Aidrik had said. *Evigbond is not the nature of our relationship.*

What, exactly, then, is the nature of our relationship? A means of satisfying your conjugal urges?

Long sigh. *Mercy. You place too much stock in physical activities which mean little.*

You dare accuse me of prioritizing physical needs over spiritual?

Another long sigh. *Are you not doing precisely that, by making them the means to address your point?*

He was right, and she hated him for it. Her desire for him

had confounded her, leaving her placing greater importance on her relationship with Aidrik than her devotion to Emyr.

She slowly withdrew from him. First, physically. Then, over time, emotionally as well. She did it in part to hurt him, but when he allowed her to do it without argument, she was the one who ended up wounded. The pain was near unbearable, but in that experience she grew closer to Emyr once more, and eventually her love of Aidrik faded to a dull scar.

One morning, he rose to attend to some business, and never returned. Aidrik was inducted into the Eldre Senetat, the greatest honor any Child of Emyr could ever be endowed with in life, and that came with his seclusion from all other Empyreans. Later still, when news of his Ascension reached Mercy's ears, she was glad for him, though she realized, in all her wandering with him, she never did quite understand the scope of his faith.

After Aidrik, she did not give her time quite so freely, or easily.

Nicolas was downstairs making tasteless jokes with one of his house staff. They were very different in ways that mattered most, but in other ways—in their quest to be alone, to trust only themselves—they were on common ground. She suspected he wasn't quite the jerk he wanted others to believe he was.

Briefly, Mercy wondered what Nicolas would think if he caught a glimpse of her Mark. From a distance, it looked no different than any ornate tattoo of Man. Close up, though, even mortals could easily spot the subtle fluttering of wings, tender snorts, and tiny billowing smoke trails.

Smiling in the darkness, Mercy closed her eyes and thought of the loving arms of Our Father, reaching out for her as she came to Him in flight.

As His face came into focus, she gasped as she realized He was Nicolas.

21- NICOLAS

*W*hen Nicolas opened the door and saw Ana's pretty blue eyes, his resolve, anger, everything, melted away. He yanked her into an embarrassing hug and clutched her tight, feeling her wilt in his arms. Behind her, Finn smiled. So, he had followed, after all.

"Nic," Ana whispered. He had to do something before she started crying. The rare sight of her tears would dissolve him to pieces.

"Invite them in, asshole, it's cold outside," Oz called out from behind them. Nicolas stepped out of the way and motioned for them to come in.

Ana looked fresh and beautiful, as usual. Her pale cheeks were flushed, her crimson hair staticky, and vibrant. Her eyes, though, gave away her distress. She looked more miserable than Nicolas had ever seen her. A small, pesky ache penetrated his cold heart. He still loved her. He didn't hate himself for it nearly as much as he had even a few days ago. Hell, not as much as a minute ago.

She wrapped her arms around herself, in a self-conscious manner that immediately bothered him. The sensation that something was deeply amiss again flooded to the surface. Images he pulled from her before danced in his head, but he shrugged them off, fearing being pulled in all the way.

"It's good to see both of you," Oz prompted, subtly reminding Nicolas of his host duties.

"Yeah, good," Nicolas added in a daze.

"Let's sit down to dinner, and we can catch up," Oz suggested, bailing him out again. He avoided looking directly at Ana, and Nicolas could smack him for it. *You're the dumbass who invited her!*

Condoleezza took their coats, taking a moment to embrace Ana, whom she'd always had an especial fondness for. Richard took off upstairs with their bags. The rest shuffled into the large, formal dining room.

After everyone had been served, Ana put both hands on the table and said, "So, who's gonna start talking?"

Oz and Nicolas looked at each other. *This was your idea, Ozzy.*

"Well," Oz said, placing his napkin in his lap, "there's a woman upstairs who's been hiding for five days. Well, maybe six or seven, if you count the time on the island, but ah, even I'm losing track of time. Mercy, she calls herself. Her story is she's on the run from an extremely abusive and terrible ex, although we've been unable to verify her story at any level. Not even her name. Nicolas met her on the island, and after a rather painful encounter with him, she subsequently tried to take her life." Nicolas issued a swift kick under the table, and was satisfied with Oz's grunt of pain. "Nicolas came to the startling realization this was *not* about him, and accepted he did, in fact, have a moral obligation to help her. He spirited her away to *Ophélie*, Aunt Colleen gave her a clean bill of health, and she's been here since we arrived, five days ago. Does that about sum it up?"

Nicolas finished off his Hennessy, glaring at him. "Yes, pretty much."

"Why didn't you tell me?" Ana asked. She looked stricken.

Nicolas didn't feel as though he owed her any allegiance, but this wasn't the time to make cruel jabs, either.

"Probably the same reason you never tell him what's going on with you, Ana," Finn pointed out. He also looked out of it. Weary. Undoubtedly, their plane ride over had been an awkward one. "I'm sure he was protecting you."

Ahh, so she hadn't told Finn about what transpired between them. What else was she keeping from him? And what was she keeping from Nicolas?

"He knows I don't need protecting," Ana said, dropping her eyes. The blood rose to her cheeks.

"I wasn't protecting you," Nicolas insisted. "I was being respectful to Mercy, who's naturally trying to guard her own privacy under the circumstances."

"You told *him*," Ana accused, poking her thumb toward Oz. "I would think his hero complex would be more of a risk to her than my pragmatism."

"Hey!" Oz said.

"I was a little overwhelmed, and let's just leave it at that," Nicolas replied, defensively.

"Fine," she agreed, but there was far more than *fine* behind it. She looked at Oz. "So what's the next course of action?" She was punishing him, by looking to Oz as the leader.

"First, she needs to come downstairs. Once she does, we can figure out where she wants to go, and arrange for it. We'll get her to a safe place and then we can work on any additional details."

"Has anyone tried to talk her into coming down?" Finn asked.

"Fuck, we hadn't thought of that!" Nicolas exclaimed, wishing they could go back in time to before Oz had invited them.

"Nic doesn't want to," Oz said in the condescending way

people say things when they openly disagree with someone and want them to feel silly. *Asshole.* "Instead, he's wasting even more of his family's money with unnecessary security."

"Should we call a doctor?" Finn asked, innocently.

"Yes, that would be great," Oz said, answering for them both. Nicolas was starting to not like him being in charge, if it meant making him look and feel like the village idiot. "Perhaps a doctor can succeed where Nic has failed."

"Aunt Colleen already examined her. She's fine." He almost added that Ana was also a healer, but stopped short of saying the words. Something told him this wasn't information Finn was privy to yet.

Ana raised an eyebrow. Finn and Oz exchanged a look. "You asked for help. This is me helping you," Oz said, and then added, "and now, this is *us* helping you."

"This isn't what I had in mind," Nicolas openly pouted. He should be grateful, but the prevailing desire was to kick them all out of his house.

AFTER DINNER, OZ DISAPPEARED TO CALL ADRIENNE, AND Nicolas walked into the den to discover Finn kissing Ana. She leaned into him as he held her close, almost too close. Nicolas caught a glimpse of her gaze over his shoulder, and the sadness in her eyes was even greater than the sadness in Finn's desperate gesture.

Nicolas had a precipitous urge to pull him away and tell him, *don't you understand no amount of love you can give will help her love herself?*

He went into the sitting room to see if Oz was finished, and stopped when he heard him still talking.

"I know... but he's your brother. My brother. I have to do this."

Nicolas couldn't hear her response, but it was obvious she was talking him into coming home.

"I have to respect his privacy Adrienne... yes, I know... I know... I don't think much longer... I'm not avoiding what happened, it's just that sometimes people need us even when we're hurting... I love you Ade, you know that... yes, I promise... yes, soon.... yes, no matter what.... I love you, too."

Nicolas didn't need a code to decipher that Oz was leaving.

"Let's go talk to Mercy and get things moving," Nicolas decided, as Oz hung up the phone and walked out. His smile was full of relief.

22- MERCY

"*R*ock paper scissors?"

"No, we will not rock paper scissors, Nic. She's your damsel in distress."

Mercy could almost feel the dirty look Nicolas gave Oz as he bent down and very gently touched her shoulder. She wanted to laugh. That wouldn't wake a puppy.

"Heaven's sake," Oz groaned, and then felt two stronger hands shaking her.

Mercy saw Nicolas first, and then to the other side, Oz. Oz had a very soothing aura about him. She was surprised how much this comforted her. Even more surprised at how happy she was to see Nicolas. She nearly blushed, remembering the image of Nicolas as Our Father.

Clearly, this Ascension was taking its toll on her. If it didn't happen soon, she'd possibly go insane.

Oz was gazing down at her, probably trying to decide if he should introduce himself or wait for Nicolas to do it.

"You must be Oz," Mercy said, deciding for him, and he smiled. He had a nice smile. The gestures that were difficult for Nicolas came naturally to Oz.

Oz nodded. "Nice to finally meet you, Mercy. I'll have to ask you for forgiveness now though, as I have two other people to introduce you to." He looked penitent.

How had she not picked up on the fact there were two new people in the house? She was deeply concerned at this lapse in instinct, but Oz's warming aura assured her she was in no danger.

"Oh?"

"Oz felt it necessary to invite my cousin and her boyfriend," Nicolas explained. "I'm sorry we didn't talk to you first."

"It's okay," Mercy said, concerned despite sensing no danger to her, "but why?"

"I don't know how much longer I can stay," Oz answered, with a touch of embarrassment. "My wife needs me."

"Oh, then you must go to her."

"Soon, but first, we have some work to do to help get you to safety," he encouraged with a smile.

She'd been waiting for this. The Ascension was taking far longer than expected, and at this point, she no longer had her earlier confidence on the timing. Her Inner Voice told her it would happen here… that it needed to happen here… and she had to make sure they didn't send her away before it happened.

"I would rather not rush it. I still don't feel very well."

They exchanged looks. Nicolas was thinking about her fictional ex-husband slitting his throat in his sleep, and Oz about the wife he was neglecting. If they knew she'd been waiting over three thousand years for this, it might put things in perspective.

"Luckily, we have a healer here," Oz said, brightening. "We can get you feeling better in no time."

That was just a little too convenient. "Your aunt?" she asked Nicolas.

Nicolas shook his head. She pulled from his thoughts the healer was in fact Ana, his beloved cousin from whom he'd been estranged for some time. "No," Nicolas said. "And Ana's not even a *good* healer. She can only heal her damn self."

Oz gave a hopeless frown. Nicolas persisted in looking annoyed. Mercy almost smiled.

"Thank you for letting me stay here," Mercy cooed, squeezing Nicolas' hand. He looked down in dull surprise. "I think another week and I'll be all set."

They exchanged looks again. "We think we can get you out of here tonight, Mercy." Nicolas tried a more determined approach. "I can understand why you're nervous. But you wouldn't have gone to such lengths to start over if you weren't really ready to do it."

For a moment, he actually sounded heartfelt. Mercy thought probably, in his own way, that's exactly what it was intended to be. "I just... I don't quite feel ready." Her struggle for words was real. Desperation was setting in. This cover story seemed so logical at the time, but now it was becoming a hindrance. If she'd known the Ascension would take so long after the process started, she would have slowed down and waited before engaging Nicolas.

But had she slowed down, he might have gone through with his plan to take his life.

It occurred to Mercy that Emyr might have another plan for Nicolas, one He wanted the Child of Man alive for. But that didn't make sense at all.

"Now that this is happening, I feel like I need to slow things down." Then Mercy added, with a twinge of guilt as she added a gentle nudge, both in words and something deeper, "if you want me to go, I can stay somewhere else."

They both tripped over their words, working to reassure her that no, she was welcome there, and they didn't want her leaving until she was ready.

Oz added, "We can spend a few extra days on it, if it helps get you ready."

Mercy smiled. This time it was real. "I appreciate everything you're both doing for me. If there's anything I can do to repay the favor…"

"If everything works out for you, then this was all worth it," Oz assured.

"Not that we mind worrying about you," Nicolas said, stumbling further as he added, "I mean, not that we want to have a reason to worry, I mean more that if we did have to worry it wasn't putting us out… ah, fuck it."

They all shared a laugh at this. In a way, Mercy liked Nicolas' cold, unfeeling demeanor more because it was real. But this confusing attempt at chivalry was nice, too, and brought out yet one more dimension to the strange Man.

"You'll have to pardon Nicolas. Despite his privileged upbringing, he's never learned to speak properly in front of other humans," Oz joked.

"Your mom sure as hell doesn't mind it," Nicolas shot back but then looked at Mercy as if worried the joke might offend her. She had heard it all, and far worse.

"Well she doesn't exactly need poetry when you're pumping her gas," Oz volleyed back.

"If by 'pumping her gas,' you mean—"

"Okay, okay, enough," Oz conceded, hands up in defeat. Mercy couldn't help it, she laughed, too.

"You always give up too soon," Nicolas said disdainfully, but his affection for his friend was genuine, maybe the purest thing about the Man. To obtain love from someone as selective as Nicolas seemed no small thing.

Mercy thought of all she'd be giving up, and reminded herself everything would be so much better where she was going. Much like Christians and their idea of heaven, life for Empyreans was preparation for their eventual Ascension. Some even believed there were multiple Ascensions, and this first one was a test to determine worthiness of future opportunities.

Everyone could agree on one thing, though: once you left this world, there was no returning.

Would she miss it? She'd fixated so much on her Ascension that she had pushed thoughts of anything else from her head. Would she miss the personal relationships? Love? Sex? Sensations, like swimming, the smell of the glaciers back home? She thought maybe she would. But no great reward ever came without some degree of sacrifice.

Oz and Nicolas were bantering again. She didn't even know what they were going on about, but it was clear Nicolas was winning.

As unexpected as the experience with Nicolas had been, Mercy didn't mind that her last few days on Earth would be spent with him.

"I'm looking forward to meeting Ana and her friend. Would it be okay if I did that after a short nap?" It took only the smallest nudge of subliminal coercion and both men left feeling as though they'd made the progress they'd intended.

23- ANASOFIYA

*B*eing home was hard. Ana had hoped returning to New Orleans would be a reprieve from the anxiety in Maine, but instead the dark hand of self-loathing gripped her heart tighter, a relentless promise that she could go anywhere in the world and nothing would change.

The darkness squeezed hardest when she saw Finn waiting for her at the Portland Jetport. She didn't know whether to be more shocked he'd found out and come for her, or that she hadn't seen it coming. In one hand, his packed bag, signaling his intention to join her, regardless of her destination. In the other, the beautiful ring she'd left on the nightstand.

What are you doing here? There was little emotion left in her that night. She'd given her tears to the evening before.

Silly girl, Finn had said, closing the gap between them. His bag fell to the dirty linoleum floor, and his strong, thick arms encircled Ana. Protectively, lovingly. Finn loved her beyond anything she deserved. He knew who she was, and loved her in spite of it. Because of it.

She allowed herself to melt in his arms, where it felt safe. One of the biggest surprises of her life had been learning she loved him back, that she'd even been capable of it. She didn't leave Maine to protect herself, but to protect *him*.

I love you, Ana, he'd said, pulling back and inspecting her tired, weary face. *You don't have to run away anymore. And if you insist you really need to leave, I'll leave, too.*

They'd stood there in the crowded airport, holding each other, both desperate for different things. His caring, pure heart beat strongly through his thin white shirt, and Ana knew for certain there was no greater man in all the world.

But she was not a good woman. Her heart was not pure. Not strong. Not loyal.

First, she'd slept with Oz. Her old friend; her *married* friend. That evening remained a blur of sensuality, and she didn't need further clarity on the matter. That horrible night was what had sent her to Maine, to put distance between who she'd been then and who she wanted to be. Then, the brief fling with Jonathan, Finn's brother. She and Finn had only been friends at the time, but the deception of keeping it from Finn had been almost unbearable.

When Finn found out, rather than turning Ana away, he pulled her closer, and then asked her to marry him. *I know you, Anasofiya Aleksandrovna Vasilyeva Deschanel,* he had said. *I know you like my own heart.*

You don't know the dark things in my heart, Finn. It's rotten, and it will poison you, too.

Silly girl. For such an intelligent woman, you say the oddest things. Your heart is dark from your own sadness. From not allowing yourself the happiness you deserve. I can give it to you, and do you know why?

I don't.

Because I know you. I know who you are, and I don't want you to change. I absolutely forbid it.

But Finn's love didn't change Jon's anger. It didn't take away Jon's ultimate act of violence against her, one that led not only to her own damaged horror, but to the sundering of the lifelong fraternity between two brothers.

When Aunt Colleen showed up, Ana couldn't hide her relief. Several of the women in the family had bonded together to suss out Ana's distress. Amelia, first, through her empathic sense, and then her Aunt Elizabeth confirmed things with telepathic snooping. All three were entirely unapologetic about their solicitous use of abilities.

But Aunt Colleen's truths about Ana's mother didn't empower her so much as solidify that her innate ability to hurt those she loved wasn't unique. She knew now she took after the mother she'd never met.

Her love for Finn was greater than anything she'd ever known, but the rift her arrival on Summer Island created, between brothers who'd once been best friends, was a guilt she could only carry if she committed to righting the wrong.

Then Oz sounded his call to arms, and while she'd intended to come alone, Finn had other ideas.

Finn slipped his arms around her waist, snapping her back to reality. He smiled, laying a kiss against her forehead before shifting his mouth lower. *I love you,* he mouthed, moving his lips to hers. That was his thing; a moment meant only for them. As if she were the only woman in the world.

She let his lips rest there for several moments. She could feel his smile as he kissed her. Love. It was not about darkness, it was about light. Ana wished she could stay in the light with Finn.

"I'm going to go find something to drink. Want anything?" Finn asked.

Ana nodded. "Water. Thanks."

Moments later, Oz walked in.

Looking at him now, Ana didn't know what she felt. Their last conversation in Maine brought them both closure, but still left much unsaid. He was as much a part of her as Nicolas, but so many things had happened. So much had changed.

"Ana," he said in her ear, brushing his lips against her. She wished things could go back to how they'd once been, the three of them against the world. When their mistakes were trivial, forgotten the next day.

"How are you?"

"I've been better," he replied, with a hollow laugh. "But I'd say you have, too."

"Is it that obvious?"

"I guess I've just known you too many years to not see when you're troubled."

Ana nodded, unsure of the best way to respond. "We've all been through a lot."

Oz let out a long, measured breath. "Ain't that the truth. Has Nicolas talked to you?"

She shook her head. Oz's lips parted, presumably to start into some heartening explanation about how Nicolas would *come around* and *things would be okay*, but he seemed to think better of it. Another sign of how much things had changed. "How's Adrienne?"

His face fell. Was it in inappropriate for her to ask about Adrienne now? She was still Ana's cousin, no matter what had transpired.

Her desire to disappear entirely deepened.

"She's been better," Oz admitted. "In fact, I need to say my goodbyes and go home to her now." He smiled sadly and pulled Ana into a quick embrace before leaving.

She found Finn in the kitchen, staring out the window, lost in thought. There were no drinks in front of him.

"Are you okay?" Ana asked, sliding up behind him. She was always a little wary of anyone when they behaved in unexpected ways.

"It's nothing."

"It's something," she said, growing worried. "Tell me."

Without turning around, he blew out a gust of air. "I was just remembering what happened in November. And I was thinking, what if Alex had gotten his hands on you? Killed you?" He turned when Ana put a soft hand on his shoulder. "I know it's not healthy to think this way, but every time I look at you...." He put one large, softly calloused hand against her face. "I love you so much already."

Ana pulled his head down to her chest in comfort, reminding him that everything had worked out. Alex was gone, and they were all safe now, all healed He didn't cry, but she felt his agony as if it were her own.

If I really loved you, I wouldn't put you through this. You deserve better than someone like me. Someone so damaged she can't help but to damage those she loves, too.

24- NICOLAS

*N*icolas snuck in a shower before Oz left. While he was sad to see him go, he was happy for the new normal they seemed to have found over the last several days.

Did it mean he was over it? Over him sleeping with Ana? It would always feel like a betrayal, but Nicolas understood now what he never could before. It wasn't about him. Whatever desperation had driven Ana and Oz into each other's arms, Nicolas had been the furthest thing from either of their minds. Forgiveness wasn't his to give, and he'd been too wrapped up in his own selfish feelings to wonder if they had, or would ever, forgive each other.

It was hard for him to believe they were all under one roof, again. The last time, gunshots rang out and a person died.

As Nicolas wrapped the towel around his waist, someone knocked on the door.

"I'm leaving," Oz called, from the other side.

Nicolas dressed and followed him downstairs, then outside to the wide front porch. Oz looked guilty at his eagerness to depart.

He expected a quick goodbye. Oz surprised him when he said, "Seeing Ana is hard."

"Fucking harder for me," Nicolas confessed, feeling the heat rise to his face. He would've been fine with going their whole lives never having this discussion. To just let things slowly dissolve into history. But Oz loved to talk about shit.

"I know."

"Did you two...?"

"We talked," Oz confirmed. "I think..." His voice trailed off, and he looked up toward the flickering gaslights with a gentle sigh. "I used to wish things would go back to how they were. But the more I think about it, the more I understand things never do. The best we can hope for is that each of our experiences prepares us for the next phase."

"I don't follow."

Oz smiled. "Our relationships... yours and mine, mine and Ana's, yours and Ana's... they've changed. They've evolved. And that's okay. I'm sorry for what happened, Nic. You're the only brother I've ever had, and I never meant..." Oz faltered again, but he didn't need to finish his sentence.

"I know," Nicolas answered. Oz was finally acknowledging how his actions had impacted him, and now he wished he hadn't. His throat felt thick, and heavy with emotion.

"Something's wrong with Ana," Oz said, breaking the fugue of emotion between them. "I don't know what it is, but I don't need to be a Deschanel to know it."

A sudden, irrational anger flew up inside Nicolas. Who was Oz, to tell *him* what Ana was thinking? His Ana? Of course he knew something was wrong with her! Why would this asshole think he wasn't already aware of it?

Nicolas pushed the anger down and asked Oz the question he'd wanted to ask all along. "Are you ever going to tell Adrienne?"

Oz shook his head, slowly. Sadly. "It would kill her. It kills

126

me everyday, seeing her, knowing what I've done. Knowing she trusts me completely. What kind of man can't fight his own demons? I'll spend my whole life making it up to her, and even that will never be enough."

Sympathy for his old friend rushed forth. Nicolas wanted to push it away, but the truth was, he did feel sorry for Oz. He wasn't a bad man. Good men could make bad decisions.

"It will be," Nicolas said, finally managing to work around the tidal wave of emotion.

"I want to believe that." Oz dropped his eyes. "I would do anything in the world to make it right."

"And that makes you a better man than ninety percent of the assholes out there," Nicolas said, slapping a firm hand on his shoulder. "People fuck up, Ozzy. It's not the end of the world."

Oz looked up and smiled. Nicolas realized it was his absolution Oz had been waiting for all along.

"Thanks for coming out, asshole," Nicolas added, to lighten the mood and restore the conversation to more familiar terms.

Oz surprised him again by pulling him into a rough embrace. Nicolas shocked himself by returning it just as vigorously.

"I'm proud of you for helping Mercy," Oz praised, and then turned to leave.

25- AIDRIK

A fine mist had settled over the house, and the river behind Aidrik. He sat perched upon the levee, watching. Inside *Ophélie*, the Children of Men slept. An occasional car passed by, but otherwise quiet prevailed. Only the sound of bullfrogs and crickets penetrated the deafening silence.

His eyes fluttered, exhaustion threatening. As Mercy's last moments ticked closer, sleep had not come easily. He did not want to disturb her until absolutely necessary. Wisdom deemed he needed rest, but stubbornness won out. He could rest later. Later was his to command, but it might not be Mercy's.

Then, he saw her. Mercy, coming toward him, through the mist, a white lace nightgown accenting the crimson waves of hair flowing over her breasts.

Aidrik rose, processing. Had she detected his presence here?

As she came into full view, a new realization came over him. This was not Mercy. This female was human, though she had an air of Empyrean about her. She stumbled, collapsing into the muddy gravel. Then, seemingly spent, she curled up in the mud and went to sleep.

Baffling. Children of Men often were, but this was especially puzzling behavior. Alcohol, perhaps.

Ulfberht tight at his side, Aidrik trekked down the levee. As he reached the asphalt roadway, mist obscured his vision, blocking her from view. Instinct carried him forward onto the crunching gravel. He knelt by her side.

Her eyes flashed open, but he knew immediately she was not of consciousness. Sleepwalking. A curious affliction unique to Men. Empyreans slept too light for such a proclivity.

Nevertheless, her eyes locked with Aidrik's. He scanned her. That she was Empyrean jumped forward in his mind again. Impossible. No, not Empyrean. Halfling, like Nicolas. With hair like Farjhem's fires. Skin like the unblemished ice of Emyr. Eyes like the North Sea. A heart of darkness.

The creeping feeling pervading him could be compared only to the moment he first laid eyes on Christiane, his evigbond of many years past. A sensation not to be confused with lust, or desire. Need. Connection. Innate, and ingrained. Indisputable.

The evigbond had been immediate; no time to ponder, or make sense of it. Nay, it would be impossible for Aidrik to experience it again.

He began as if to speak, but realized waking her could be traumatizing. She was lucid enough to find movement, but engaging her in speech would break the trance. He did not wish for her to discover him just yet.

He slipped an arm under her waist, lifting her in one swift movement. She swayed, favoring her left foot. Balancing her with one arm, Aidrik knelt and examined her right ankle. Injured in her fall. Possible sprain. A bruise would form forthwith.

Though she was no wraith, this Nordic Princess felt light as a feather as Aidrik lifted her into his arms. Mud dripped from her white gown as her long legs dangled, dirty toes bouncing gently as he paced toward the estate. Her hair fell in limp waves, tickling the ground like molten lava pouring from a gap in a mountain.

The tiny pearl buttons on her gown had come undone, exposing one delicate, pale breast. Her nipple stood erect in the cold air, framed by tiny, rebel bumps. He frowned at the instinctual stirring under his robe. Quickly, he tugged at her nightgown, covering her again.

Aidrik reached one hand toward her troubled ankle and passed healing to her. When she woke, she would feel nothing. He could do nothing for her dirty nightgown, which would hold its own untold story.

She stirred, mumbling things unintelligible against his woolen cloak. He wanted to wake her, to palaver, but knowing she resided here, under the roof of Aidrik's descendants, gave him a hopeful pause. He would see her again. Tomorrow. On equal footing.

Tomorrow. It was decided. He would announce his presence, regardless of Mercy's progress.

Reading this Child of Man's thoughts would be a simple matter, but the dreams of Man were mired with pointless images. Through her head flashed waves crashing against a shore, shattered Christmas ornaments, names carved in oak trees, and the ripe scent of sexual desire. No coherence among them, and no meaning other than her memories converging together in nonsensical torment.

"Nicolas," Aidrik heard her whisper. Her sleepy tone masked any emotion. Nicolas, his descendant. The owner of this manse. This Daughter of Emyr was somehow a relation as well.

Rain slipped through the clouds, penetrating the mist around them. He hurried under the cover of the ancient oaks, shielding her. Instinctively, she pressed tighter, and his heart lurched as one of her arms slid around his waist.

A powerful, languid peace stole over Aidrik. Unfelt since Christiane.

No. Weariness was getting the best of his judgment. He knew he must get her to safety. She could wake at any moment, and he did not want her first image of him to be one of unexplained terror.

He moved swiftly through the grove of oaks, toward *Ophélie*. With the moonlight shining through the mist, the path before them seemed sinister. Ominous. He knew it was not true; his protections ensured evil would be kept from this doorstep. He must not let confusion further cloud judgment.

As they approached the door, Aidrik slipped the dagger from his bootstrap. Long and thin, like a shiv, it gleamed with the same magic infused in Ulfberht. In a flash, the row of locks came unlatched, and the door swung open. The house was entirely silent, save the light, laborious, ticking of the old timepiece in the study.

Aidrik reminded himself to wipe the mud from his boots before entering, avoiding evidence of trespass. His heavy steps labored across the creaky old floors, but he did not detect anyone waking. The Daughter of Emyr's soft snores told him she had slipped back into the comfort of deep rest.

Ophélie had many rooms. He closed his eyes and inhaled, drawing upon his deeper senses. Many Empyreans' heightened senses had dulled over the years, but Aidrik had never allowed his connection with nature to wane.

Ascending the stairs to the second floor, he came upon a wide, central hall with rooms on either side, and a set of double doors straight ahead. Nearly two centuries since he had walked these halls. Before what his descendants had called the War of Northern Aggression. Many inhabitants occupied it since. Generation upon generation of Halflings, entirely unaware of the loins from which they sprang. Proof he did not hold to Emyr's decrees.

Once again inhaling her scent, Aidrik memorized it, then searched for its match.

He carefully nudged open a heavy, oaken door. Her bed lay before him, the blanket turned back just slightly, evidence of her departure. But the bed was not empty.

On the left side, a large, sturdy, Child of Man. Not Halfling, like her. Good. Pure. Oblivious his bedmate had embarked on an unexpected voyage while he was lost to his dreams of salt and sea-foam.

Thoughts of her in his arms pulsed through Aidrik's head. Jealousy was not an emotion he indulged in often, and not since he'd learned of Christiane's marriage to the Marquise Deschanel. Unflattering, and mildly annoying, this sensation of begrudging others for having that which you also wanted.

No matter to trouble over tonight. He laid her gently between the emerald sheets, and she folded into the bed naturally. As if she had never left.

As an afterthought, Aidrik decided to leave her with some peace. He gently pulled the filthy nightgown up and over her head, tucking it under his robe. She might wonder at waking in the nude, but it was preferable to dwelling over a muddy nightgown she could not explain.

He allowed himself to take her in once more before leaving. Her glacier skin shone, soft and smooth. The small triangular mound of crimson between her pale legs glistened. Her roulette wheel of dream images now included Aidrik. He was not the only one with impure thoughts.

It would be nothing to take her. To ease her beau deeper into sleep with dream suggestion. Then, spread apart her legs and drive into her, taking his fill. Even if she were to wake, he could quell her fears with persuasion, and leave his seed indiscriminately, forcing the evigbond.

But his honor prevented it. His willpower, ironclad.

Folding the blanket over her, Aidrik leaned in. Whispered in her ear, "Tomorrow, my Nordic Princess. My eyes-like-the-sea."

A small smile spread across her glacier-skin. His heart again lurched, defiantly. He had more pressing matters to attend under this roof.

Yet only a fool would hold to the premise that Mercy's passing remained his only interest.

26- ANASOFIYA

*A*na distinctly remembered putting on the old nightgown. It wasn't hers. She'd packed in such a rush she'd forgotten both pajamas and a hairbrush, so was forced to comb through the old rooms looking for both. Condoleezza rummaged up the old lace relic, claiming it had been among Nicolas' late mother, Cordelia's things. *Belonged to 'er ma or nana, I 'spect.*

It certainly hadn't belonged in this century. From the shearing lace at the cuffs and hem, to the thinning of the fabric throughout the chest and waist, it was likely an heirloom Ana had no business wearing. But she was grateful for something to change into.

She recalled buttoning every last pearl button, save the one missing at the top. Not the usual, habitual memory of going through the motions. The tiny bits of oyster creation, and even tinier holes, had been no small chore.

So where had it gone? Ana knew it hadn't been thrown aside in some fit of passion with Finn. She didn't want to make him promises, and sex was Finn's way of showing his commitment. She smiled in spite of herself at the memory of his odd look when he woke her up. He understood her nakedness wasn't an invitation, and that confused him further.

Answers started assembling as Ana noticed the mud around the soles of her feet. On the palms of her hands. She must have fallen, outside. Sleepwalking was nothing new to her. She'd been scaring the family for years with her midnight treks across the neighborhood. But what on earth could have happened to the nightgown?

As she stood in the shower, earthy mud swirling into the drain, her dream from the night before came back. A hooded, robed man carrying her across the stormy grounds of *Ophélie*. His hand brushing against her breast, as he moved to cover her, then winding around her ankle. It was one of the most erotic dreams she'd ever experienced, and there wasn't even any sex.

It wasn't unusual for Ana's sleepwalking dreams to be interspersed with images she'd come across in her rogue evening jaunts. But she had no idea who the enigmatic hooded stranger was. Or what had become of her nightgown.

In the end, Ana decided both mysteries were better left unsolved.

OZ WAS GONE. NICOLAS WAS UPSTAIRS WITH MERCY. FINN AND Ana were alone in the parlor, playing the waiting game.

He'd tried to engage her in conversation, but Ana's stilted answers told him she wasn't in the mood to talk. Without pressing it, he retreated to the library and emerged, moments later, with a very old copy of *The Lord of the Rings*. Tolkien was his favorite. In Maine, she'd often found Finn curled up by the bay window, reading *The Silmarillion*.

"This looks like a first edition," he muttered, turning it over in his hands as he dropped down into the armchair.

"It probably is," Ana agreed, distantly, gazing out the

window. The morning sky was clear, crisp. A beautiful winter day.

It was impossible not to love Finn, or to prevent her mind from wandering back to moments she still cherished, regardless of her fears. She returned to the night they'd connected, really connected, talking for hours in conversation that ended with mutual, affectionate understanding. She recalled with perfect clarity the way his hands felt across her skin; like safety and sensuality. How Finn insisted on taking it slower than the day on the cliff where they'd traded passion for abandon, instead tracing his lips over every inch, every contour of her body.

Ana's heart would never forget the way his muscles trembled under her hands as he took her slowly, rhythmically, controlling his motions so as not to finish too soon. How the slight stubble on his chin brushed across her forehead, and breasts, as his kisses landed with each stroke of his lovemaking.

Finn had loved Ana that night with impressive self-control, and as she allowed him his release and reward, he recovered quickly. Before slipping off to sleep, he'd whispered, against her collarbone, "Ana, you're the first safe place I've ever had."

For so long, so many years, Ana had believed Nicolas was her safe place. But his safety was a false economy, only shielding her from a world she'd eventually have to face. What Finn gave her, and what he believed he got in return, was so much more. It was real, a two-way mirror reflecting at each other the good, the bad, and everything in between.

Love. That's why I can heal him, when I've never been able to heal another before.

Love.

"There's a storm coming in," Finn said, nose in the book.

"I don't see it," Ana replied, taking in the unusually bright sunshine. She had an impulsive urge to be outside, breathing in the slightly humid river air.

Finn shrugged. He'd been predicting weather his whole life.

Just like he always instinctively knew where the lobster would trap. He couldn't explain it, nor could anyone else, but people never doubted his uncanny connection with nature.

And, of course he would be right this time, as he always was. Ana decided to go out and enjoy the sun, while it lasted. When she stood, Finn instinctively rose with her, and then stopped, hovering over his chair. He seemed to understand she was after some privacy.

Ana slipped through the kitchen, and then out through the back door nested between the dual butler's pantries. The back of the property faced Brigitte's Garden straight ahead, with oak groves flanking either side. If she were on the upper balcony, she'd be able to see the large oil machinery churning off in the distance. From her vantage point, the antique beauty of the Deschanel home land was all that lay before her.

She wandered to the left of the garden, gliding through the oaks. Their roots were so large and deep that, even over twenty feet apart, some were beginning to overturn due to their close proximity. The original Charles Deschanel had planted these in the 19th century, after he purchased the property, but time had turned them into something bigger than he ever could have imagined.

Ana knew exactly where she was going. Her feet steered her true, and she found the oak she'd spent so many summers, and weekends, reading beneath. The oak where she and Nicolas hatched their most devious childhood plans. And where they'd shared an innocent, childhood kiss; a gesture which had simply been exploratory then, but led to a lifelong tether between them.

Muffins + Nicolas, a deep inscription read. Nicolas carved it with Richard's pocket knife, when they were just eleven. Then, they'd sliced their palms and joined their blood together, transferring the red bond to the deep grooves of the words.

Ow! What the hell? Ana had cried, shaking her hand.

I saw it in a movie, okay? It's legit! Besides, you'll heal yourself in seconds, silly.

In their youth, Ana had deferred to him always. Let him lead wherever they went, and in turn, he protected her from the wider world. But illusions didn't last forever. Childhood dreams faded, only to discover the boogeyman was real after all, hiding within you all along.

There was little left of the blood now except the hint of rusted brown in the deepest grooves. Ana traced her finger over the rough bark, wondering, if she had to do it all over again, would she rather go back to a time where she didn't understand who she was?

A warm breath against her neck startled her. Strong hands slipped around her waist.

The sensible thing would be to protest, as she had last night, but instead, Ana arched her back, feeling him grow hard against her backside. She moved his hands down, into her panties. Fingers slid inside, awakening her.

In one move, Finn turned Ana and lifted her into his arms, his hands cupping her bottom as he pressed her against the tree, roughly. Nicolas and her words burned hot behind her, but the thoughts were driven from her head as Finn pushed up the hem of her dress and impatiently tugged his panties aside before driving himself in, filling her. His small, tender grunts against her neck, along with the sharp cuts the bark made in her back, drove Ana mad with a desire so potent it temporarily shelved her fears.

Ana wrapped her legs around his waist as his strong hands slid down to grip her thighs, the cold steel of his father's watch marking her flesh.

No amount of self-awareness could overcome her desire for Finn, and she was completely vulnerable to this welcome attack. When he was inside of her, there was nothing she could do to convince herself this was wrong, even though she knew his insistent lust was his helpless way of pulling her back to him, showing his devotion and fears in the same gesture.

After, Finn gently laid her down against the dirt and grass beneath the tree. Watching her. His eyes were filled with mixed love and desire.

He slid Ana's panties down her legs, and crawled up between them, flashing a sly grin. Always an unselfish lover.

As he pleasured her, another, recent memory flashed through Ana's mind.

Two weeks ago, just days before the big explosion of truth and violence. It was evening, and she was fixing herself some tea. Finn had come up from behind her; the sneak attack, one of his signature moves. Whispering his affection in her ear, then promptly lifting and settling her on the counter. Her pants were off before she could protest, *What if Jon comes in?*

He's working late, Finn insisted, though she could hardly make out his words with his face nestled between her legs.

She relaxed, allowing the loss of herself in the moment. The pleasure mounting, she closed her eyes to shut out everything else from the sensory overload. The risk of detection only heightened her need.

When Ana's eyes opened next, Jon stood in the doorway. Watching them. She very nearly jumped, but the shock was quickly overrun with rage knowing he remained there inten- tionally. He was *challenging* her. To do what? To stop? To call him out? She wouldn't give him the satisfaction. She was tired of his selfish, hurtful games.

Ana dug her heels in, meeting his challenge in obdurate determination, fixing her eyes on his as she grew closer to conclusion. Jon's lips twitched as he watched. He had done this to himself, and his own stubbornness kept him firmly rooted in place.

Squeezing her thighs against Finn's head, bracing herself against the oak cabinets, she bit her lip, prolonging the moment.

She wanted to punish Jon, the way he'd unfairly punished her, although she could never match in her own revenge the violence he'd wrought upon her.

In that moment of increasing intensity, Ana hated him with a passion that rivaled any she had ever known.

As she shuddered in release, cries of pleasure filling the kitchen, Jon's face tensed. For one moment, his eyes betrayed his pain, but then a slow, cruel smile spread across his lips.

Shaking off the memory, Ana looked up to see Finn eyeing her, confused. "What's wrong?" he asked.

"Let's finish later," she coaxed gently. She let him pull her back up, and dust her off.

"That's not why I came out here..." Finn wondered in a distant, contented voice, as they walked back toward the house. His ruddy cheeks were flushed in satisfied bliss. For now, he was happy, their problems forgotten.

Ana didn't say anything. She let him pull her close, protectively, and even smiled when his lips touched her forehead. But once back in the house, Ana excused herself and found privacy in the small bathroom near the butler's pantry.

Once behind the closed door, the dam broke. She gasped, heaving against the door, biting back the tears, knowing if she did not they would never, ever stop.

Maybe it was true, what her aunts all said about the Deschanel Curse.

Ana had a secret.

The result of Finn's passion had become effective shackles, binding them together, no matter how much pain she was bound to cause him. She was trapped, and lost, and her entire world was about to crash down around the shoulders of Ana and everyone she loved.

27- NICOLAS

*M*ercy had been in the shower quite a while. He wanted to check on her, but it would be entirely inappropriate to walk in there while she was naked.

Nicolas had given away all his sisters' clothing when they died, but kept some of his mother's. He didn't know why, exactly, although he was sure a shrink would have plenty of conclusions to draw from it. Mercy was tall, like Cordelia. He was certain the clothes would fit.

The pipes creaked as she shut the water off. Nicolas' heart skipped. *What the hell is wrong with me?*

A few minutes later, Mercy emerged dressed in a loose fitting black cotton shirt and probably the closest thing Cordelia Deschanel had ever owned to sweats—some red yoga pants. Her wet hair spilled down over the shirt, and where the silvery-red stopped, the red from the pants began. She appeared before him, a flaming torch.

She stole his breath away.

"I feel much better," Mercy said. He observed the way her cherry-red mouth formed the words. How she favored one leg over the other as she glided toward him. The slight cock of her hips. The way the water in her hair brought out that astonishing chromatic effect.

She rubbed her lips together, slipping her tongue slightly through the gap.

Fuck's sake, Deschanel. Pull yourself together!

"Are you up for meeting the others?" he asked, attempting to regain some composure and dignity.

She hesitated. "Would it be bad if I said I wasn't?"

"Would it be bad if I admitted I didn't really want company either?"

"I'm fine on my own," she offered.

Nicolas threw his hands up. "No, I wasn't saying…. I guess what I meant was I would prefer if it were…"

"…just the two of us?" she finished for him.

"If that's okay?" Nicolas wasn't sure whether to be grateful she'd bailed him out of his hormonal awkwardness, or concerned she was finishing his sentences. What he didn't like was the feeling of his beloved control slipping.

"It's okay," she demurred, looking down. Her sudden bashfulness was even more of a turn-on.

He needed fresh air. He gestured for her to follow him out to the veranda. The door from the bedroom faced the rear of the property and its vast fields, most of which had been sold off over the years. The Deschanel Trust had ruled the land unnecessary, and with the financial gain to the estate, worth the loss. If it were up to Nicolas, and he supposed it was, they'd never sell off another inch of Deschanel land.

It was raining, but the veranda had partial cover. Nicolas pulled her chair out first, then sat next to her. The fire inside him began to die down, as the breeze and comfortably soothing sounds of the winter raindrops in the eaves relaxed them both. A fine mist settled over the grounds, visually splitting the great oaks in half so their heavy branches seemed to float above the haze.

"I can't quite figure you out," Mercy ventured after a comfortable silence. A small smile hinted at the corners of her lips. The way she looked at him then—the way she always looked at him—made Nicolas feel as if he were nothing more than a social experiment to her.

"There's not much to figure out," he insisted, after an intentional pause. "What you see is what you get."

She shook her head. "No, you'd like for me to think that, but it isn't so."

"If you say so." Nicolas rolled his eyes.

"You want people to see you as carefree, not giving a damn. For people to assume you're unaffected by everything that comes your way. You diligently maintain the claim of having virtually no cares, no direction, and no goals except to live each day to the fullest. Am I right so far?"

"I didn't know you were capable of sarcasm, Mercy."

She laughed. "Except none of that is entirely true. You do care about things. There are people in your life you would die for. Your confidence is real, but easily shaken. Rather than admitting a weakness, or letting it be seen, you instead shrug it off as yet another thing not to be worried about. You've never been in a real relationship, but you wear the absence as a badge of pride. As if it makes you some sort of ultimate bachelor, when in reality the reason you've never opened yourself to love is your very real fear of losing control. You're also in love with your cousin, primarily because it's easier to be in love with someone you can never have, than potentially put yourself out there and get hurt. Am I still on track?"

Nicolas gaped her. What the hell was he supposed to say to that? And who the hell told her about Ana? "Bartender, I'll have what she's having," he quipped.

She didn't laugh back. "No one else has ever said anything like this to you before. Most people accept what you present, at face value, and assume you're a professional asshole. I would guess maybe Oz, and Ana, have a slightly better understanding than most, but they let you live the façade because they love you too much to actually hurt you by exposing the illusion."

"You don't even know me," Nicolas objected, tensing. He shifted in his seat, wondering how the conversation had so swiftly moved in such an uncomfortable direction. The soft sounds of rain were no longer soothing, but grating. The mist separating the treetops from the grounds made him think of unpleasant scenes from horror movies.

"I've always been a particularly good judge of character," she said, without elaborating.

"Oh? Then explain to me how you managed to marry a psychopath?"

Amazingly, she didn't skip a beat. "We're often blind to our own relationships, but I have a pretty keen sense for others. I could see right through you almost immediately."

Mercy was backing him further, further against the invisible wall. "If that were true, you would have left my fucking island as soon as you met me!"

"I'm not trying to stir your defenses," she backed off, dropping her voice.

"Then why *are* you saying all of this? Is there a point? Huh?"

"I don't know. Because you're helping me. Maybe I want to help you, too," she said.

"And exactly how the fuck is this helping me?"

She put her hand over Nicolas', and his heart leapt again. This time the feeling wasn't unpleasant, but it was immensely confusing. He didn't particularly *like* when women got all feely around him, but especially not hot on the heels of an unsolicited, unwanted psychoanalysis session.

"Isn't it nice, for once, to just be yourself?" she asked, gently. The heat from her hand, still attached to his, scalded him.

Nicolas started to form a stinging retort, but then realized he didn't know what to say. He supposed there was truth in all she was suggesting, but to acknowledge any of it meant climbing the wall he'd built for himself long ago. He liked the wall. It was a handsome, sturdy one. He had built it, after all. He wasn't sure breaching it was such a good idea.

When he opened his mouth, what traitorously came forth was truth. "I suppose so."

Mercy's hand squeezed his again, and then she intertwined their fingers. Sighing, she dropped her head on his shoulder, beginning a moment he would look back upon for years and wonder about. One surprise after another, one heartbeat skipped after another. It couldn't possibly have been Nicolas who squeezed her hand back, and rested his head atop hers. He'd maintained the Nicolas illusion for so long, to act outside of it felt decidedly foreign.

"You're going to miss me when I'm gone," Mercy stated confidently.

"You'd sure like to think so."

"You will."

"Maybe."

"If it makes you feel less silly about it, I will probably miss you, too," she said.

"Well, who could blame you?" Nicolas teased. The tension was receding, and he was gradually returning to a place that was comfortable, no longer pondering the best way to jump off the balcony without breaking too many bones.

Mercy sighed and let the silence hang a moment before she said, "I can't really decide which side of you I like better: the witty asshole or the awkward, sensitive hero. "

"I think I liked *you* better when you kept shit to yourself," Nicolas bantered back easily.

She chuckled and leaned further into him. Her hair had a scent like nothing he had ever smelled before. Like honey, glaciers, and eternity.

Before Nicolas could persuade himself not to, he kissed her.

The shock of her warm lips against his nearly made him recoil, but then her mouth parted in welcome, her tongue lacing around his own, and he pressed further into her.

"This isn't a good idea," she whispered, their lips still lightly touching.

"Right," he politely agreed, stiffening. "Sorry."

Mercy put her hands on the back of his head, forcing eye contact. "No. Nicolas, you know what I meant. Want has nothing to do with it."

Want had *everything* to do with it! Nicolas wanted her. He knew it now. More than he had ever wanted anyone else.

He was furious, all at once, with everyone. Oz, for leaving him here to face these realizations. Mercy, for forcing herself into his life, and then under the surface. Her husband, for laying hands on her. Himself, for allowing his casual desire to encroach on his better judgment.

No, fuck that.

"Calm down, Nicolas," she whispered, pulling him out of his angry trance.

This time, she kissed him. He was drawn to her as if being led by invisible hands, out of his chair, sinking to his knees at her feet, in submission, years of feigned indifference gone, in a moment of need which defied reason. His illusion no longer mattered when measured against the sum of him and her.

He had never felt more vulnerable, or more alive.

"Mercy," he began, voice cracking, heart on fire, "I'll tear the world apart with my own hands to protect you."

Tears pooled in Mercy's brilliant gray eyes, and though he wished he could read her thoughts, he didn't need to. Her lips traveled to his cheeks, chin, forehead. She laid kisses atop his head, then grabbed hold of his hands, pressing those to her lips, too. He didn't understand this tenderness, nor the startling realization he needed it. He closed his eyes and let it happen, lost in a moment he never could have predicted.

Mercy remained in charge as she pulled him to a stand, leading him back into the bedroom. He was hers; in a single moment, he had surrendered everything to her. His vulnerability. His fears. His heart.

Mercy gently pushed him down on to the plush bed, working on his pants, then shirt. Her fiery hot lips burned as they excited parts of Nicolas he'd shared with many others, yet never like this.

Removing her own clothes, Mercy climbed on top of him. Her wet heat brushed up against his now rock-hard cock, and he nearly lost it. But as she looked down on him, Nicolas knew then that he had never seen anything more beautiful, or more real, than this. He had never before trembled with such crippling humility, or allowed himself to be this helpless.

Nicolas reached up and seized her hips gently, but firmly. Entering her felt like something transcendent. Ethereal. It was as if she wasn't even human, but some warm, beautiful creature he had dredged up from the sea. Her heat swallowed him whole, scorching him, a brand upon his heart and soul.

She closed her eyes as she rocked rhythmically, the glow of her body matching her flaming hair. He guided her, fearful he wouldn't last, and afraid of it ending. "Mercy," he whispered, as he spilled inside of her, unable to contain it any longer. His cock pulsed as her muscles seized upon it, finishing with him.

Mercy fell softly down on his chest, whispering, "Emyr help us both, Nicolas." Her tears trickled down his chest.

Nicolas was utterly lost.

28- MERCY

"*W*hat...?" Nicolas pointed at the Mark upon Mercy's breast. The tiny wings fluttered.

"Never mind that," Mercy moaned, distracting both him and herself. She could deceive herself into thinking this sport was intended as a distraction for him, but it wasn't true. She wanted him inside her again. She wanted him to fill her, again. Emyr, help her, but she did.

Desire flashed through his eyes. His thoughts were plain as day: *This time, I will not be so gentle.* Good. She was not after gentle. There was nothing gentle could do for Mercy in these final hours, as she frivolously allowed herself this one, final distraction...

Nicolas' soft hands turned her around, flipping her to her stomach in one swift, shocking move. She gripped the sheet to steady herself as his hands roughly tugged on her hips, raising them to meet him. There was no warning; he entered her, beginning his thrusting in desperate, but practiced moves. The tenderness from earlier was not gone entirely, but the submission was; it was his turn to dominate. This was his territory.

Mercy moaned as she was rocked back and forth from the

shock of his forceful lovemaking. His fingers dug into her thighs, bruising, and his hips smashed into hers with such force she feared he might break one of his precious, human bones. But oh, how the blood rushed to her face, filling her with such a longing as she had never, ever known.

She nearly laughed as she remembered Aidrik's warnings. *Men are... smaller, Clementyn. The punishment of such an offense would far outweigh any reward.* Ahh, her dearest Aidrik. Even Empyreans were not impervious to silly rumors. She would be adequately sore after this.

The pleasure in being so filled drove Mercy mad with wanting, and she spread her legs wider to receive more of him. His thumbs pulled her further apart, and as she pushed back into him, she was rewarded with another powerful, shuddering orgasm, perfectly in synch with his.

Nicolas didn't hesitate to take her again, and then again. He stopped only to taste her; not a selfish lover, as she might have expected. He grew harder at observing her pleasure.

She had always heard Children of Men tired easily at sexplay. Not Nicolas. Was there any end to his desire? Was there any satisfying him?

His soaking, throbbing cock thrust into Mercy once again, silencing her question.

MERCY'S MIND PICKED UP BITS AND PIECES FROM THE VISITORS downstairs. Concern, curiosity. Glancing at the grandfather clock, she saw why. They'd been lost to their desires for hours.

What do you think they're doing up there? the one named Finn was asking.

Each other, obviously. Ana, the woman, responded without sarcasm. Ana, the cousin Nicolas was in love with.

They all loved her. Nicolas, Finn. Even Oz. Mercy had to meet the woman who could capture the hearts of this dynamic group of men. She came from a family of magi, though. Perhaps her ability involved enchantments.

No, it was not that, she realized with a burst of insight. Men were drawn to Anasofiya with a need to save her. Change her. Understand her. Fulfill her. But Ana believed herself incapable of all those things. She felt utterly alone. Worse, she believed she should be.

"We should go down now," Mercy whispered to Nicolas, lips pressed against his forehead. He was curled in her arms, breathing softly against her Mark. He wanted to ask more about it, but his thoughts were more deeply consumed with the moment.

Nicolas grunted, then nodded. As he slid off her, across the bed, a keen sense of loss struck Mercy. Would they ever be locked in embrace again? Worse, would the Senetat somehow find out, and punish her? Or him?

She had never taken the man's measure before, because it had not mattered. But now she allowed herself this final diversion. He was tall, though about half a head shorter than her; his muscles were cut lean, showing he took care of himself, but not too much. His skin, which had a slight permanent darkness about it from living in the South, was ruddy, yet somehow also pure. Unmarred. A lovely mouth, gently arced, always at the ready. His dark brown hair curled around his forehead from the sweat and exertion. Pretty. Yes, Children of Men would call him a pretty boy.

Mercy was startled with the realization that, very shortly, she would never see him again.

Nicolas worked around the bed, retrieving clothes, then sidled up behind her, still nude. His hardness pressed into her back, awakening her once more. Selfishly, she could remain in this bedroom with him until the end. For his sake, she would not.

"Change of plans," his deep, exhausted voice purred in Mercy's ear, "stay with me, here. I can protect you."

"Yes," Mercy whispered, weakly, the lie reverberating through the quiet room. She was once so sure of everything.

Emyr, what have I done?

INTRODUCTIONS WERE HARDLY NECESSARY, AS SHE'D GLEANED most of what she needed to know from their thoughts, but she allowed Nicolas to introduce her, finding his fumbled attempts at playing host endearing.

Mercy politely returned the greeting, reminding herself that while she knew something of both, neither knew anything about her.

Ana watched her closely. Her mind was well-guarded now, and Mercy wondered if she somehow knew she'd been listening in, the way her aunt had. This put Mercy at an uncomfortable disadvantage. Was Ana angry for what happened between Mercy and Nicolas? Or was she protecting her cousin? Their relationship confused Mercy.

She didn't know why she'd allowed the union with Nicolas at all. She tried to convince herself it was a means of thanking him for his help. She imagined herself teaching him some valuable lesson about tenderness. But none of these things were true, they were simply thoughts meant to restore her pretense of control.

Why now? she wanted to ask Our Father. *Why now, when I am about to achieve that which I have wanted for so long? Is this a lesson to me so I can feel something beyond my desire for Your love? Are You reminding me there are things I will miss in this world? Or is this a test, to see if I can withstand the trial of doubt?*

Mercy didn't want the answer. And if she didn't stop dwelling on it, she'd slip and this whole ruse would come crashing down...

...and yet, somehow she didn't care if it did. She no longer had the same enthusiasm to carry it through.

I am Yours in the flames... I am Yours in the flames...

"Are you going to get transportation arranged tonight?" Ana asked. Tonight! No, that was impossible.

"She isn't leaving," Nicolas quickly affirmed. "Sorry Oz wasted your time."

Finn and Ana exchanged looks. Finn was confused, but not Ana. Her eyes narrowed.

"What do you mean, not leaving?" Ana demanded.

Nicolas rolled his shoulders in a shrug of indifference. "She's not leaving. If her husband shows up, I have every legal right to blow his fucking head off for trespassing. Problem solved."

"We have your back, Nic," Finn said.

"That isn't why we came here!" Ana exclaimed. "I'm not going to sit back and accept you putting yourself in danger for someone you hardly know."

"We came to help," Finn said. "Not to take over. Right?"

"He's going to get himself killed, getting involved in this domestic crossfire!"

The bickering continued. To fight, or not to fight. For Mercy, there would be no fight. Her cells were slowly dying. She felt the call now more strongly than ever before.

A rippling, burning sensation rolled through her entire body. She gripped the table, throwing a searching glance out the large bay window. She couldn't do it in here. She had to find somewhere else. Outside.

"I know this sucks," Nicolas consoled, misinterpreting her body language for emotional distress. When he slipped his hand over her shoulder, his touch was tender. Protective. "But it'll be over soon."

Mercy nodded, wincing. It *would* be over soon, just not in the way they were expecting.

29- AIDRIK

*A*idrik rapped his knuckles against the large, oaken door. A home fit to house the entire Deschanel clan, yet his descendant, Nicolas Deschanel, had chosen a singular lifestyle. It defied comprehension.

An aging Child of Man answered his summons. His countenance reflected complete shock at Aidrik's appearance. Leather jerkin armor, battle-worn. Charcoal cloak, hood pulled back to reveal an avian-shaped scar. Violet eyes. Ulfberht dangling loyally at his side.

Being fair, he had not dressed for the occasion.

"Nicolasssss," the Man called over his shoulder. His eyes never left Aidrik's.

"I told you, let me answer the door, Richard." A swaggering Man trudged forth. His eyes, like his servant's, took Aidrik in. A smirk played at the corner of his Halfling mouth. Even had Aidrik not been watching him since the day of his birth, he still would have known him as part of his line.

Nicolas Deschanel was his progeny. His powers, either unknown or unrealized. Squelched by the shield Aidrik created to protect his descendants. This shield held strong over *Ophélie* after nearly two hundred years. By extension, protecting Nicolas as long as he never encountered another Empyrean to amplify what was in his blood.

But, he had. Mercy. Through Aidrik's gentle nudging. Was it possible, then, her presence had weakened the barrier?

Nicolas Deschanel and I, face to face, at last. The younger Man continued to watch in growing amusement. It would not be the first time, this standoff between Man and Aidrik. He was impervious.

"Please extend invitation," Aidrik declared.

"Yo, the LARP club is several plantations down the road," Nicolas replied. He nodded at Ulfberht.

"I have no time for games, Brother of Emyr."

"I don't know anyone named Emyr. Where did the security team go?" Nicolas queried, stepping outside and past him.

"Dismissed," Aidrik replied. "A task easier than it should have been."

"What the hell do you mean, dismissed?"

"I am Aidrik, of the Farværdig. Son of Emyr. Friend to Mercy. Your ally. Extend invitation."

The Halfling's attentions were no longer humor-filled. Taking in Aidrik now, slowly. Assessing the threat. Eyes narrowed, fists clenched at his sides. He meant him harm, though his reasons were as yet unclear.

Aidrik added, attempting a gentler tone, "Child of Man, there are powers beyond your understanding. Our goals are in accord. Time is running out, and I must palaver with Mercy."

His eyes widened in furious comprehension. "I promised Mercy if you showed up here, I'd kill you." Flashing, boasting eyes. Hesitant heart. He would do Aidrik no harm, despite his intention.

"That won't be necessary," Aidrik assured him. "Nor is it possible she was expecting me."

"Look, motherfucker, you're on *my* property now. This ain't

New York. We don't lay hands on our women. Ever heard of Southern justice?"

His defense of Mercy, simultaneously baffling and endearing. Halfling perhaps, but his Empyrean blood ran true. Amusing under better circumstances. "You may yet get your chance at exacting it. But not this day."

Nicolas's mind searched for a proper response, but it would wait. For, before Aidrik's eyes, stood Mercy. His Clementyn.

"*Aidrik?*" Her childlike wonder rooted him. Standing before her confirmed his worst fears. Undetectable by Man, but clear as crystal ice to him: Mercy would perish from this Earth. Soon.

"Aidrik?" Nicolas repeated. "Who the fuck is Aidrik? I thought your husband's name was Andrew?"

Nicolas was confused beyond measure, but explanation was unimportant. Time was of the essence. He must proffer truth and comfort to Mercy while she still lived.

"It cannot be," Mercy's voice called out, in little more than a whisper. It struck him her zealot heart might interpret his arrival as a sign from Emyr. For a brief moment, he considered changing his plans and playing to her heart's desire.

"But it is," he assured her. "I have much to share with you, and little time in which to do it. We must make haste."

More confusion. Explanations demanded from Nicolas. Insufficient answers from Mercy. Unimportant in light of what lay ahead, but Aidrik reminded himself these gestures were necessary.

His eyes scanned behind them and came across the Halfling from the night before. Her eyes grew wide at the sight of him. Recognition, though she remembered nothing real of the night before. His Nordic Princess had a flood of confusion and unasked questions. He forced himself to set aside the growing fondness, lingering in her luminous gaze.

He sent his thoughts silently. Direct. *Sister of Emyr... your name?*

What? How? Her eyes-like-the-sea further widened. Surprise. Telepathy, then, new to her.

Your name.

Ana. Anasofiya.

Anasofiya. We must palaver.

Do I know you? I do. I know you.

Yes, though not in the way you might expect. Is your sojourn here permanent?

No.

You will wait? Long enough for us to talk?

Small hesitation. Eyes-like-the-sea searching for understanding, and explanation. Fear. *I leave when she does.*

Unexpected, piercing warmth stole through Aidrik's core. The strength of connection from the night before magnified to a near painful certainty. *Evigbond.* The evigbond was not like the romantic love of Men. It was instant. Immediate, like a gust of mighty wind. Unseverable, like the Gordian knot.

Anasofiya.

But first, he must attend to Mercy.

PATIENT, THOUGH NOT IMMUNE TO FRUSTRATION, AIDRIK WISHED Clementyn and Nicolas shared his urgency instead of their heated discussion. His will was lost as his eyes continued to fall on Anasofiya. Another Child of Man now present, holding her from behind; the one from her bed, the night before. A clenching, iron possessiveness stole over him. Not a flattering trait. Instinctively, he unsheathed his steel.

"Is that...?" The blonde Child Of Man gestured at Ulfberht. "God, that is one hell of an Ulfberht replica!"

"Replica?" Aidrik raised eyebrows at the young Man. He emitted a bright, shining light. Innocent. This did not quell the unbecoming jealousy at his familiar touching of Anasofiya.

Physical connection meant little in the face of evigbond.

Aidrik would not feel this if it were one-sided. The evigbond only happened when two beings fused equally. The only unknown was the potency in which Men experienced it. For Empyreans, there was nothing stronger. In Men, their human side fought for equal footing. Even Christiane's heart had been torn in two. Was Anasofiya's?

Evigbond could be achieved in two ways. The first, through intimacy. This way was not guaranteed, except when Empyrean mated with Man, yet another reason the Senetat had forbidden this act. The second was chemical; innate. No connection necessary. Fate is the word Man might use to describe it.

This second, more sacred form was almost certainly at play now.

"Where do you even buy such a thing?" The Man approached Aidrik with wide, curious eyes. Small pride swelled within him. Many, many years had passed since any Man recognized his steel with such immediate ease.

"Finn," Anasofiya cautioned, in a small voice. Lyrical and smooth, like honey. Spindles of heat coursed through Aidrik again. *Anasofiya.*

"Ana, have you read the stories about this thing?" the one named Finn asked. Anasofiya dropped her eyes. *Avoiding me.* Yes, that would be easier. But impossible now.

"Well, it's similar to Damascus steel, but better. It's from Viking times, and no one was able to replicate how they made it until recently. Hell, no one even knows *who* made them!" Finn reached a hand toward his crucible blade, then thought better of it. "This is the best replica I have ever seen."

"It was made for me," Aidrik explained, to Finn. Finn, like the mariner. A man of the sea would recognize a sword wielded by Vikings.

After Aidrik ignored his query, "Who made it for you?" Finn continued his education of Anasofiya. Crucible steel. Charcoal and steel, forged at 3,000 degrees. Made for strength, lightness, flexibility. Minimal slag, to reduce brittleness. A history book lesson, and only a sliver of the truth.

History books did not tell of Blacksmith, one of the first Empyreans. Not Crucible Steel, but Empyrean. Forged high in the mountains of Farjhem. Man vied to wield them, but they were crafted for Empyrean hands.

Finn's interest and education on the matter was a first in Aidrik's modern wandering. He was undeniably surprised. Moreover, delighted. An unexpected respite in an otherwise somber journey.

"It's not a replica." Mercy's voice broke into Finn's excited tutelage. Weary. Weak.

"But... how?" Finn wanted to believe. Perhaps did.

Surprising himself even more than Finn, Aidrik tilted the hilt his direction. Offering. Large, innocent eyes grew wide as Finn accepted, slowly. His strong, labored hands sagged slightly as he bore the full weight of Ulfberht. Aidrik felt his wonder and marveled anew.

Never before had he allowed any Man to wield his steel.

Finn. Anasofiya. His sense of charity toward the former, his connection to the latter. Pondering this would come later.

Mercy could not wait.

30- NICOLAS

"*L*et them have their privacy," Ana chided him, as Nicolas paced outside the study where Mercy and Aidrik were "talking." Or whatever the fuck they were doing.

Finn had escaped to make a phone call. Ana leaned against the back of the armoire, gazing out the window. The rain and wind lashed violently against the panes of glass.

"Excuse me if I feel the need to know more about the warlock cosplay fuck who just came into my home," Nicolas snapped. "And Mercy, how the fuck does she know him?"

"There's a lot you don't know about Mercy," Ana reminded him. Her calm rationale threatened his irrational anger only slightly. When he'd assumed the role of Mercy's protector, it meant not letting ridiculous-looking fucks into the house to toy with her.

"I don't need to know her life story to be concerned about whatever the hell just walked in to my home." Nicolas continued to stride around the hall, needing some sense of action. It was killing him not knowing what was going on in the next room.

"She wasn't concerned. Maybe that's reason enough for you to calm down?"

"I didn't ask for your advice," he spat. He stopped moving, as it occurred to him this was his first moment alone with Ana since he banished her from his life.

"No, I don't suppose you did," Ana replied, her voice sad and distant. She was only half-present in her gentle admonishments. Her mind was drifting elsewhere, and for once, he wished he could force this strange new mind-jumping ability and dive in.

He had wanted her to suffer for what she did. It was easier to punish Ana than to accept his own twisted feelings.

Nicolas no longer wanted her to be in pain.

"I forgive you," he blurted. Did she even require his forgiveness? Had she ever?

She turned her head, her attention now focused entirely on him. "Okay."

"Fuck's sake, Ana, let me try that again. Will you forgive *me*? I've been a selfish son-of-a-bitch. I put expectations on you that were unfair, and wrong, and fucking unhealthy. I don't really want to go into it, but I think you understand what I'm trying to say."

Her eyes glistened. Her face was impossible to read, as always, though he studied it intently, trying anyway. "I came here to help you, but I also came to say goodbye."

"Where the hell are you going?"

She shook her head, wringing her small, delicate hands in anguish. "I don't know. But when I get there, I'm never looking back."

Errant foolishness drove Nicolas to rush toward her, and take her in his arms. He crushed her to him, desperate for words he couldn't begin to suitably articulate. In his arms, her demeanor crumbled. *Oh, my Ana.*

Further senselessness led his lips to hers. The unexpected kiss choked her sobs, and she returned his foolish gesture, sobbing into his mouth as he consumed her. Thirty years of angst-filled love passed between them; all his frustration, pain, sadness, and desire. His Ana. His first love.

He came alive in her arms. He was an unnatural abomination, and no longer cared to deny it.

It was Ana who chose to end their foolish self-indulgence. "We can't live trapped by this," she whispered, burying her tear-stained face in his neck. "We've held each other back our whole lives. Love disguised as salvation."

Nicolas knew whatever happened here, whatever was said, it would be permanent. "You *are* my salvation," he insisted. It sounded like hollow begging.

"Mercy is your salvation," she corrected. "I'm your undoing."

"Mercy—" he started to protest, then stopped. What was his objection? That Mercy was just another passing fancy? That she meant nothing? Ana's words unsettled him, for reasons he didn't fully understand.

"Ana. What happened after I left? In Maine?" Nicolas demanded. Images from his voyage through Ana's thoughts still flickered through his head. Her sorrow now had nothing to do with what transpired between them.

Ana shook her head. "It doesn't matter now."

It mattered. It mattered enough that it had turned Ana into a former shell of herself. But Ana was no longer his, if she ever really had been. When he'd let her go in Maine, it was as symbolic as it was literal. When she released him moments ago, the decision took a deeper hold. There was a wall between them that would never again come down. His heart ached to think of it, but it also felt liberated. Pain in freedom.

"Finn is a good man," he said, finally. "He's good for you."

She swiped the back of her hands across her eyes. "Yes, he is. And he'll be back soon, so you should pull yourself together."

Nicolas hadn't realized he was crying, too.

31- MERCY

*M*ercy hadn't yet begun to process Aidrik's startling appearance. Now, alone with him in the large study, she was forced to.

He looked no different, really. His violet eyes still pierced directly to her soul. His soft, beautiful face remained unlined, despite his age. Most of the red was purged from his hair now, and he wore his chromatic silver locks shorter. The soft strands went in all different directions, making him appear a man in his twenties, though he would be pushing four millennia. He was handsome, and commanding, as he always had been. Perfect.

No, not perfect. Where the Mark once lay beautifully at his temple, a white, scarred outline remained. Mercy gasped. Was this a result of his Ascension?

"I razed it from my flesh," his soft voice explained. Was he in her thoughts? She did not think so. Her eyes had betrayed the question.

"But, why?" She could think of no better question to start with.

"I am here to tell you," he replied softly, gesturing for her to have a seat.

Mercy sunk down in the large, leather armchair, slowly. "You're alive," she breathed, voicing the most prevalent thought running through her mind. "You... are... alive."

"For the time being," he agreed. His sad, resigned smile, so achingly familiar, pierced her heart. What had he been through? And where, on this Earth, had he been?

"How, though? How did you survive it? Aidrik, I *saw* my parents die when their Marks were removed! Saw it happen to others!"

"It was not the Mark's removal which killed them," Aidrik revealed. "It was the sundering of it using black magic. I removed mine beyond the knowledge of the Senetat. Your mother and father's were removed by the Lion itself."

Mercy didn't understand his bitter words towards Our Father's revered Senetat. "How did you find me?"

"I never lost you," he replied. Simply, as Aidrik always spoke.

She took a deep breath, and the phoenix on her chest fluttered at the disruption. Two statements, two surprises, and only the beginning. "I'm listening," she said.

Aidrik did not sit. But then, Aidrik never did. He preferred the freedom and flexibility of standing, always being at the ready.

"You are evigbond with the Man," he said, with a disapproving frown. "Unwise, but likely irrelevant now. We will discuss at the end."

There was no point in arguing with him, or in telling him her time with Nicolas was an unexpected distraction, nothing more. Any feelings she had for the Man held far less sway than what lay ahead.

No point in explaining either, that had she met Nicolas before the Ascension started, she might have thrown everything aside for him.

No, there was no point in discussing or dwelling on anything of this Earth. But she would listen to Aidrik's story, out of love, and relief that she could see his face one last time before her departure.

"The Senetat revealed itself to be less than honorable, early in my tenure," he began. He stood near the door, as if expecting an unwelcome visit. Ulfberht hung close to him. She was still shocked at his willingness to hand it over to Finn earlier. Very unlike the Aidrik she had known.

"No form of government is without fault," Mercy replied, defensively. She was not of a mind to listen to one of his lectures about humanity. "Empyreans are no exception, old friend."

"Genocide, from any governing body, is unpardonable," he countered. "The Mark is their vessel for this destruction."

Mercy couldn't help herself. She burst out laughing, harder than she had in some time, and so much it actually felt cathartic. Genocide? The Mark was an ancient, enduring symbol of Our Father! Wherever Aidrik had been all these years, it had not done him favors. Why, he was as crazy as Old Aita.

He ignored her and continued. "In the beginning, I was an eager disciple of their teachings. Like you. I absorbed everything. I believed only the most wise and venerable could rise to such ranks. To be included among them was life's greatest honor. My hubris at being inducted to such a status, then, understandable.

"We were faced with many challenging decisions. Discussions often led to heated debate. I was reminded of my disdain for their rulings, in my youth. Now one of them, I sympathized with the untenable burden.

"But always, always I believed it was in service to greater good. In veneration of Our Father. It did not once occur to me there might be more sinister forces at work, until I became witness to them."

"Really, Aidrik? Still... after all these years? I can already see where this is going, and you needn't bother!" Mercy exclaimed.

"It was during a jesting discussion about Old Aita I first suspected the truth," he continued, ignoring her. "One of the old ones joked it was a far worse punishment allowing her to live than to activate her and end her suffering.

"'Activate?' I asked.

"'Son of Emyr, we chose you for your healthy skepticism. Do you really believe it is Emyr who calls you home?' One of the elders cajoled me.

"Yes, I had believed it. Like you, Clementyn, I had trusted the Mark as a physical manifestation of Our Father's love. But it was not until I witnessed their destruction of my beloved kinsman, Galon, that I knew the Mark was false."

"Aidrik—" Mercy started, but he continued his story.

"The Marks are indeed magic, though a more sinister form. When bound through incantation, the Mark becomes an instrument of the Senetat. Any Empyrean can be tracked at will, and when the Senetat deems it so, their Mark is activated. Death comes swiftly."

"*I'm* still here," she said dismissively. "What you are suggesting is blasphemy! Clearly, they were toying with you. Our Father would never allow anyone, not even His beloved Senetat, to assume such control over His people!"

"Free will," Aidrik said, by way of explanation. "Our Father gifted us the choice to believe as we wish. It was not his will we be subject to the Senetat's self-serving laws. It is our own fault for letting them rise up in His name."

"Lovely sentiment," she hissed. "No wonder they kicked you out."

"I removed myself. Had I not, they would have likely sent me to Farskilt for my burgeoning dark thoughts." He pointed to the scar at his temple that she had been eyeing in a vague curiosity. "I cut this from my being, without fore-knowledge of the result. I did not know if I would survive it, or if it would do as I intended, and sever my indenture with the Senetat. At the time, either outcome meant freedom. Fortune was on my side."

"Or folly! You have eradicated the most sacred connection to Our Father! Your actions are an affront to him and... and ... to me!"

Aidrik's stone-still hands finally moved, folding over his mouth. "I do not wish to affront you—"

"Three thousand years, Aidrik. That is how long I have been alive. How long I have subscribed to the theology—"

"Zealotry."

"My *faith*! You knew... wait, you knew I wouldn't believe you," she said, slowly, as this realization stole over her. He had known her too well to believe his words would sway her.

"Yes," he confirmed.

"Why are you only now coming to me?" she demanded. Suspicion edged with doubt. She'd once trusted Aidrik, but the years dulled her unwavering loyalty.

"It was unsafe."

His judicious use of language was still frustrating.

"And now it *is* safe?" she pressed, annoyed.

"Safe or not is irrelevant now," he said, with a near imperceptible shrug. "The risk is no longer present."

"I don't understand..."

Slow, sad smile. "You never did."

Mercy's pride flamed forth. No one had ever been able to make her bury her tail quite like Aidrik. "You haven't answered my question. Why now?"

"To offer you some small comfort as you die."

"Ascend," she corrected. "Your heretical story taught me nothing except confirmation of your apparent insanity."

"I know."

"You know?"

"Clementyn. I embraced false hope for years, praying you would find enlightenment. Watched sadly as you blindly followed errant wishes of the heart, rather than face reason. In part, your accusation of insanity is correct. My fondness for you kept me watching far beyond what could reasonably be termed sane."

"If you were so fond of me, why did you not attempt to rip the Mark off my breast like you savagely did to your own?"

"I think you know the answer."

She smiled crudely. "*Enlighten* me."

Aidrik's sigh spoke of his further disappointment in her, but he went forth with explanation anyway. "Had I believed there was even a small chance you would accept the truth, I would have ripped it asunder without hesitation. But I am living flesh, as you. My instinctive need for self-preservation is strong. I could not risk detection for what was destined to be no reward."

She laughed in offended frustration. "Then why tell me at all!"

"A parting gift. A chance it may help you in whatever after-life awaits."

She wanted to scream, but feared Nicolas might come in bearing some crude weapon of Man, constructed from his vast kitchen apparatus. Aidrik had always condescended to her beliefs, and now he sought to ruin the one thing, in all the world, that held meaning to her by tainting it with *truth*? "What-ever awaits? So, Aidrik the Wise does not *know* what awaits?"

"No," Aidrik said, simply. "And it matters little."

"You never did have faith," she accused. "You danced around it with reason, never even trying to believe, even for a moment, you might have been created by something, someone, greater than you—"

"—I doubt not Our Father, only his misguided minions—"

Mercy threw up her hands, silencing his interruption. "You questioned everything, always! You could never just accept the plan Our Father laid out for you! Never!"

His face was, as always, impassive. She hated him for it.

"Faith and blindness are often confused. Ignorance is not permission to loiter in darkness," he said.

She balled her fists at his slur, but his hand reached to steady her. Within moments, his face had taken on a softer countenance. "Mercy, accept my apology. I did not come here to insult you."

"I still can't believe you are actually here," she mused, more to herself than him. Her anger was dissolving slowly, replaced by wonder her old friend had somehow cheated death. She did not, for a second, believe any of the nonsense about the Senetat, but she didn't doubt Aidrik had somehow escaped his fate by removing his beloved Mark. However, while Aidrik saw this as a vehicle of freedom, she knew it to instead be the destruction of his very soul.

Death would be a mercy for him.

"I am not so eager to meet my maker as you," Aidrik said with a sly smile, reading her mind. In her anger, she had let her guard down, but it didn't matter. Anything he would read in her thoughts she would just as quickly speak aloud.

"Assuming that's whom you will meet when you die," she retorted, but this time there was no venom in her words. She was genuinely dismayed to know her old friend would die a death of the unknown.

"We should discuss the matter of your evigbond," he changed topics. His tone was almost fatherly, reminding her time had dulled any real passion between them.

"Must we?" she moaned, playing the part he assigned her. "And I would hardly call it evigbond. Sex is sex."

"Unwise," he scolded, gently ignoring her futile denial. "You've put his life in danger."

It was Mercy's turn to frown. "How so?"

"Suspend your disbelief on this matter, if on nothing else. You've defied one of our most natural laws. The Senetat does not take well to disobedience, and will not shy from meting appropriate justice."

"The laws state I am the one who has disobeyed. Not Nicolas," she replied. "Which matters very little given the time I have left."

"Mercy," Aidrik said, "have you not wondered why this law exists?"

"I suppose you're going to tell me."

"Mating between Man and Farværdig creates a permanent, unbreakable bond. Evigbond, every single time, without fail," he explained.

"That is not how evigbond works," Mercy argued, thinking of the hundreds of years she'd spent with Aidrik. "It is not a guarantee."

"Between two Empyreans, no," Aidrik agreed. "Between Empyrean and Man, the cohesion of mating results in evigbond in every case. You are confusing it with the biological evigbond that can occur between two Empyreans, without conjugal relations."

"I don't understand where you're going with this."

"Any offspring from the unions between Empyrean and Man result in an unnatural Halfling, who is neither truly Man nor Empyrean. Unwieldy, reckless, unsure how to handle the power they possess. Their very existence threatens the secrecy and solitude of our race." Aidrik paused. "Even you can grasp the danger in this."

She snorted. "Well, he's safe, then. Conception is irrelevant at this stage in my Ascension."

Aidrik eyed her, his raised eyebrow indicating she had missed the point. "You may not be with child. But you have exposed yourself, and thus our race, to a Child of Man. The bond you created was permanent, and he will not forget you. He is vulnerable by it. This puts him in danger. Your Mark, the conduit through which he will be revealed."

She shrugged, as if it could not matter less, but his words strangled her. She felt as she did when she'd nearly drowned, panicked and flailing in the cold dark water. She wanted to continue refuting everything that fell from Aidrik's lips, but his admonition rang true. What if they did come for Nicolas? She would not be there to protect him, to shield him. She had possibly sentenced him to death with her weakness.

"He is protected," Aidrik assured her, once again reading her thoughts. "I have guarded him all his life, as I shielded his ancestors. Your arrival at *Ophélie* was no mere coincidence. Did you never wonder why your 'Inner Voice' began only after I was no longer counted amongst our ranks?" When Mercy started to speak, he held one hand up, gently silencing her in typical Aidrik fashion. "Do not request explanation yet, Mercy. We have little time, and I'd rather not repeat the story."

Without saying anything further, Aidrik moved toward the door. "Where are you going *now*?" she asked.

Aidrik smiled at her, but his smile did not reach his eyes, displaying rare proof of his age and weariness. "To *enlighten* you and your bonded mate."

32- NICOLAS

*I*n the long moments before Finn reappeared in the central hall, Nicolas tried desperately, and failed miserably, to dive into Ana's thoughts. Her demeanor chilled him, and he was convinced something was horribly wrong, but he needed to confirm what she wouldn't tell him.

It had to do with whatever happened in Maine. It was the same thing that turned strong, confident Finn into a clingy teenager whenever he was around her. But worst of all, and at the front of Nicolas' mind: whatever it was, it was killing her.

In that desperate, crazy moment where he finally kissed her, wrought with years' worth of stored love, grief, longing, and frustration, he didn't feel nearly as sorry as he should. For more than a moment, he'd wished desperately everyone would leave the house so he could take her, right there, just as he'd always secretly desired, somewhere well under the surface of his conscious existence. He would have, too. Even now, with the fog of desire cleared from his thoughts, he would still do it. She was the only woman he had ever loved, and he'd reached acceptance on the indisputable truth that he would desire her until his dying day.

Quite frankly, he didn't care what that said about him.

Beyond all his illogical desires, though, Nicolas just wanted her to be okay. He wanted to see that beautiful, secret smile of hers again. He'd even be happy to see her light up in Finn's arms, as he had in his first vision of her. He could celebrate in his irrational jealousy if it saved her.

Nicolas didn't like the way she smiled with her mouth, but not her eyes, as Finn embraced her this time. Nor how, as soon as her head was safely over his shoulder, the tears welled in her eyes and her lips twitched in pain. Why had he not demanded the answers from her? He let her get away with "it doesn't matter," when he knew better. Shit, *she knew* he knew better!

Nicolas hated feeling as though he'd failed a critical test. He worried what that failure might mean for Ana. A sense of dread he couldn't set down.

He hadn't missed the way that cosplaying fuck had eyed her either. In his long, thrift-store cape and that ridiculous white stencil of an ugly bird on his face. And now, that same asshole was in Nicolas' study, alone with Mercy. They must be conducting their business in whispers, too, because he could hear nothing at all beyond the doors.

Mercy. He hadn't thought of her once while he was with Ana. His feelings for her weren't something he was prepared to analyze. Love was such an unappealing thought. Loving Ana was okay because she was off-limits. Even if he couldn't control himself, she could. Nicolas had told many women he loved them in the throes of passion, knowing it would build the climax higher and higher, only to never return a call from them after. Much as he wished to fool himself, Mercy was not one of those women.

She possessed an unsettling understanding of who Nicolas was, and was not the least bit put off by it. She handled his embarrassing vulnerability with astonishing finesse, letting him then redeem himself by showing off his unparalleled domination skills. Hell, he was surprised the chick was walking.

Then he invited her to stay here. Like a chump. And though Nicolas was sure he could find a smooth way to take it back, he didn't want to. He wanted that woman, as he had wanted Ana moments before. His head spun to think of it.

"Want me to go in there?" Finn asked, snapping Nicolas back to the current reality.

Nicolas shook his head. "No. But if Mercy looks the least bit upset when they come out, I'm going to rip that ugly, Viking replica piece of shit out of its plastic scabbard, and slice his fucking head off."

Finn nodded appreciatively. "Fair enough."

THE RAIN CONTINUED ITS MERCILESS STACCATO OUTSIDE. FINN held Ana like he feared she might sprint off into the woods at any moment. She'd fallen asleep against his chest. Or, was pretending to sleep. Nicolas knew her mouth gapped slightly when she was really sleeping. It was currently pressed tight.

Without warning, the study door flung open and Aidrik marched into the foyer. His presence immediately overwhelmed Nicolas, and he was suddenly conscious of his every flaw. Weirdo or not, the man knew how to work a room.

"We must palaver," he demanded. His voice was so strong and commanding Nicolas almost followed it like an obedient puppy. "Privately," he added.

Instead Nicolas said, "Go fuck yourself. Privately."

"No time," the man responded.

Mercy spoke up. "Nic, please. Aidrik has some things he'd like to tell us, and at this point I'm tired of mysteries." When Nicolas narrowed his eyes, she added, "You have nothing to worry about. Aidrik is a very old friend. That's all."

Nicolas wanted to argue she'd never mentioned this "old

friend" before, but even he knew that was an unreasonable response. He'd only known Mercy for a few days, even if it felt like an eternity.

"Fine. But the cheap, shitty sword stays with Finn."

Aidrik scoffed at this, looking nonplussed for the first time since Nicolas greeted him at the door. "Ulfberht is not meant for horseplay."

"It's also not meant for grown-ass men trying to overcompensate for other disadvantages I won't mention in front of the ladies. I'm not going into a closed room with you and that ridiculous Halloween prop."

Aidrik unlatched the sword belt, and handed it to Finn. It looked light in Aidrik's hands, but as soon as Finn bore the weight, it nearly clanked against the floor as he adjusted to its heft. Nicolas was stunned it had been that easy to get the man to relinquish it, and clearly so was Finn. He looked so excited Nicolas was almost happy for him.

"Incredible," Finn whispered. "Did you know the biggest advantage of the Ulfberht was its flexibility, which helped to ensure it didn't stick in shields during battle?"

"It's fake, and I don't care," Nicolas snapped. "Shall we?"

Nicolas gestured toward Mercy and her "old friend." He didn't have the faintest idea of what lay ahead. He only hoped that, once over, it would mean the guy could go back to wherever he came from.

33 - ANASOFIYA

*T*he grandfather clock gonged the hour painfully in the otherwise silent hall. The sound caused Finn to jump, nearly dropping the book he'd been pretending to read. Ana clasped her hands together, trying to stop their ceaseless shaking.

"I suppose you were right about the storm," she said, as the rain beat down on the fertile land outside.

"Yep," Finn replied, with a slightly cocky, and more than a little miffed emphasis at the end. She knew he was confused at her hot-and-cold behavior, and afraid to address her about it. He believed his promise to understand her meant giving up the right to probe into her gloomy moods. He was wrong, but talking about her problems had never resulted in anything good, so it was just as well he was disinclined to ask.

A part of Ana wanted him to sense the cruelty in her. She'd never directed her hurtfulness his way, because hurting Finn felt like hurting herself. A psychiatrist might say she was deliberately pushing him away, giving him cause to slowly stop loving her. It would be easier in the end, if it were his idea.

"I have a confession to make," Finn blurted, breaking the silence.

"Okay," she replied, tentatively. In her experience, confessions never ended well.

"When I told you lobsters can't feel pain, I lied." With that, he blew out a long-held breath, and awaited her reaction.

"Wait... what?"

"Do you remember me telling you that, when I met you on the beach? After you'd accidentally broken the cord to your fridge?"

"I remember," Ana said, as her mind attempted to puzzle out his intent, "but I'm not sure why you're telling me this."

The slight ruddiness in Finn's cheeks darkened. "Most scientists believe lobsters don't feel pain, and that's why animal welfare groups allow us to catch and prepare them the way we do," he continued. "Lobsters don't have a very complex brain or nervous system, so it's believed they aren't capable of feeling pain in the way creatures with a vertebrae do. But the truth is, they do feel pain. Maybe not as intensely as we do. I mean, hell, lobsters are known to rip off a limb if it's injured, and you'll never see a human do that. But they absolutely understand and feel it, in their own way."

"Finn—"

"I'm not a marine biologist, but even if I was, that isn't how I know. I know because I *know*. Do you understand what I'm saying?"

Ana nodded. Finn's connection with nature had, more than once, reminded her of the unique way a Deschanel was able to interact with the world around them. Inexplicable, but indisputable.

"I'm apologizing because..." When he looked up at her, she had to bite back a giggle. Seeing him distraught over something so silly was, unfortunately, a little amusing. "That was a line I used on women all the time, when I wanted to get them in bed. I thought it showed my sensitive side, and made me look smarter than they thought I was."

This time, she did laugh. "I would've eaten the lobster regardless."

"My point is, you deserve better than that, Ana."

That was debatable. But it was very apparent this confession was not easy for Finn, and it meant more to him than just a silly fib about a crustacean. Everything he'd been trying to tell her for the past month had all lead to this deeper, more intense message.

He was powerfully in love, and it was turning him inside out.

Suddenly, the confession didn't seem so funny.

If only he'd allowed her to come to Louisiana on her own. She could've made a clean break. He might have hated her for her cold defection, but hatred is quicker to heal than heartbreak.

But then, Ana hadn't known what she knew now. What had been weighing heavy on her heart since she arrived, though so far she'd willfully ignored it.

The conversation with Aunt Colleen from the day before played in her head, over and over. She'd met Ana and Finn at Louis Armstrong International Airport when they landed in New Orleans.

Darling, when I said I hoped you wouldn't be a stranger, I was not implying we needed to see each other every few days, Aunt Colleen had teased.

Nicolas needed me.

Yes, I know of Nicolas' delicate condition. But I'm not sure how I missed yours.

Excuse me?

Why, you're with child, dear, Aunt Colleen had whispered in Ana's ear. Finn was across the crowded room, awaiting their bags. The room started to spin.

I'm not, she'd insisted, but her aunt's knowing eyes studied her. If anyone would know, it was Colleen, the healer. Her senses were uncanny.

You are. Her delicate hands smoothed Ana's hair back from her face in a gesture so tender a sob caught in her throat. *But it doesn't have to be the end of the world, Ana.*

Oh, but it did. But it was. Then a deeper fear hit Ana as she realized the child could just as easily be Jon's. Colleen allayed those fears with an additional bit of information. *Three weeks, at most, my dear. Too soon to show up on any test. Unless you've revisited your affections with Jonathan since that first time, your child is Finn's.*

Of course, the possibility had always been there. Ana had been near to running out of birth control even before her fall had landed her at the St. Andrews house for over a week. And then, she'd stayed at Finn's bedside for two more weeks. By the time they'd returned home, in mid-December, she'd long forgotten the need for it. Too many other things clouded her mind.

And now, she would pay for that lapse in judgment. How could she make a clean break with Finn's child growing inside her? Especially knowing how much he wanted it; how much he craved the idea of being a father. She knew he would make an excellent parent, but she could not confidently say the same thing about herself.

The last twenty-four hours had been a complete whirlwind. From her aunt's revelation, to Nicolas' pent up passions spilling through; to meeting Aidrik, whose presence alone set her entire body on fire in a way that was not, entirely, unpleasant.

In fact, it was more than not unpleasant. When her eyes locked on Aidrik's intense gaze, pulsing shivers ran rampant along the length of her spine. She was frozen in place, first by his piercing eyes, and then his telepathic messages. She had never, ever before communicated with anyone that way. Ana was a healer, not a telepath, and while she had learned to block her thoughts from others, she had never been able to share them.

The enigmatic hooded stranger, from her dreams. Somehow real.

Who was this man? Not a Deschanel, certainly. But then, how had they communicated that way? And why did it feel as if he were still inside her, connected to her very soul?

Wait for me, he had said. *For now*, she had replied. Lied. Her response had been autonomic, as if it were not her mind but soul responding to him. What she should have said was: *It's too late for me.*

Love. Want. Need. The three words were so easily confused. Ana loved Finn. She loved Nicolas. Had loved Oz, at one time. She'd wanted Oz that night, just as she'd wanted Nicolas moments ago in the parlor, and had let him, just once, kiss her.

But what she needed was in direct conflict with all three. She needed to have never acquiesced to Oz's affections. She needed to have been more firm in the wall she put between herself and Nicolas. She needed to have never caved to Jon. She needed them all to love someone else, so she could let them go.

And, she needed *both* Finn and Aidrik, all at once. In a visceral, fundamental way, just as people need oxygen to breathe, and water to live. She didn't even know Aidrik, and his presence did nothing except complicate things. Worst of all, wanting him didn't feel like a choice. It was as if her body and soul formed a mind of their own, making the decision for her. She'd never felt so disconnected from her own free will.

She didn't understand it even a little, and chose instead to ignore it.

What she needed most of all was to be alone. To be away, and to know the darkness inside her was far enough away from her loved ones it could never hurt them again.

"Do you really think his sword is real?" Finn asked, breaking her train of thought.

"You would know better than me," Ana replied. She didn't want to talk about Aidrik, or his Viking sword, but she couldn't help smiling at the memory of Finn's wide-eyed innocence when he laid eyes on both of them.

"It certainly looks real," Finn said, more to himself than to her. He put the book down, finally shrugging off all pretense of reading. "If it is real, it held up remarkably well over the years..."

Finn continued rambling to himself, but Ana's mind was drawn elsewhere. A shocking, piercing pain in her belly. A wave of sickening nausea swept through her and the blood violently rushed to her head. Ana quickly excused herself, and rushed to the bathroom.

She knelt before the toilet, vomiting the jambalaya from the night before. A series of rippling sensations coursed through her and she realized, with an unexpected wave of regret, what was happening. *My child.* The child she had never wanted was now, in these final moments, *my child*, and she was overcome with torment.

There were no visible signs, nothing a doctor would notice. She knew because of the innate connection she had with her body. Once Aunt Colleen had opened her eyes to it, she could sense every cell, every growing fiber. Her body went into healing overdrive, trying to correct this expulsion of life.

"No," Ana whispered, to herself, to no one. She wanted to plead and beg to God, but her faith in Him had never been more than the dutiful kind. If she really believed in God, she might not be who she was today. She might not bring sorrow with her wherever she went, would form meaningful, healthy connections with people. She would be capable of settling down with someone as kind, and good, as Finn. She would still be carrying his child. They'd be celebrating the inception of a miraculous new life, rather than mourning the passage of it.

There would be no "we" in this mourning. Ana would endure this alone. Yes, Deschanels were cursed.

The sound of the door opening and closing startled her, but when she looked up, it was Condoleezza standing before her, not Finn. Condoleezza, who had delivered Nicolas, helped raise him, and attended the births of Nicolas' four sisters. Condoleezza, who had been the only maternal figure Nicolas had ever known, and who, though sharp of tongue, would die for any of the Deschanel children.

"Shh, now, child," she said soothingly, as she gathered Ana in her arms. She raised a shaking hand toward the older woman and she grasped it, laying it back over Ana's chest, planting a light kiss on her forehead. Condoleezza was a woman of few words, but her actions were always front and center in every important moment that passed under the roof of *Ophélie*.

Her generous, unselfish love only made Ana spiral further down into her despair. There was nowhere she could go, physically, to escape the darkness spreading further across her soul. The only escape final enough would be to escape from herself.

34- AIDRIK

"**W**here to begin…" Aidrik started.

"The fucking beginning would be nice," Nicolas said.

"Mercy has told you about the Farværdig?" Aidrik asked.

"Farfuckwhat?"

"Empyreans," Aidrik clarified, but knew the answer to his question already. Of course she had not. Her fearful squirming confirmed it.

"Aidrik, no," Mercy warned, eyeing him. "Don't say another word."

"This is not to torment you," he assured her. "The relevance will be revealed shortly."

Nicolas, his descendant, stood with a drink in one hand, and the other resting against the oak bar. Watching them both. Proud. No doubt this one was a Deschanel.

His mind was bare to Aidrik. This was not a Man who was equipped for, or accustomed to, protecting his thoughts. That he was without ability surprised Aidrik. But no, he picked up flashes of something. Latent abilities, coming to life. Empyrean presence. More specifically, Mercy's presence. In Aidrik's protection of him, he had stifled his strength. Mercy, then, surfacing it.

Nicolas was troubled by these newly discovered abilities. Troubled further by Aidrik's appearance. Wondering what he meant to Mercy. Loathing his noticing of Anasofiya. Plagued by his own love of his blood cousin. Aidrik nearly smiled at this last, a nuance of Man. The Farværdig saw all individuals equal. Sharing blood was an honor. Only the bond with Emyr was sacred.

But, Nicolas had experienced evigbond with Mercy. And Anasofiya belonged to another.

"Get on with it, before I call the police," Nicolas snapped. "I doubt these good ol' boys would appreciate a dude running around dressed like a wizard and flashing around a fake sword."

"It is no accident Mercy showed up at your hearth."

"No shit. And if whoever hurt her shows up, what happens to him will be no accident, either." Clearly a lie Mercy told to protect her secret.

Aidrik caught the small, hidden smile from Mercy at Nicolas' protective outburst. Evigbond, after all these years. A small tragedy for it to come so late.

"Mercy believed she was following the instincts given her by Emyr, but it was I who sent her here."

"Nicolas, don't listen to him—" Mercy interjected.

"I am nearly four thousand years old," Aidrik said, silencing her.

Mercy held her breath. Nicolas snorted. Knowing disbelief would be his first reaction, Aidrik had not bothered with explanations, yet.

"I was one of the first of the Farværdig," he continued, but Nicolas interrupted him.

"Mercy, seriously? Is this a joke? I mean, did he suggest you play a prank on me, and you went along because, what, you're bored from sleeping for a week?"

Mercy wouldn't make eye contact with him, as he continued to gawk at her. His thoughts told Aidrik he was tottering between anger and frustration. Questioning her. Her motives. Her sanity.

"Hello? Earth to Mercy? Or, are we not on Earth, anymore, but in the realm of His Majesty Cockandballs?"

Modern slang vernacular was beyond Aidrik's comprehension, but he admired his colorful nature. "Nicolas, please. Let me tell my tale, without interruption. Then you are welcome to poke holes in it, or me, or whatever your pleasure," he insisted, politely.

Nicolas, realizing Mercy was beyond his reach in her shock and embarrassment, flopped back in his seat. His arms folded tersely over his chest. Aidrik sighed, grateful. He did not have time to reason with him. *Mercy* did not have time.

But he would keep her occupied here until the time was upon her. He would not risk her running off. She would die here. Amongst his people.

"There is much I would wish to tell you about us, but we have time only for the shortest of versions," Aidrik began.

"By all means, regale us," Nicolas retorted, with a flippant wave. Aidrik knew he would listen, though. If he had to use persuasion to keep him quiet, he would.

He went on. "Ancient texts tell us Father Emyr created all in this world billions of years ago. The fossil record confirms that with fantastic skeletons. Though I am old by your standards, I have only seen four thousand of these years pass. Watching other Empyreans guide Man in construction of the pyramids was satisfying, but I regret never seeing the mammoths roam the earth. Never seeing the moment of life's conception.

"It took millions of years for cosmic and living forces to meld Earth into the idyllic Farjhem Emyr envisioned for us. As He created all the other creatures of the Earth, Emyr crafted two final species: Men and Empyrean. Men were created two hundred thousand years ago, in the blueprint of animals. Some say Father immediately regretted creating a small-minded, two-legged animal. Others believe Father intentionally created Man first to test the mold, and to create a special species for us to look after. As Man considers the beasts of Earth his charge, Empyreans consider Man theirs.

"Theology aside, Emyr assuredly rejoiced when he created His Children. Similar in appearance to Man, but gifted with power, intelligence, and great strength. If you require a scientific explanation, then it is as simple, or as complicated, as this. Beyond the same Creator, we share the same DNA, the key difference being there are genes dormant in Men which are active in the Farværdig. Those genes gift us our long lives, and special capabilities. Our perfect cell replication.

"At nearly four millennia, I am one of the oldest living. Most Farværdig, through the manipulations of our Eldre Senetat, never live past two thousand years. They die believing they will meet a fate far more satisfying than the one reality gives them.

"Early in our common history, the Farværdig mixed more freely with Man. The results were unpredictable. Sometimes gifted in magic, offspring of the inevitable mating filled the role of healer, or shaman, in their simple society. Other half-breeds were of great size and strength. Those are the giants of legend, veritable gods to the Norse and Viking Man colonies. The Ispolini of Bulgaria. Daityas of India. Empyreans traveled the globe, spreading our knowledge and seed indiscriminately. Even the Christian Bible documents these children mixed of Man and Farværdig, Nephilim, as 'sons of God, daughters of Men.'

"Our race, as a result, became heavily diluted.

"Several thousand years ago, a group of power-thirsty Farværdig rose up, declaring a governing body was needed to regulate such events. Initially cloaking themselves in ideals of democracy, as later the Romans would with their

Senate, most believed their intentions pure. Farværdig royalty had never served a purpose beyond their mark of distinction. Their desire was not to govern, but to enjoy the luxuries afforded their position. Grand Emperor Seti was among the strongest proponents of a neutral, benign Senetat.

"In the early days of the Senetat, democracy was not an illusion. The ruling body of Eldres listened to the concerns of Farværdig across the globe. Their edicts were a direct result of this collection of feedback.

"Several subjects, specifically, were polarizing for our people. Of the utmost importance was the fading of our Empyrean attributes. In some births, the blessing of Emyr was lacking entirely. Beyond our striking red hair, there were more subtle gifts which marked us as special. His chosen Children. Many Farværdig expressed concern regarding this thinning of the race, and strict reproduction standards were enacted by the Senetat in order to protect our society and return purity to future generations. Copulation with Men became a crime punishable by death.

"This, and other edicts aimed at restoring Empyreans to our once former glory, were incorporated early in the Senetat's history. But without a structure in which to regulate and monitor these rules, they meant nothing. Thus, the Senetat introduced the concept of Emyr's Mark.

"Many already believed the Senetat was ordained by Emyr himself. Certainly, that was their abiding claim. So, it was no stretch for many to believe Emyr had appeared to the Eldres, much as Christians of Men believe their God appeared to Moses, and decreed each Empyrean should be infused with a piece of Emyr."

"Aidrik, that is preposterous. It is not *presumed* the Mark was ordained by Emyr, it is a fact," Mercy interjected. "Yes, some complained at what they considered overly intrusive restrictions, but only Runean heretics ever doubted the purity of the Mark."

Nicolas' posture had changed, subtly. At Mercy's interjection, he looked bewildered.

"Yes, I believed that once, too. Like you, I was raised on the story of Runa, the ancient who rose up defiantly in the early days of the Senetat. Our history paints her as a godless rebel. A heretical enemy of Emyr. Defeated in the First Runean War, thwarted by Emyr Himself. But history is written by the victors. Reality is, Runa and her rebels were put down like feral animals.

"In my youth, many thousands of years after Runa's fall, I joined with the Eldres when Erikr rose up with his small rebel army. He was intent on unseating the demigods, in the name of Runa. I sounded the battle cry with devoted fervor, believing implicitly that the Empyrean blood running through my body was not in vain, and served a higher purpose. Watched as Erikr was dragged across the glaciers and encased in ice. As he cried, 'For Runa!' before the last of his ancient breath left him. I still see his frozen expression in my nightmares.

"Within days of our victory in the Second Runean War, I slipped into a fugue of self-doubt. How could Our Father, the very source of goodness and love, want this? Why would he endorse a body of individuals who sought to destroy His children? My faith was interlaced with questions there could be no satisfying answer for. Each unanswered doubt spiraled into four more, and there was no end to the debate raging in my head. I tabled my concerns, for lack of any better direction, and focused my energies on being a good citizen.

"I celebrated the victory alongside the Senetat. Years later, I was inducted into their ranks, in recognition of my 'unwavering faith.' Though my beliefs were shaken, I yet hungered for truth. I believed, as many politicians must believe when they are still innocent to the world's ways, that I could make a difference. I could help restore faith to the rebels, named Runeans after their 'true goddess of Emyr,' Runa. That peace was not simply a fruitless ideal.

"But, Empyrean truth is elusive. The Eldre Senetat has cloaked it well in crafted history and comforting ritual. Uncovered lies wrought only more pain. Sometimes I envied your innocent faith, Mercy.

"To quote the venerable Plato, 'Strange times are these in which we live when old and young are taught in falsehoods school. And the person that dares to tell the truth is called at once a lunatic and fool.'"

At this, Nicolas rolled his eyes. But Aidrik was heartened that he was listening.

"My foundation was chipped with doubt, yet stable, until my last visit to the sacred caves at Farjhem," he went on. "Searching out Blacksmith for a minor Ulfberht repair, I overheard two Eldres in plot. A respected community member, an uncle to me, had become difficult. Their tone became conspiratorial as they suggested his Ascension was near. Galon 'flew' to Emyr less than three days later.

"Knowledge is a cruel mistress. More so when you realize only the tip of the iceberg has been revealed through a fog of superstition. Thus began a century-long search, beginning with the lands Galon favored. My horror increased with each discovery. Using pretty words does not mute the brutality of our Great Cleansing. The Senetat, hungry to maintain their inherit and stolen power, imposed further laws. Laws many ancestors saw no value in. Those who refused compliance were murdered, under guise or sword. Empyreans consider themselves more civilized than Man. I know better.

"After excising my Mark, I wandered without a destination in mind. Despite the hopelessness of my discovery, I did not wish to die. Nor did I wish to return to my people.

"I came across others in my wandering. Runeans who gave me a hope that fed my secret, wishful suspicion: an Empyrean could be immortal if not bound by the controlling shackles of the Council's Mark. That it was, in fact, the black magic of the Mark which caused us to age at all. This included the process by which the crimson left our hair, and was replaced by silver.

"Dagr was my first exposure to this. He claimed an age of nearly double mine. Insisted he was born without the knowledge of the Senetat, which we were taught to believe was impossible. The Scholars always insisted the Senetat knew all, and saw all, with Emyr's blessing. I was shocked Dagr had no Mark, nor signs of one ever existing. Stood in awe of his flaming red mane, not a single silver strand marring it. He was entirely 'off the grid,' as the contemporary colloquialism of Men goes.

"He told of many others, most living individually or in very small groups. Other Runeans, but they didn't use that name. Some, as ancient as Runa herself. He claimed to have met Brynja and Einar, the ancient, mythical outcasts rumored to have escaped when Runa was captured. 'Adam and Eve,' some rebels dubbed them. The Senetat maintained the duo had met their demise with the rest of Runa's rebels, but, without proof, legends grew. Dagr was the only one I'd ever met who claimed to have laid eyes on them.

"*We can live forever*, Dagr told me. *We can live in truth.*

"I burned to see the Runeans band together and rise up once more. But they lacked clear leadership, or even direction. They scattered in fear, unwilling to cohabitate for fear of arousing suspicion. Most were content simply to exist, and did not seek to replicate the Empyrean society they once loved.

"So I did as the others, and wandered. Solitude was not a completely unwelcome concept to me. Most of the beings I came in contact with were a disappointment, in one way or another. Too pious on one extreme, too atheistic on the other. Though I was now awake to the realities of the Senetat, I was still a faithful disciple of Emyr. It was never His love, or existence, I questioned. My disenchantment lay only upon those parading as vessels of His word. To put it in terms you might understand, Nicolas, I was the equivalent of an excommunicated Catholic; no less devoted, but forever jaded by the leaders chosen to represent Our Father.

"I watched as empires rose and fell. Entire societies phased in, only to die out. Though tall, I did not look entirely inhuman, and I blended in, living amongst Men for years on end. Inevitable disappointment with their ways would set in, and I would retire reclusively. Later a burst of misplaced optimism would compel me to rejoin society. It was a never-ending cycle, without purpose, direction, or desire.

"I had been walking the earth over three thousand years when I met Christiane de Laurent."

Coming upon the history most relevant to Nicolas, Aidrik stopped long enough to ensure his attention. He no longer felt threatened; instead his mouth twisted in bemusement. Mercy showed no signs of her imminent demise. He continued his narrative.

"Christiane was a peer of Catherine de Medici, and a courtesan of the French court. I arrived to attend the wedding of Catherine's young son, Francis, to the child Scots Queen, Mary, in the year 1558 Ano Domini. I was a frequent guest of Catherine's Florentine Medici kin. I had attended her birth, though she did not know it.

"I enjoyed the patronage of many royal families over the years. As my agelessness became a concern, I would move on, enjoying the fruits of a different court. At least once a century, though, I would return to France. A piece of my heart lives there still."

Nicolas made a crude hand gesture at this, but didn't interrupt. Mercy continued to look away, but her head tilted up slightly. Angry, but listening.

"It was at the French court I met my evigbond. Whimsy is

impractical, but flashes of Christiane de Laurent haunt me to this day. The long, curling blonde hair she wore defiantly virginal, even after marriage to the honorable Marquise Deschanel." Nicolas' arrogant smile dropped at the name, his brow now furrowed in a mix of concentration and recall. Aidrik continued, "How radiant she looked compared to the aging and venerable Catherine de Medici. I had never before been taken so deeply with another living soul."

Aidrik offered an apologetic smile to Mercy, but she still refused to look at him.

"I knew coupling with a Child of Man was an incomparable sin. It went against the most sacred of our tenants. True, I was no longer bound by the Senetat's rules. But it was well-documented, both in Empyrean and Runean lore, that mixing of DNA resulted in unpredictable, even dangerous, spawn. Knowing all that, I wanted her still. Millennia of wisdom and wandering were little defense in the face of blind desire. In some ways, Man and Farværdig are not so different after all.

"Claude Deschanel, then, was the result of that union. The lovely Christiane's death, another result. Children of Men are not as lenient in matters of the heart. We were discovered, overconfidence on my part sealing her fate. Had I known, I would have spirited her away, but her infidelity was revealed by a disgruntled servant. I observed helplessly as she was shaved, whipped and paraded through her husband's village in shame, with a rare dignity far less heathen than the Men arranging the sport. Finding her later, bleeding and maimed by her own hand, I answered her desire to end it all. I held her as the life passed from her small, strong body. Choice had nothing to do with it.

"She did not ask anything else of me, except that I ensure Claude did not suffer the same fate. I would have done it regardless. He was my son.

"Convincing the scorned Marquise Deschanel to accept Claude as his heir was no small feat. My long-held patronage with the Medicis was an asset I had no remorse in leveraging. I employed persuasion when even that was not enough. A viscounty bought my only son his future. A small set of lands, then, started an entire dynasty of my progeny.

"What I could not tell the Marquise? Claude was also his. His and mine. For, unlike Men, Empyreans could have many fathers. And if an Empyrean were to mate with a female already with child, that Empyrean would fuse their DNA to the unborn child. It is called Sveising, and is our most sacred ability. Christiane was already with child when I lay with her."

Nicolas blinked indulgently, but said nothing.

"From the mingling of our blood stemmed a unique hybrid group of individuals who were Men, but also Farværdig. Men who possessed my extraordinary gifts.

"I observed Claude grow to manhood. He lived a short life, the Viscount Deschanel, born in 1559 and dying just after the turn of the 17th century, nary a year after the passing of the English Virgin Queen Elizabeth, Gloriana. But, he had five sons, and those five sons begat many more sons, over the course of many, many years of Man.

"But, as with other Men who have been fused with the gifts of Emyr, the Deschanels grew greedy. They passed edicts through generations, demanding brother marry sister, and cousin to cousin. They sought not just to protect, but to increase their powers. Not satisfied to be superior to other Men, they would be kings among them.

"There's much I could tell you of your ancestors. Much I may, yet, tell you. But I must approach the end of my story, as time is not a luxury we're free to enjoy at present.

"I experienced shame in the dereliction of duty to my descendants. Even a minor interference into their doings would have directed a wiser path. Finally, as behaviors grew more concerning, I decided upon a course correction.

"I purchased the plot of land *Ophélie* sits on. I strongly encouraged Charles Deschanel, your ancestor, to leave France and emigrate to America. Made the prospect of doing so too rich to pass up. I told him nothing of who I was, or of his family's origins. By the 19th century, there was no longer anyone living who knew about Christiane and her powerful lover. Charles knew only he had a mysterious benefactor, whose gifts came on the condition of no questions asked. Charles' greediness outweighed his curiosity on the matter, and thus your family came to New Orleans.

"Prior to Charles and his family taking ownership of the land, I placed a Farværdig protection on the earth itself, and all buildings upon that stretch of land, cloaking anyone who lived there from the eyes of the Senetat. Contributing, most likely, to your abilities being stifled all these years." Aidrik paused, briefly. "Only the presence of another Farværdig can weaken the protection. You have Mercy to thank for enabling these latent talents to surface." He let out a small, measured breath. "Those are the essentials you need know."

A pregnant pause filled the room for several minutes.

"Soooo…" Nicolas said finally, leaning forward in his chair. His eyes flashed with collective amusement and fire. "You're saying I should call you grandpa?"

It was apparent he did not take Aidrik's revelations seriously. He could not blame him, though it did complicate matters. Surprisingly, it was then Mercy who spoke.

"Nicolas, it's the truth," she said, barely above a whisper.

"Oh, so, you were there, in the sixteenth century, when he boned my eighteenth great-grandmother then, is that it? Oh, no, maybe you were the midwife who delivered this… Claude? Is that right?"

Mercy ran a weary hand through her silvery red hair. "I wasn't there. It's the first I'm hearing this story, too. But Aidrik is who he says he is."

Nicolas snickered, shaking his head. "Mercy, you don't strike me as an idiot, so either this dude has a really large cock, or—"

"Stop!" She screamed the word defiantly. "Nicolas, I'm Empyrean, too."

Nicolas's rough laughter continued, but he started to pull away. His thoughts were a confusing collage. Angry. Annoyed. Slightly afraid. He was remembering all the things about Mercy that didn't ring true. Pieces of her story which did not add up. His unaccustomed submission to her in the bedroom. The cautious words of his empathic cousin, Amelia. Mercy's strange expressions and disconnect with modern times.

"I think you both should leave," he said, very slowly. His smile was gone. "Whatever fucked up sexual games the two of you are playing, I don't want any part of it. This isn't going to end in some costumed threesome. Y'all need to find a bigger sucker."

Pride coursed through Aidrik as Mercy bravely stood and rent open her shirt, baring her breasts. Her phoenix, proud and alive, fluttered. Closing her eyes, she balled her fists and a slow ember glow began radiating from her pale skin. At first, a mere tint. Then, as it rose to crescendo, a pulsing light emanated from her chest, illuminating the entire room.

Aidrik had never seen her shine so bright.

Nicolas, shielding his eyes, yelled at her to stop. Defiant, angry, and resigned to the course of the discussion, she continued her glow, humming the song of Emyr under her breath.

Her high pitch slowed, and then she began the prayer of Our Father: "Our Father of Light, Our Father of Fire. I am but a vessel of Your Love. I am Yours in The Flames!"

Nicolas curled into the chair, cowering in fear. He continued his screams at her to stop, but her episode was so intense she could hear nothing but her own prayer. Reaching out gently, Aidrik beckoned her to calm. Slowly, the room dimmed.

Nicolas unfurled himself cautiously. "Jesus fucking Christ," he whispered, still pressed into the back of the leather chair.

"I'm sorry," Mercy said, sounding not the least bit apologetic. "But we don't have all day. My Ascension nears." Her look to Aidrik was unnecessarily defiant.

"Get the fuck out!" Nicolas said. "I've seen a lot of impressive shit in this family, and that does *not make you three thousand years old!*"

"Just do it," Mercy said to Aidrik, already knowing where his thoughts were going. As he moved toward Nicolas, the young man shrunk back, but Aidrik continued forward, undeterred. Placing both hands over his head, he fought his thrashing, focusing on forging the connection. Once linked, Aidrik began the transfer of thoughts. Nicolas was flooded with images of Aidrik's youth in the northern lands of Norway, his years with the Scholars, his first hunt. His love of Mercy. His wanderings across the courts of Europe. His first image of Christiane.

When tears formed in the trembling young Man's eyes, Aidrik stopped, realizing he'd gone too far. Scolding himself, he remembered Nicolas was not equipped for such a connection, even if he was a Halfling.

"Please," Nicolas whispered, gripping the chair, panting. "No more."

Mercy rushed to his side in loving concern, but he shrugged her off. His pale face looked stricken. "Don't *touch* me," he hissed. Thinking again of Amelia's warnings. *Nothing. Absolutely nothing.*

"This isn't how I wanted you to find out," she was saying.

"Oh? How were you planning to break the news to me you aren't fucking human?" He jumped to his feet. "Out of my way."

Then, Nicolas slumped back into his chair as if his soul had departed his body. He erupted in violent convulsions.

"Aidrik, do something!" she cried, flinging herself at Nicolas. Aidrik threw out one arm, halting her.

"He's having a nested vision," he said, in shocked wonder. "If you intervene, he could die."

Her wide eyes looked at him as if he'd lost his mind. "He looks like he's dying now!"

"The best we can do is wait," Aidrik reassured, wondering how this Child of Man had been a mystic and he had not known it until now.

35- NICOLAS

*N*icolas had wished for Ana, only to find himself thrust violently into her mind.

The now-familiar waves of confusion passed, replaced by paralyzing dread.

She was in trouble, and he was frozen in place, observing.

Ana had known all along things couldn't go on forever like this. Eventually, whatever life she chose would end in fiery flames of regret. Her current situation, though, went beyond fate. She was being punished, and there would be no greater punishment than the one she could give herself.

She deplored cowardice, but found she couldn't escape this abhorrent trait in her darkest hour.

Ana wished she had never gone to Maine. That she'd never met the St. Andrews brothers. She'd entered into her relationship with Finn knowing it wouldn't end well, but had selfishly indulged in the comfort of security anyway. Worse, she'd fallen desperately in love with him, forming an unexpected bond she could neither ignore nor continue to cultivate. Ana could forgive herself wrongdoing, but she couldn't change who she was. This winter had been a farce; one more experiment in normalcy gone horribly wrong.

She thought of the diamond ring, still sitting in Finn's pocket. Finn's gesture had come in a moment of blind panic. Afraid of losing her, and not thinking about the fact that, perhaps, Ana's departure would have been the best outcome for everyone.

Ana's tears blinded her, but her body felt weightless. She was unable to control her stumbling as she made her way through the left parterre garden and off toward a building she had once loved as a child, the old livery.

The livery had not been active in over a hundred years, but it was still mostly intact. It had two floors, the top meant for an overseer, and it was that upper floor she'd often escaped to when she really didn't want to be found. She went there instinctively as she fumbled down the old path, losing herself to her misery.

Ana wiped her tears on her sleeve, leaving a dirty slash of mascara on her white shirt. She slowly climbed to the second floor of the livery and the old mattress, the one she used to sometimes sleep on. It was still there, with the same old blue knit-acrylic blanket, the edging present though tattered. Hers from many years ago. A childhood escape from her dark thoughts, now a final comfort.

She slid the satin binding between her fingers as memories flooded through her. Even as a child, she'd never been whole.

That one, intense moment with Aidrik pervaded her thoughts. The electricity that stole through her as he sent very direct, very comforting thoughts. For now, she had promised, knowing it was a lie. Knowing it was already too late. Knowing he couldn't save her from her own decisions, just as Finn couldn't, just as Nicolas couldn't.

Opening the large, red cabinet in the corner, she was relieved to see what she came for was still there.

Ana did not know whether it was cowardice, or courage, that bade her reach inside.

*N*icolas fumbled back to consciousness. Mercy reached to steady him, but he swatted her hand away. He was sick with the vision, still wavering between the two realities.

"You are a mystic," Aidrik observed.

Nicolas eyes rolled back and forward in his head, and his mouth hung slack. He snapped his head forward, and then coughed. "Ana," he whispered.

"You can see her thoughts, through her eyes," Aidrik said, confirming. "When did this start?"

"Very recently," Nicolas panted, leaning forward. This new ability took much out of him. He pointed an accusing thumb at Mercy. "Not long after *she* showed up."

Mercy looked at Aidrik, eyes wide in fear and panic.

"Yes. Her presence surfaced them," he agreed. "I believe the protection I placed on *Ophélie* may have dulled the ability over the course of your development."

"Protection?" Nicolas asked the question, clearly not remembering that part of the narrative as his mind was split between the present and whatever he'd witnessed in Anasofiya's mind.

199

"The Eldre Senetat remains unaware of your presence. It must continue that way," Aidrik clarified. "But there is little time to explain now, and later will be better."

"What the hell is a mystic?" Nicolas was confused. Still processing. Aidrik resisted frustration at his slowness to absorb. "And why can I not control this shit?"

"The most powerful of all magi," Mercy explained. Her voice was small, childlike. She was hurting at Nicolas' defection. Aidrik regretted his reveal had caused a rift between them, when they had such little time left together. "As for why you can't control it, it's simply that you have not learned to. The nested visions are only the beginning. You've been persuading others in the household, without realizing. It's why Oz stayed as long as he did." She paused. "I'm ashamed for not seeing it earlier, but the abilities are so uncommon. Even for Empyreans. Aidrik is the only mystic I've ever known."

"Indeed," Aidrik affirmed. "And I recall only one other Deschanel. I daresay, I am shocked to find you with it."

"Stand in fucking line," Nicolas snapped, but the virulence was gone from his voice. Worry creased his brow. He was reflecting on what he'd seen in Anasofiya's head, his thoughts catching up with him. Moving from processing to a need for action.

"What is it?" Aidrik pressed. A darkness crept into his chest.

"Are we done?" Nicolas asked, eyes on the door. What lay beyond? Aidrik could not see what Nicolas had seen because the Man had pushed it from his mind. Knowing Aidrik could read his thoughts, he had willed himself not to think it.

"For now. But you must learn to control this violation of others. You must never use it to spy, no matter how pure your intention—"

"I wasn't spying! I can't stop it from happening!" Nicolas defended himself as he moved toward the door.

"I will teach you," Aidrik promised to his retreating back, but instinct drew him far from the conversation at hand.

A shocking pull, his senses immediately alert. No danger to him. No danger near. What then? Mercy started to follow Nicolas. He forestalled her motion on instinct.

Anasofiya. Aidrik could see her in his mind's eye. Hanging, from a rope at the neck. Some kind of granary or barn? No matter. He knew the direction.

"Where are you going *now?*" Mercy's words lingered distantly in his mind as he fled in search of Anasofiya.

37- MERCY

*A*idrik flew from the room, and Nicolas followed.

Mercy understood very little of their exchange but the pressing message was clear: Ana, Nicolas' beloved cousin, was in danger. She understood Nicolas' concern, but Aidrik's equal urgency left her baffled.

She was still processing his story of the Deschanels, though she had no reason to doubt the truth in his statements. She was troubled by the notion Aidrik had somehow brought her here, to the home of his descendants, in order to die safely. Disguised as her Inner Voice, he'd led her down the path of his choosing. And she'd blindly, foolishly, followed.

Mercy exited the study, and Finn stood before her, concern in his eyes. He looked from Mercy, to his hands, where Ulfberht presumably lay moments before. "Where did Nicolas and Aidrik rush off to?" he asked.

A sharp pain moved through Mercy's chest, and it took all her willpower to stabilize herself. The hour was upon her, finally. She couldn't dally while the two men were off running errands. There was no time to waste.

"Where's Ana?" she demanded, more rudely than he deserved.

"She went for a walk," he said, wide-eyed. "What's going on?"

"No time," Mercy muttered, sprinting away from him. She stumbled, realizing she could not, in her final hours, move the way she once had.

Finn rushed up behind her, and she nearly stopped him. It would be a kindness to keep him away from whatever waited, but perhaps a greater compassion to not leave him in the dark. Whatever the case, she was too exhausted to put up resistance and she needed to say her final words to both Aidrik, and Nicolas, before it was too late.

Another pain shot through her and she had to stop, clutching the bark of an ancient oak for support. Finn scooped his arm under her in concern, but she waved him past. "Go," she whispered.

Finn stopped, propping her in his strong arms. This was a good man, a rarity. "Whoa," he coddled, gently. "Let's get you back to the house."

"I'm okay," she said, forcing a smile she did not feel. "I'll be right behind you."

He paused, trying to gauge whether to believe this. His thoughts showed he was worried about her well-being and hesitant to leave. She passed a comforting thought of her own making, a kind manipulation. *I'm perfectly okay. Never been better. Go on. Go to your Ana. She needs help. I do not.* He smiled then and released her carefully. She waited until he was a hundred yards ahead before standing slowly.

The pain grew in intensity with every passing moment. She gazed ahead in the direction Finn had run. He was naught but a speck, and she couldn't see Aidrik or Nicolas anymore. Her chest seized with gripping agony, and she realized, with a sinking sadness, there would be no goodbyes.

Whatever words they'd said last to one another would be counted as their parting words. They weren't the words she wanted to leave him with, but there was nothing to be done about it now.

Mercy curled in anguish around the base of the mighty live oak, its leafy branches spreading over her in protective comfort. In the course of her wanderings, she'd envisioned, many times, where the location of her final rest and rebirth would occur. She felt a small comfort in knowing she was amongst Aidrik's descendants, despite his manipulation. Wincing, she smiled as she thought of Aidrik the Wise lovingly watching over his progeny for centuries. His unexpected story proved that even your oldest friends could still surprise you.

The oak shielded her from the pelting rainstorm, but the property lay before her in an iridescent brilliance. *Ophélie*, Nicolas' beautiful home, Aidrik's legacy, standing guard like a broad, ivory tower. The flora and fauna flanking the home startlingly vivid, like the personality of its owner.

As far as last visions went, she could do worse.

Any moment now, Emyr's Mark would emerge in its final song, taking flight from her breast. Her breath would cease, and her physical body would die. Then, she would merge with the Mark, rising from the ashes like Emyr Himself, and fly into His loving arms. *I am Yours, in the Flames.*

In her flushed, rising excitement, she couldn't resist looking down at the Mark in action. Even as she lay dying, she focused not on what she'd leave behind, but only what lay ahead.

As Mercy's eyes locked on her breast, she jumped in blinding fear at the sight of the Mark. It had faded to black. Shriveling, shrinking. As her parents' had looked when they met their punishment before the citizens of Farjhem. Dying.

No. This was impossible. No, no, no, this could not be! Emyr was supposed to grow and burst forth, taking her life force so that she may live on in His image. How could she do that if the

Mark was shrinking... disappearing... dying? How would she make it home, to Him, without it?

She gasped for air, panic rising up from her chest, to her throat, choking her. She needed Aidrik. Aidrik would know what to do. He would be able to impart reason, to assure her this was part of the process. Aidrik would say this was supposed to happen, that the lovely imagery of the Mark bursting forth was simply exaggerated folklore. Aidrik would know what to say.

Mercy's tears of confusion flowing freely now, she knew that hope was in vain. Aidrik had spent what precious time they had left convincing her the Mark was a lie, that it was not a vessel of Emyr, but of the Senetat. An assertion of control.

She couldn't think of that now! Not as she lay dying, in His final test. She could not entertain Aidrik's blasphemy!

Daring herself to look down once more, the dread and disenchantment rose higher as she realized the Mark was nearly gone. The outline, a withered, dried up version of its former glory. Something had gone horribly wrong. Mercy knew it. She was sure of it. This was not supposed to happen, not like this, not this way! Somewhere, she'd gone utterly off course and now was being denied!

So, Aidrik the Wise does not know what awaits?

No. And it matters little.

The darkness enveloping her Mark now spread outward from her chest, in jagged, pointed distress. She scratched at it, willing it to stop, to go back. This was wrong, all wrong! This was not how it was supposed to be, she was not supposed to die like this! Not the death of a heretic! Not like her mother and father!

The blackness continued its malicious spread, and her hands flew across her skin in a panic, clawing, unable to keep them still despite knowing they could fix nothing. Images flashed through her mind. Memories. Stilted ones. Missed ones. All the things she had given up to be a devout follower of Our Father. Telling herself fleeting experiences mattered nothing compared to a lifetime in His Arms.

As she lay dying—a real, final death, not the Ascension she had, for centuries, envisioned as her ultimate redemption—the only arms she longed for were Nicolas'.

38- AIDRIK

*A*rriving in a blur, Ulfberht already drawn, Aidrik severed the woven cord in one swift motion. Ana fell into his arms, limp. Blue. Warm, but not hot.

Nicolas drew to her side as Aidrik searched for what nearby threat caused this. Ulfberht's steel rang in the silent barn. A dusty crate was tipped askew in the hay pile. Frowning, he understood the only threat to Anasofiya was herself.

He had but two options. Allow her to die, as she would certainly do without his intervention. Or, transfer a vital piece of himself through to her, infusing her via the Sveising. Changing her. The latter option would save her, but the exact results were unknown. Linking DNA between races was a volatile, inexact science.

As the last of her life force passed through her, Aidrik knew there was but one choice. From the moment he had first laid eyes on her, there was only one choice. He would not stand by again as he had with Christiane. As long as he took breath, there would *always ever only be one choice* where Anasofiya was concerned.

He placed his thumbs against both of her temples. The

Sveising was nothing new for mystics, but performing it on Children of Men was dangerous, and unprecedented. Even more so, now that he knew she was his evigbond.

Forgive me, he said to her, knowing she could not hear him. *I know not what will come.*

The transfer of power was magnetic, his thumbs fusing to her flesh. Quick, powerful. He knew the Sveising had worked, for he could *see* her life force returning. The Men could not. Their grief was palpable, keening.

Ana was at once confused. Then, furious. Then frightened. She opened her mouth in a silent, horrified scream. Aidrik leaned over her and pulled her to him, holding her tight against her resistances, ignoring the two Men fighting for their right to comfort her.

I am here, Anasofiya.

Why?

Because of you. For you.

I don't know who you think I am, her tormented mind responded.

You are exactly who you are.

You don't know me. You don't know what I've done. What I'm capable of. Why didn't you let me go?

Aidrik's heart caved in his chest. Not since Christiane had he been so consumed. This, though, was somehow different. Stronger. Infinitely more potent. Unending, and undeniable. He stroked her brow, a gesture far less than what he wished to display, but the only one appropriate for the moment. *You have never felt you belonged with the Children of Men.* It was not a question.

I belong nowhere.

You belong with me.

Nicolas sobbed inconsolably at her side. Finn, removing the rope from around her bluish neck, suspended disbelief through assumed command, demanding he move aside. Shocked, indignant, that Aidrik refused to budge.

Her eyes still closed, the Men did not know of the power he'd transferred to her through the sacred Sveising. That, though she lived, she was changed.

Ana attempted to sit, and both Men cautioned her, handling her with extreme care. Aidrik smiled. They did not know what he knew. That their Anasofiya, once broken and disconnected, was now whole. She was an extension of him. Her power, her strength, would eclipse even the most powerful of Men. Perhaps many Farværdig as well. He could not prevent his thoughts of a future with her, linked forever, armed against the world. He no longer wanted to prevent them. He was now whole as well.

If evigbond were not present before this moment, it had unequivocally been decided with the Sveising. Ana was his, and he was hers.

"Jesus Christ Ana, what the fuck," Nicolas cried. This time, Aidrik allowed himself to be wrested aside. Nicolas pulled her into his arms, rocking her tight to his chest. She lay limp in his embrace, like a child's doll. Not for lack of physical strength, but emotional. Aidrik had not the heart to tell him this love, this suffocating obsession, was among her final thoughts before she stepped into the noose.

"Nic, are you gonna call the hospital or what? Where's your phone?" Finn was demanding, frantic. Aidrik realized he had been asking this, repeatedly, though was only now processing it.

"That won't be necessary," Aidrik replied. Ana's eyes studied him curiously from over her cousin's shoulder. Her mouth parted, ever so slightly, red slowly replacing the blue. Tears of confusion streamed down her pale face.

"Not necessary? You can't be serious!" Finn exclaimed. "She just tried to kill herself, are you mad? Doesn't need a hospital?" Finn rushed from the barn in indignant rage, off for help. In a flash, Aidrik was before him, hand against his chest.

"It won't be necessary," he repeated. "She is fine."

Finn looked to Nicolas for help, so flustered with Aidrik's apparent daftness he was lost for words entirely. *Get your hands off me. I'll kill you. You won't stop me from protecting her.*

Separating her from this Child of Man would be no easy feat.

Nicolas, though, knew better. He knew who Aidrik was now. Who *he* was. And he knew, at least in part, what Aidrik had done.

Why? Anasofiya asked him. The telepathy was easy for her now. Many other things would come just as easily, from here on out.

You know why.

Pause. *I don't understand.*

I wish I could explain it to you. But I also lack understanding.

The tears dried in her eyes. Nicolas cried into her fiery hair, but Anasofiya simply watched Aidrik from over his shoulder. *You are very old.*

I am.

You shared some of that with me, didn't you? Somehow?

Aidrik filled with pride at her awareness. He was bursting to know the full extent of what he had passed to her. *That remains to be seen.*

I had an ability before this. To heal. It's more than that now.

You undoubtedly have many new abilities.

This is different. I could heal before, but it was unreliable. I think... I feel, I'm capable of so much more.

A shaman's powers magnified could do spectacular things. What power had he given her? *I will help you, Anasofiya. I can teach you.*

The questions in her heart could build a mountain. He heard them all, rushing from her mind in an anxious jumble. *Why has this happened? What does it mean? Who are you? What am I feeling, what is this? Am I free?*

We *are free,* Aidrik corrected. *And this is quite real. Perhaps this is Ascension.* The last was his own thoughts getting away from him.

Ascension?

Something I have misunderstood all along, the realization only coming to him as he formed the thoughts. *Something all of us have.*

I don't know why I need you, she thought in a rush of emotion. *It makes no sense to me. I don't know why, or where it came from. It doesn't feel like a choice.*

As I need you, he replied. Aidrik knew the adjustment for her would take time. Evigbond was challenging enough to understand as one born Empyrean, and now she also had to contend with Sveising. She would struggle between her love for Finn and her need for Aidrik, but he would assist her through the transition.

Aidrik's heart was at peace for the first time in nearly two thousand years. He wished to tear her from Nicolas' embrace. He'd wanted Anasofiya in his arms since the moment he discovered her eyes-like-the-sea, hair of flames, and heart of darkness.

Nicolas and Finn need me, she reminded him.

The pragmatism of his own soul, reflected in her understanding.

39- NICOLAS

*D*eep down, Nicolas had seen it coming. From the moment Ana stepped through the large, oaken doors of *Ophélie*, it was written all over her face. She was dying, and he'd ignored it. First, out of pride. Later, out of selfishness. And God, had it been his actions earlier that drove her over the edge? Had his single stolen moment been the catalyst for his Ana stepping off a dusty crate to her intended demise?

She lay in his arms, as if dead, but he had a sense of her thoughts. This time, it wasn't an accident. She *willed* him into her head, for the first time having control over this bizarre ability.

Rather than finding her confused, however, he found her thoughts contained surprising amounts of clarity. And she was somehow communicating with Aidrik.

He was torn, then—no, *removed*—from her thoughts, and thrust, without warning, into Finn's. So much for control.

Finn's mind was awash with so many emotions he hardly knew what to do. He thought of the events leading up to this act. Specifically, the last, big blowout in Maine, with Jon, that led to Ana packing her bags. Then, he shut it out, unwilling to force a painful memory open on top of so fresh a wound.

Had he somehow driven her to this, with all his talk of being unable to live without her? Proposing to her? Maybe she didn't love him the way he loved her. She was taciturn and distant. He was so used to that demeanor with Jon it never frightened him away the way it might other men. Instead of wanting to change her, he only wanted to be with her. He understood her, or tried to. He had not, ever, loved a woman as he loved Ana, and he was horrified to consider his love may have stifled her, rather than soothed her.

Nicolas tumbled out of Ana's arms as this last episode left him. Finn blamed himself, just as Nicolas did. He couldn't say which of them was right. Perhaps both. Probably neither.

Only one thing *was* clear in this mess: Aidrik saved Ana's life. Either through that fact, or through some other revelation yet to be uncovered, Ana flourished in his presence.

Nicolas watched her, still traumatized by the image of her lying on the floor with the rope strangling her. This Ana was the complete opposite image. Her hair, skin, and eyes all seemed to glow brightly. She was radiating health and energy and... power. Yes, power.

She was alive with it.

What did that bastard do to her?

Ana surprised him when she reached her pale hand out to touch his face. He flinched; her skin was so hot it nearly burned his, reminiscent of Mercy's touch. "I'm okay," she assured him. She'd read his thoughts, he was sure of it. She was no telepath before her accident, but clearly things were different.

"You are *not* okay," Nicolas whispered. But she was. What bothered him was the difference in her. What he saw before him was a woman more at peace than he had ever, ever seen Ana. This should have filled him with warmth, but instead, there was sinking dread, as he sought to understand what price had been paid to achieve it.

She leaned forward and kissed him on the lips, lingering a moment. She was confident in this gesture; it was a kindness. It completely lacked the desire they'd shared for one another earlier. "You're going to be fine, too," she stated confidently.

Out of the corner of his eye, he saw Finn's jaw drop. Clearly, his first time at the rodeo as far as Nicolas and Ana were concerned.

Nicolas loved her still. That would never change. But where his passion for her once burned so hotly he couldn't function, it dulled now to a distant, lukewarm awareness. She was no longer his, and never, truly, had been.

But he wasn't sure she was Finn's anymore, either. Everything had changed, in a single, terrible moment.

Nicolas' unanswered questions would stay that way for now. Aidrik became suddenly alert, his face creasing in growing concern.

"Mercy," he intoned. "It is time."

"Time for what?" Nicolas snapped, tired of riddles and half-stories. Exhausted from watching Ana nearly die before his eyes.

"She is dying," he responded. The look on his face silenced any further imminent objections; the sadness in his eyes confirmed the truth of the completely illogical statement.

"She said she was okay," Finn said, distantly, as if recalling a moment that no longer seemed quite real. "I saw her. She was…"

There was no time to explain all of the insanity in Aidrik's story to Finn. And before Nicolas could try, Aidrik was striding, with purposefulness, out of the barn. All three followed, without hesitation.

IT WAS IMPOSSIBLE TO SEE THROUGH THE RAIN, NOW COMING down in relentless sheets.

"This way!" Finn yelled as he took the lead, racing through the muddy, flooding grass.

But it was Ana who spotted her first. She ran ahead, faster than Nicolas had ever seen her move before. Faster than he had seen *any* human move. She was already kneeling beside Mercy by the time he caught up.

In one swift move, Aidrik produced a tiny, sharp blade and was at Mercy's side. He pressed it against her bosom, as if to cut out her phoenix Mark.

"No," Mercy croaked. A weak hand clamped over his wrist, before falling away. She looked horrible. Dying. There was no doubt in his mind at all. But they had called it something else... Ascending.

"It is the only way," Aidrik insisted. His voice was strained, almost cracking. Nicolas would not have thought this stoic being capable of such raw emotion.

"Please," Nicolas begged around the growing lump in his throat, dropping down into the mud next to her. He gathered her hands. As he did, her full appearance revealed itself, and a gasp rolled up within him. The beautiful red was completely gone from her hair now, replaced instead by a dull, muted silver. Her gray eyes faded to the color of decaying flesh. But her skin was the worst of all, covered entirely in black mud, and it sagged, as if no longer attached to anything. *Oh god, Mercy.*

"I am... sorry," she struggled, each word taking considerable effort. Nicolas squeezed her hands tighter.

"Do something!" he screamed at Aidrik. "Isn't this what you fucking came for?"

Aidrik dropped his eyes, and the blade disappeared into his robe. "The choice is not mine," he said sadly. "I cannot make it for her."

"Mercy, please, darling, my dear, I'm *begging* you, please let him do it!" Nicolas rambled his pleas, kissing her limp hands, rolling forward on his knees, crying, begging. She did nothing but smile through her blackened, cracked lips.

He turned to Aidrik. "I'll do anything you ask! I'll believe anything, anything at all you tell me, just please, I am *begging* you, do this!"

"Our Father, Emyr…" Aidrik began, in a low voice. A prayer. A fucking prayer. Some fucked up version of last rites!

Small black bubbles surfaced through Mercy's lips. She closed her eyes, taking in Aidrik's words of dying comfort.

Nicolas continued to scream, beg, and plead with her, and with him, but he knew it would do nothing. Change nothing. She had made her choice, and her peace. Mercy was going to die.

40- MERCY

*M*ercy's heart was torn in two.

On one side, she heard the beckoning voice of Our Father. It was not the same as she'd been led to believe, all her life. It was deeper, final. Not a rebirth, but a true and real death. Yet, somehow there was a comfort in this, despite that it was not at all what she had hoped for.

On the other side, Nicolas. Her heart. Her evigbond. She had given a part of herself to him without knowing it. Without realizing her heart could, or should, be given to any living thing. Evigbond was a powerful, infinite thing, but this went beyond that, and she knew it.

All these long years she'd believed her heart belonged to Emyr. That her love would be repaid, a thousand fold, when her days on Earth were at an end. To know now she was wrong was indescribably more painful than the sensation of all her cells dying.

Her life, all of it, had been scripted as a part of a powerfully false illusion. Flashes of late evening arguments with Aidrik popped into her head. How sure she'd been. How absolutely positive he was wrong, and that it was he, in the end, who would not be saved. She had spent many sleepless nights pondering his fate, wishing there was something, anything, she could say to sway him to the truth.

Likely he had done the same. But only one of them could be right.

Mercy thought then of Old Aita. The oldest Empyrean still walking the Earth, by far. She was old when Mercy was born, even. Many, many times she had thought of her, and was filled with pity. Poor Aita, whom Emyr had forgotten. Wandering, unloved. She feared becoming like her, as most Empyreans did. As they were taught, by the Scholars in Farjhem. It was preached, passed down, and ingrained. She could find it almost humorous now, as her phoenix withered on her chest in cruel defiance, that Old Aita was the most fortunate of all.

She remembered the image of the phoenix rising from the ashes in Rome. How sure she had been it was a sign. How sure she was now it was, in fact, just a bird.

Mercy's dying thoughts shifted then to her parents. Her mother and father, who had been braver than she realized. *Runeans,* she had said of them, disdainfully, when asked of their fate. *They were trying to give me the gift of truth. They loved me enough they had risked their own lives.*

As her eyes fluttered closed for the last time, her final vision was of Nicolas.

In his eyes, home.

41- ANASOFIYA

*A*na was different now. Not simply in the way she responded to the world, but also in how the world responded to *her*.

She crackled with newfound power, and energy, as if she could conjure a ball of fire and hurl it at the livery, burning all memory of her selfish choices to the ground. She thought if she ran up the ramp of the levee she could scale the entire width of the Mississippi in one, long leap. She was certain she could sprint the fifty miles to New Orleans.

With this came the promise of unrealized abilities. She told Aidrik she believed her existing powers were amplified, but she didn't know how she knew, only that something had shifted within her, giving her this new confidence. It seemed to Ana there was no malady, no matter how great, she couldn't remedy. Even her broken soul no longer seemed so far out of her reach. Whatever happened in that barn, the past no longer mattered.

Most importantly, her mind was able to touch the child still thriving within her.

My child is still alive, she'd said to Aidrik, in wonder.

Our child, yes.

Mine and Finn's.

It is all three of ours now, he explained. *It is yours and Finn's. It is yours and mine. In saving you, I infused a piece of myself into you, which passed on to the child. Sveising. There was no other way.* This last he communicated with a mild hint of apology, but also a touch of arrogance.

That's not possible. Children can't have more than two biological parents.

For Man, no. But for Empyrean, it is not simply possible but desirable. The strongest Empyreans are born of many fathers.

You're Empyrean?

As are you, to an extent. A distant descendant of mine. Through Sveising likely even more so, now. Our child will be very strong.

There was no point in asking the dozens of questions which followed such a conundrum. Why he'd saved her, or why, despite not knowing him at all, she suddenly needed him as much as she needed Finn. And two fathers? A mother that was more Empyrean than human now? Whatever it meant, it would need to be deciphered and pondered, but now was not the time.

Mercy had died. Nicolas' salvation had died. Despite Ana's intense focus, she'd been unable to save her. She'd watched, hollowly, as Nicolas threw himself on top of her, prostrate with grief. Finn stared slack-jawed at the once beautiful woman who, in death, was covered in black rot.

Ana's shaking fingers intuitively fluttered out to touch her. and Aidrik's strong hands landed atop Ana's.

Focus, he said. *Focus.*

I've been focusing!

Focus harder.

Aidrik, she's dead, I can't—

FOCUS! His fingers gently laced through hers. *Anasofiya, 'can't' is no longer in your construction.*

He was wrong. Doubt would always be a part of her, no matter what he'd done to alter her.

She knew the words. *Resurrection shaman.* None existed within the family, except through legend. It never occurred to her that the shift within her might come with such an elevated power. But Aidrik's own powers were so much greater than hers, and yet he wouldn't attempt to revive Mercy, so who was Ana to try?

Aleksandr, she thought, out of nowhere. *My son's name is Aleksandr. Like my mother's father. Like her brother.*

This realization of the strength growing in her womb gave her unexpected courage as she reached her hand further and connected with the remnants of Mercy's rotted flesh.

With a surge of maternal power, Ana closed her eyes and fixated on seeing her whole again. Beautiful... alive. She focused without fear or doubt clouding her. The ground trembled beneath her confidence.

Yes, that's it. Focus, Anasofiya. All of my experiences, memories were transferred to you. Use them now. You were made for this.

No, she thought, diverting her focus for a split second back to the child growing within her. *I was made for Aleksandr. I was made for this moment when suddenly everything makes sense and I'm not simply the broken daughter of Augustus and Ekaterina, but Anasofiya, the unbroken, the one made whole.*

"Aleksandr," she whispered, and let the power flow through her fingertips, into Mercy.

42- NICOLAS

*N*icolas' gut twisted in a desperate agony which had no cure. So many feelings rushed to the surface, he couldn't take the time to address each one properly. The evolution they'd taken, from the moment he'd laid eyes on Mercy, to their unexpected intimacy, and then, to her death, felt like being drop kicked into a brick wall. Repeatedly.

All his life, Nicolas believed the only woman he could ever love was Ana. His unobtainable soulmate. He had never, ever met a woman who threatened this. Mercy jumbled everything, including his heart, upside down. He didn't know if he loved her, but for the first time in his life, he'd been willing to find out. And now, she was gone.

He threw his head back and screamed into the endless void of driving rain. The sound was lost in the storm, though he felt Finn's strong hands, and Ana's soft ones, laying comfort on his shoulders.

But there was no comfort from this.

The purpose Nicolas felt in saving Mercy had dulled his desire to check out. The sensation grew distant, and unimportant. Stupid, even. But it was back now, with an undeniable vengeance. Life had been throwing opportunities at him for years, chances to change and be a better person. To be someone who would put others first without hesitation. One who would think less of the inconvenience helping others placed on his own life. He'd risen to the occasion, only to fail. Utterly.

Nicolas wanted to throw himself in the raging current of the Mississippi. He could, too. It was only a hundred yards away.

Aidrik and Ana were whispering to one another. He couldn't hear them. He didn't care what they were saying. Nothing mattered except his grief, his sagging regret. He should have sliced the Mark off her breast himself, even if it meant risking an eternity of her hatred.

With arms like steel, Aidrik pulled him away from Mercy, tossing him aside into the mud, like a rag doll. Ana then leaned over Mercy, obstructing his view. As Ana raised her hands above Mercy, they first started pulse, and then to… to *glow*. It was almost indiscernible, but Nicolas saw it, just as he'd seen the same light from Mercy.

"Go on," Aidrik urged, gently. Ana lowered her quaking hands and placed them on each side of Mercy's face. As she did, Mercy's blackened skin emitted tiny sparks, her body jolting crudely and bouncing sideways into the mud.

"Stop!" Nicolas cried, then realized his protestation was ridiculous. She was dead. Nothing could hurt her anymore.

But Ana wasn't giving up. Her whole body quavered, the blaze from her hands radiating out through every tip of every finger. The ground beneath them erupted in a low tremor, as leaves from the rows of trees shimmered and sighed

Nicolas knew what she was doing. She was trying, for his sake, to save Mercy. But that was wholly impossible. Ana's healing abilities were timid and unpredictable, and this was a mountain higher than any healer, even the best ones, could climb. *Oh Ana,* he wanted to say, but had no energy, *bless you for trying.*

Finally, Nicolas' mind caught up to what his eyes were seeing. The black rot pervading Mercy's flesh was receding, slowly. Beneath it was an ashy, graying color that reminded him of rotting flesh, and he winced. But then, that too, subsided. Mercy's prior pale, vibrant skin revealed itself as Ana continued to tremble and glow above her.

Then, Mercy's eyes flashed open. In one jarring move, she shot upward, gasping and heaving. Breathing. Alive.

"Jesus Christ," Nicolas whispered. Finn stopped breathing beside him.

"Jesus has nothing to do with this," Finn said reasonably, as he struggled to regain his senses.

Ana tumbled back into Aidrik's arms, spent. He held her close, whispering into her ear, soothing her. Finn started as if to take over for Aidrik, but then stopped, watching them with painful curiosity.

"Mercy," Nicolas ventured, tentatively, still not understanding the breadth of the reality. Her beautiful, pale skin was as radiant as the day he'd met her. The red hadn't been restored to her long hair, but the silver now had a brilliant sheen as inhuman as he now accepted Mercy to be. Her chest moved up and down, clean breath flowing in and out of her lungs. Upon her breast, the brilliant phoenix was gone, and in its place was a dull, white outline, resembling a white tattoo. Less jagged than Aidrik's, but equally void.

Nicolas gaped in complete, indescribable shock. Ana had done it. Mercy was alive.

"Nicolas," Mercy whispered, equally awed. She turned her hands before her eyes, studying them. Pulling the strands of her hair forward, she eyed them, unable to form the questions they both had.

There were so many things he wanted to say to her, but they seemed unimportant. Mercy had died, and she was back. And he wanted her more than he had ever wanted anyone in all his self-ish, spoiled years.

Nicolas pulled Mercy into his arms, crushing her. He worried for a moment he might be hurting her, but she responded by holding him even tighter, burying kisses in his neck, her warm breath soothing. He inhaled the scent of her hair, and skin, but it wasn't enough. He needed to absorb every last inch of her.

In that moment, with the rain pouring down at eventide, and the world on fire, there was just Nicolas and Mercy. He could see, feel, or hear nothing but her, and he knew, Mercy was everything he needed. Ana had been right. Mercy was his salvation, and just maybe, he was hers.

43- MERCY

"You are Farværdig no longer," Aidrik said.

Though Mercy now appreciated Aidrik's authority in a way she never could before, she didn't need him to confirm this fact for her. She required no formal diagnosis to understand she had died Empyrean, and was reborn a Child of Man.

The disappearance of the Mark was not as startling as the other clues, nor would it have been enough to curb Emyr's gifts, as Aidrik's removal had not quelled his own immortality.

Emyr had gifted Man in a way Mercy had been blind to before. Mortality was a treasure, reminding you to savor each moment. Her awareness of it came with an appreciation of this new life. Something she'd railed against for millennia now had urgent and tangible value. The blood coursing through her veins was mortal. If she were to sustain a wound, she would be pained. If a blade passed through her flesh, she could die. And, if no tragic accident were to befall her sooner, die she would, in another threescore years or so.

She had the body of a healthy, mid-twenties human female, and the mind of the ancients.

Mercy didn't know how she felt about this, yet, but she would process it later.

"I don't understand," Nicolas kept saying, shaking his head, staring at his cousin. Mercy thought she understood, but kept silent. *Let Aidrik explain it. Seems that's why he's here.*

Aidrik's hand absentmindedly brushed Ana's cheek, passing back and forth in gentle tenderness. Mercy was taken aback by this uncharacteristic show of affection from someone she'd believed, before now, that she'd known better than anyone. But then. most of what she'd known and believed was a lie. This physical rebirth came with a spiritual one as well.

"I revived Anasofiya through an ancient ritual, Sveising. Only before performed on the Farværdig," Aidrik began. "The results were unpredictable but the alternative was to let her die. This infusion of my DNA to hers brought forth abilities she did not have prior. Strengthening others."

"Okay, but even the best fucking healers in the family cannot bring back the dead!" Nicolas exclaimed. His shoulders tensed under his thin, soaking shirt. A heat stirred in her new mortal flesh, and Mercy scolded herself for wanting him under such conditions.

"But there are Farværdig who can," Aidrik explained. "Though, not many. I am pleased Anasofiya inherited the power of resurrection. Even I cannot do that." Aidrik gazed at Ana, protectively. "It implies Sveising is more powerful on a Child of Man."

"So, what, she's Empyrean now?" Nicolas asked. Mercy slipped her hand through his. He was shaking. She frowned when she realized she could no longer read his mind. *Are all my powers gone, then?*

"I know not," Aidrik admitted. "I believe I have given her more than the power of resurrection, though."

"She looks evanescent," Mercy said. Without the ability to

read Ana's mind, she could only guess at her jumbled, confused thoughts. The girl looked dazed. "As I once did, in my youth."

"Without fear of the Council's Mark, the Farværdig may live forever," Aidrik said. "I cannot know for sure, but I believe Anasofiya shares this gift of Emyr."

"Can someone please tell me what the hell is going on?" Finn chimed in. The poor Man, eyes sagging, face unnaturally pale, looked as if he might dissolve into helpless hysterics at any moment.

"Anasofiya's metamorphosis of Farværdig and Halfling joins our two worlds together," Aidrik continued, ignoring Finn. "Impossible to know what it means, but I must protect this secret from the Senetat for fear of dangerous reprisal."

Finn reached for Ana, but she pulled away from both him and Aidrik. She had the look of a feral cat, seeing everything around her as a potential enemy.

The pain in Finn's eyes was almost heartbreaking. With Mercy's old powers, she could have sent him soothing thoughts. Now, all she could do was watch, helpless.

"Ana," he pleaded. "Please explain this to me."

"I can't," Ana replied, in sad, strained tones, breaking her silence. Her wide eyes regarded Finn with love and fear, as she pressed herself against the tree. She was very clearly over-whelmed with all that had passed in the last hour. Aidrik would need to guide her carefully, or she was at risk of losing her mind.

Mercy understood now. Ana and Aidrik had evigbond, and theirs was a more ancient, chemical kind than the one she'd shared with Nicolas. Where theirs had been forged through consummation, Ana and Aidrik's was forged through fate. The creation of the Halfling Deschanels by Aidrik was more than a sin against the Senetat. It was also the creation of a new race of half-supernatural beings linked to the Empyreans. Mercy realized now why Aidrik had stayed away from his progeny. There had always been a risk he might evigbond with one, as he now had with Ana.

Mercy could see Aidrik embraced this new revelation, while Ana was terrified of it.

Finn walked back toward the house, his pride, and heart, broken. Ana let him go.

"You are safe now," Aidrik concluded, looking at Mercy. "In the eyes of the Senetat, you are dead. Emyr help you if they ever learn otherwise."

Mercy thought of how he'd led her here. To *Ophélie*. To his descendants. To Nicolas. In all her wandering, Aidrik was the only true friend she'd ever encountered. The only one to ever challenge her beliefs and push her toward a deeper truth. He cared for her, watching over her even after she'd turned her back on him.

Mercy's wandering was over now. Her zealotry sated, eyes opened. She no longer lived in the shadow of her dogma, and could do as she pleased, where she pleased, with whom she pleased.

A once-welcome weight had been lifted from her soul. The gift of freedom, once scoffed at, was now hers.

"Where will you go?" Aidrik asked.

"Nowhere," she said, looking at Nicolas. Her first death had severed the evigbond between them, but what remained felt somehow more real. She wasn't drawn to him by some ancient tie beyond her control. She wanted him, through the gift of free will.

At the very least, she wanted to explore what that meant.

AIDRIK AND ANA RETURNED TO THE HOUSE, AFFORDING NICOLAS and Mercy some brief privacy. A ray of ivory moonlight beat down through gaps in the leaves, forming a meteor shower of brilliant drops along the ground.

Nicolas' wet, dark hair matted against his forehead. His chestnut eyes were wide and vulnerable as he studied her. By instinct, Mercy searched for his thoughts, but again found none. It was okay. It was easier to love him when the playing field was equal.

"I just realized something," Nicolas said, staring toward the sky.

"Hm?"

"You don't actually have a husband."

Mercy laughed. "No, I do not."

"And you're definitely not from New York."

"Definitely not."

"I knew it! I fucking *knew* it! I told Oz that I could smell the bullshit a mile away with that story you told me."

Mercy tried to stop laughing, as Nicolas rolled around these genuine revelations in his mind. "I felt bad lying, but you didn't exactly make it easy on me, either. You and Oz with your research, and questions. How was I supposed to know a lawyer and a rich kid were going to be my ushers? I have to admit, I didn't expect to need so many details, and I wasn't entirely prepared for it."

"That and you were hoping to Ascend sooner." Nicolas grimaced. That word would always have a sinister meaning to both of them now. She doubted Nicolas would ever forget the image of her crying for Emyr as she died before his eyes.

"That too," she said, with a smile. She hoped her visible joy would at least temporarily push away that memory.

Mercy chuckled then, thinking about their first meeting. "That day on the island feels like an eternity ago. I couldn't even believe it when you turned out to be such a jerk."

Nicolas gasped, feigning offense. "Who? Me? Fuck, lady. You do know I went out there to off myself, right? Before you rudely interrupted me."

Mercy's smile faded. She'd nearly forgotten what his plans

were, and it was finally sinking in that she almost let him die. "We were both very misguided. For a long time."

He nodded. A lump formed in her throat, as she digested both of their words. Humor was always his first response, but there was nothing funny about the fate they'd both nearly met.

"Well," Nicolas began, making an attempt at restoring levity, "it's a good thing I realized what a badass I am, so we can put that nonsense behind us and get on with shit."

"A good thing indeed," Mercy humored him. "How are you processing all this?"

His brows knitted together in a hilarious gesture. "My mind is *blown*, girl," he said finally. Mercy laughed again. What other response was there?

"I believed for so long I knew all there was to know. Now I see I've been wrong about so many things…"

"We both have," Nicolas conceded. "But I don't think it matters much anymore."

"You're a mystic," she said in wonderment, watching him. She didn't even think it was *possible* for a Child of Man to possess such powers. "How things changed in a week. I've lost my powers, and you've discovered yours."

He kissed her. The gesture was firm and possessive, but also kind. Mutual care was as new to Nicolas as it was to Mercy. With their evigbond forfeit, they would need to find their way through whatever this now was, together.

"I have no idea what any of this means, Mercy," he said. The contrast of his dark hair and eyes against his pale skin gave him a purity which made him seem more beautiful than anything in all her wandering. "All I know is I want you, and I don't care how ridiculous that sounds."

She smiled. "It doesn't sound ridiculous."

"I do have a reputation to maintain," Nicolas replied with a sly grin. "And I have a three date rule."

"Oh? And what is that rule?"

His eyes twinkled. "Either stop fucking her, or marry her."

Mercy threw her head back and laughed with a renewed joy at being alive. "Is that supposed to be a proposal of marriage?"

"Well," he teased, "it's really a self-defeating rule because I'm not the marrying type."

"Marriage is such a human notion anyway," she concurred with feigned disgust. "So what *are* you saying then?"

"My mind is still spinning with all this supernatural bullshit," Nicolas said, throwing his hands up. "I can't focus on anything except this really bizarre emotion... love, I think? No, can't be. Doesn't exist."

Mercy envisioned a lifetime of laughing beside this man. "Charming, but I still don't understand your point."

His smile faded and he took both of her hands in his, looking down in thought. When his eyes met hers once again, there was no longer any humor in them. "I would like you to stay here with me, for as long as you can put up with my bullshit."

It was Mercy's turn to kiss him.

44- AIDRIK

They had to depart swiftly. The unknown was Anasofiya's willingness to join. Logic told Aidrik yes. The evigbond was undeniable. Unbecoming insecurity left him in the dark. An unfortunate side effect of love.

Though her physical prowess and beauty had grown following her transformation, her wandering thoughts made her seem like a member of the undead. Stumbling, fumbling through her new self. She swayed and he moved to catch her. Guide her. She would require his guidance in a great many things now. In return, there was much she could teach him about humanity.

He wished to know what she was thinking in her silence. Pulling the thoughts from her head would be simple, but it felt now like a violation. Anasofiya had allowed many Men to commit trespass upon her, believing she deserved nothing better. Never again.

Entering the house felt unwise with Finn inside. His demand for answers would be unsatisfied. Aidrik was weary of unproductive discussion. Eager for palaver with Anasofiya.

He led her instead to the other side of the house. They

entered a garden maze of green and blossoms. A parterre. Much beloved of the French.

Aidrik steadied her, and she jolted from the loss of forward momentum. Her movements had been instinctively carrying her forward. They were alone, so he could speak aloud and freely. "Are you all right?"

She turned toward him slowly. Her pale face was blank, then suddenly spread into a wide, lovely smile. Blossoming. "I don't know. I think so."

Her hands drew to the purplish ring around her neck. It was thin but garish, his healing curing her of all other ailments but this. Perhaps a reminder of where they had come from, and why, was not such a bad thing.

Anasofiya's eyes-like-the-sea watched him. He feared losing himself in their depth. Her hair-of-flames glistened in the moonlight. Her heart of darkness beat strongly.

Later, he could allow himself this departure. Not now, with business still unattended.

"Aleksandr has to come first, and I don't know the first thing about protecting him." Her voice was soothing, brave, like the imposing saltwater of the North Sea. "From whatever it is I am now... what he will be." His Anasofiya sighed. "You wanna know if I'll come with you. Do I have a choice?"

Aidrik laughed. She was in his head, when he'd agonized over affronting her with the same action. "Here I worried I might offend you by being in *your* head," he teased. *Teasing.* What had become of him? Further, why did it not bother him?

"I don't understand what I'm feeling. What's happened," she said, moving closer. Her smooth hands rose up to touch his face. They were on fire, as an Empyrean's skin always was. "What are you?"

Aidrik's lips found hers. His tongue, breaching the opening, forcing it wider. This tenderness was as refreshing as Farjhem's gentle breeze on a summer day.

She pulled away, dropping her eyes, severing the physical connection entirely.

"I know this must be confusing for you," he conceded.

"Confusion. That's one way to put it," Anasofiya replied. "There's so much swimming around in my head. Your memories, my past, my feelings. None of it feels real. Nothing except the love I have for my son. And Finn. That didn't change when you changed me."

"It will take time," Aidrik assured her, closing the gap forming between them. "I will help you."

"I've never felt more alive in all my life," she said, tilting her head back, raising her closed eyes to the sky. Something in the way she did this made Aidrik feel like an intruder, in a moment meant for her alone. "But I've also never been more lost."

"I know not what you are," Aidrik said in wonder. He had broken free of her intoxication with a willpower born of evigbond. He studied her, his creation. Still Anasofiya. Also more. "Or what you will become."

"I used to wonder who I was, or who I would become," she said. He was hypnotized by the sound of her honeyed voice. She sounded so different in his head. "But wondering is what got me where I was when I stepped into the noose. I've lived my whole life in darkness, Aidrik, and I never want to be there again. I want my son growing up knowing he is safe, and loved. Knowing it can be different for him than it was for me."

"Without doubt, he will," Aidrik replied. His lips found hers again, willpower be damned. Though he noted a rough stirring beneath his robes, it was less blind desire than an insistence to be buried in her. He craved her. Wanted to consume her. Mind, body, soul.

Again, it was Anasofiya who broke the tether, lowering her face away from him. He scolded himself. *Take it slowly. She is not yet ready.*

"Where will we go?" Anasofiya asked. Studying her confused

expression, he was again reminded she still had so much to learn. It would require patience. He was a willing and eager teacher.

"Far from here," he replied. In truth, he had not given their destination the thought it deserved. Had never foreseen this voyage would end with Mercy's resurrection. The discovery of a powerful mystic Halfling. A princess with eyes-like-the-sea. A son. His plans to wander in solitude would need amendment now that they had a child to consider. A child who was an affront to the Senetat many times over. A child who would, most likely, grow to be even more powerful than Anasofiya or Aidrik.

"I guess it doesn't really matter, as long as Aleksandr is safe," she said. As she turned from him again, the light breeze carried her scent. Her hair smelled like the blossom of a magnolia. Her skin, milk and honey.

"But," she continued, a new thought occurring to her, "how will we protect my son from the entire Senetat?"

Aidrik again breathed in the scent of her. Nearly lost himself in it before regaining his sanity. "My plan is not fully formed, but we will not remain without allies for long," he assured her. "There exist others, like me, who wish to see the Farværdig race restored to its former peace. Who would fight for it." His mind went to Agripin, the rogue son of Grand Emperor Aeron. Suspected of having ties with the Runeans, and a vision Aidrik believed in. Dangerous to approach him without confirmation, but a risk was needed if the tides were to change.

"Fight," she said thoughtfully, mulling the word over. She pulled away. "I feel like I could equally destroy what I could heal."

"Yes, destroy. But also, create. I have so much to show you," he marveled, thinking of the eternity ahead. Of their son. "Both of you."

"If it was possible to defeat them, why hasn't it happened?"

she asked. The question was more human than Farværdig, and he found it simultaneously beautiful and devastating at once.

"Possibility was not the obstacle," Aidrik admitted, after a brief pause. "It was I who was not ready."

She pulled away then, looking toward *Ophélie*. Her thoughts were undoubtedly on the Man inside. Aidrik's memory of his recognition and exuberance at Ulfberht would be long-lasting.

It pleased Aidrik this wholesome Man would be his son's First Father, a role only one male could ever assume in a child's life. The concept strengthened him, but he was yet in the dark how Anasofiya would feel as this arrangement played out. Evigbond in a Child of Man was conflicting. As such, her heart, and soul, might always be torn between Finn and Aidrik.

"Finn's coming with us," Anasofiya said, with a confidence born of her new self. "I left him before, and it was a terrible mistake. I won't go anywhere without him, unless he chooses otherwise."

"Impossible," he replied.

She spun on her heels, fire burning in her face. "Why? Because you say so?"

Aidrik could argue that evigbond was for two, not three; that he already loved her too much to share her. But she would understand neither of those things so early, and he feared losing her before she could come to terms with it. Shamefully, he played upon her worst fear to convince her. "He will be in grave danger. He wears his heart openly. He would get himself killed."

Doubt washed over her face, and so he sent her persuasive thoughts, deepening his dishonor. Realization then replaced that doubt, followed by a despairing sadness.

"I love him. With all my heart," Anasofiya said finally, her light breaths ragged. Her gaze lingered toward the house, away from him. He could not see her face. "I finally know it. There's a goodness in him I can't even begin to understand, or appreciate, the way he deserves. I wanted so badly to share it with him..."

Aidrik wished he could quell her pain, but he knew better than to think he possessed such a power. Nor did he have the right, after his deception. He promised himself her emotional scars would heal once she adjusted to her new reality. "It will be a kindness to leave him," he coaxed, finally. "He is suffering now."

"But I can't leave him, not entirely. Things are different now."

"Yes," Aidrik agreed. "They are."

"And Nicolas," she said, voice fading. She needn't say more. He gathered her meaning.

"A kindness to him as well," he replied. "And relief, perhaps. He has found purpose in Mercy. Your formal release of his heart will allow him to give it freely."

She began to argue. Likely to insist, indignant, that she had never held Nicolas' heart. Weighing her fears, she finally asked, "Mercy… she'll be good to him?"

Aidrik nodded. "Nicolas is safe with Mercy. Just as you are with me."

Anasofiya twisted her lips together. The defiant gesture made Aidrik desire to tear the dirty clothes off and have his way with her. "And how do you know you're safe with *me*?" Her pert tone matched her expression.

"Safety is a subjective sentiment," he replied. "And potentially overrated."

Her sigh pierced his heart. "I need to talk to him," she said. "To Finn."

"Yes," he agreed.

"I don't think I can do this. I don't think I can say goodbye to him." Her breaths grew ragged and pained again. "I can't do this."

"You can," he urged, gently. *Careful. Do not hurt her further than is necessary. She is your evigbond, not your slave.*

As she closed her eyes, Aidrik laid his lips atop both lids, blessing her with courage. "I will be here, waiting, *Kjære*." Kjære; *my Dearest*. A word he had never before used. Never had cause to use, until now.

As he watched Ana move toward the house, he sighed in contentment.

45- NICOLAS

*S*ex had always been a means to an end for Nicolas. When his cock was hard, he found a willing partner. If he only wanted a beautiful woman on his arm, that was no difficult matter, either. Both suited him just fine. Love was far more hassle than it was worth.

He wasn't ready to fall in love, but his mind wasn't wandering toward his next encounter, either. He liked Mercy. Wanted her here. It wasn't as demanding of a feeling as it had been before she died, but it was more real. There was no going back to the days of cheap thrills and careless encounters, and somehow, he was fine with it. Besides, Mercy was the hottest woman he had ever been with. Waking up to her each morning, even after the dreaded third date, wouldn't be especially challenging.

"I can't read your thoughts anymore," she said. Her head rested against his chest, her silver hair scattered over him like haphazard branches.

"Excuse me? Anymore?" He feigned offense, but had suspected it all along. Her knowledge had been all too convenient at times.

"Crap," she offered in lieu of an apology, and they both laughed.

"Why do you wanna know what I'm thinking anyway? I guarantee you won't like what you see."

"Yes, I already know about your bizarre fantasies involving the blonde bartender at the Monteleone, your cousin Ana, or both at the same time," she quipped. "The downside to telepathy is you can't always guarantee when or where you'll be jumping in."

Nicolas shook his head, laughing. They were covered in mud, having given into their need of each other in an entirely inopportune place, but he didn't care. He was at peace, for now. "So, then, what is it you're so eager to know?"

"Nothing I can't wait and find out on my own." She dismissed the question, as she flipped over the top of him. As she slithered up his torso, he wondered if there would be any end to his longing for her.

Nope, he thought, as she enveloped him. *Probably not.*

RELUCTANTLY, THEY RETURNED TO THE HOUSE. MERCY SEEMED to think Aidrik was eager to be on his way, and she wanted to extend proper thanks and farewells. Nicolas had a sinking feeling he wouldn't be the only one leaving.

As they crossed the property, that familiar flipping sensation rose up. Nicolas groaned as it took hold. One day, he would learn to control this, fully. Aidrik promised to teach him, but if he was leaving, Nicolas did not know when that would be.

Finn. He was standing in the study, where hours ago Aidrik vomited up his crazy story. This seemed to be a popular spot for confessionals.

He was thinking about The Lord of the Rings. *His favorite book; for many reasons, not the least of which that was the true heroes of the story always did the right thing. Friendships never wavered, even in the deepest adversity. And, despite the evil all around them, goodness prevailed. Being loyal, and good, paid off.*

Middle Earth was filled with exemplary examples of bravery, and loyalty. Samwise. Faramir. Eowyn. Gandalf. Legolas. Gimli. Merry. Pippin. Eomer. The list went on and on and on. In fact, Finn could name more role models in The Lord of the Rings *than he could from all the people he knew or had known in real life.*

Finn fancied himself a little bit like Samwise Gamgee. Unfailingly loyal, even when others ridiculed him for it, or when those he was most loyal to pushed him away. To Finn, it was Sam, not Frodo, who was the real hero. Without Sam, Frodo never would have made it to Mt. Doom. The Fellowship would have failed, and Middle Earth would have fallen to Sauron.

Ana was on a quest of her own, to make peace with herself. She believed this to be impossible, and expected to fail. Finn knew she couldn't do it alone. He desperately wanted to be her Sam.

That night on the cliff side in Maine was the first time he thought, maybe, he could be. He'd made love to her there, her cheeks and hair aflame as water crashed on the rocks below. They both lay there, breaths ragged, remembering the cold. But there were words on Finn's lips, and he would not let them die there.

Placing his hands gently against the sides of her face, he pressed his forehead to hers and whispered, "Ana, this is love. This right here."

She said nothing for the longest time, but then her eyes blinked with pools of tears, and she nodded. "It is, isn't it?"

The object of his thoughts appeared, startling him. Ana stood before him, her radiance only slightly covered her awkwardness, and pain. No, pain was not all Finn was seeing. Also, guilt. Regret.

"What have I not given you?" Finn asked, coming to the point immediately. He was near to pleading, though men like Finn didn't often plead. His desperation was completely overwhelming. The inevitable loss of Ana was weighing on his heart like nothing before ever had. The inevitability of it frightened him.

"You've given me everything," she replied. Calm, controlled. Differ-

ent. Finn hardly recognized her. *"But I can't give you the same things in return."*

"I've asked nothing of you in return, Ana!" Finn exclaimed. *"I've known who you were since the day I first saw you on the shores of Summer Island. I've never expected you to be anyone you're not, and I've given you safety in being who you are."*

NICOLAS WAS MERCILESSLY PULLED BACK TO HIS OWN REALITY. Mercy steadied him, her expression one of concern. "Are you okay?"

"I don't know," he replied, shaking his head. He was standing in the muddy grass, also in the study. He was Finn, and he was himself. *This must be what a schizophrenic on meth feels like.* "We need to get back to the house. Ana and Aidrik are leaving."

Mercy didn't ask further questions. He loved that about her. Instead, she took off in a sprint, and Nicolas followed.

"*T*here's a child," she said, letting out a breath of combined relief and fear.

Finn's face lit up. Then fell. "Jon's," he speculated, eyes narrowing.

She shook her head. "No, not Jon's. Yours, but—"

"I'm going to be a father," Finn whispered. His hands slowly went toward his head, and he sank into a chair without looking. "Ana, why tell me this if you're leaving? You aren't thinking of..."

"No, I want this child more than I've wanted anything, ever." *My son*, she almost added, but didn't yet trust her newfound abilities. She'd love the child no matter what, but had already bonded to the idea of a son, of Aleksandr.

"I don't know how to even begin explaining things," she said. She took a seat across from him, but was careful to avoid close proximity. No matter what Aidrik said, she was vulnerable in her love for Finn. It was bigger than anything else that had happened to her, even the Sveising. Always would be.

"I just saw you bring a woman back to life, Ana. I hardly

think anything you're going to say will be shocking in comparison," he replied, weary.

"I did tell you my family was different," she reminded offhandedly, but she needed to at least try to explain this to him, in earnest. She told him Aidrik wasn't human, and the Deschanels, through descent, were also not entirely human. She told him Aidrik's healing had involved an augmentation of her DNA, but also the child growing inside. The child now belonged to all three of them.

When Finn finally looked up, his face appeared to have aged ten years. The fine lines around his eyes were deep grooves, his five o'clock shadow, dark and menacing. "You mean, Ulfberht is real, then?"

Ana blinked in shock. *"That's* what you took from the story?"

He laughed, then, rolling back against the couch. "Jesus, Ana, what the hell else am I supposed to say? You tell me you love me, but then hide from me you're pregnant. You then meet this... whatever Aidrik is, and suddenly you try to kill yourself, but no, it can't be that simple either, can it? Then he revives you and whatever he does somehow also makes him the father of *my* child. Finally, though you supposedly love me, you're leaving with this man you only just met earlier today, and the two of you are going to raise *my* child together? Do I have it about right?"

There wasn't anything she could say. It did sound ridiculous. But it didn't change anything, either. The two people she loved most in the world, her unborn child and Finn, were both in danger. Aidrik would teach her how to protect Aleksandr, but she could only protect Finn by letting him go.

"The child will be in danger if we stay here," she pleaded, wanting Finn to understand. No, *needing* him to. She loved him more as each second ticked closer to her unavoidable departure. *My heart.* "The Senetat will never allow our child to be free."

Finn laughed again, this time with drops of derision. "Did you even think, for a second, that maybe I would come? That I would have gone with you, anywhere?"

Oh, Aidrik, what if you're wrong? The thought of being torn from Finn now was more acute than the pain she'd felt stepping into the noose.

If I'm irrevocably bound to Aidrik, then why is my heart still aching so desperately for Finn? Why does this feel like I'm ripping my heart right out of my chest?

Strength, Ana. Remember Aidrik's words. Bringing Finn will get him killed. This is how you protect him.

"I'll bring our child back as often as I can," Ana promised. "He'll be raised knowing both his fathers. Not just one."

"Oh, thank you for allowing me to share my child with another man!"

"I can't change the way things are," Ana whispered. Oh how she wished, desperately, that this wasn't true.

"You make no sense," Finn said, coldly. His eyes filled with tears. The sight of it caused Ana's heart to drop to the floor. "I see now that accepting you, and understanding you, are mutually exclusive experiences."

She'd been so determined not to cry, but it was impossible. She broke down, burying her face in her hands, as if that, or anything, could contain her grief. Her heart broke as much as his. Her love for Finn had never been the problem.

Finn softened, somehow surprised her humanity was still intact. "Did you ever love me?" he asked, gently, his voice that of a child.

"I love you now! If love were the only thing at stake here—"

"Tell me, Ana, what else is at stake?" Finn demanded. "If not both of our damned hearts!"

"Our child's future," she replied, unwavering.

Finn opened his mouth to object, but then turned away from her. He struggled with himself to maintain control, but she didn't miss the light tremor in his hands as he locked them over his head. "Don't you think I deserve a chance to protect our child, too?"

"You can protect our child by protecting yourself," Ana said. She moved to touch him, but he recoiled when her hand brushed his arm. "If something were to happen to me—"

"Don't even say things like that," he snapped, but then turned back toward her, softening. "Ana, why him, and not me?"

The answer wouldn't satisfy him, but she answered anyway. "He can teach me about who I am, and who our child will be. I don't know exactly what's ahead, but I do know our child is is in danger, just for existing. Aidrik will know what to do."

"You don't even know him," he protested, but his rebuttals were weak now. He was resigning himself to the reality that her departure was imminent.

"I have to do this," Ana said, resolutely. She swiped at her eyes, pushing aside tears for strength, and turned to leave.

Finn ran after her, spinning her around as he pulled her into his arms. His kiss was desperate as the first of his own tears spilled. His lips felt as amazing, soothing, as they always had, but her mind was already closing its doors. She had no choice. *My heart cannot, so my mind must.* "I'll do anything to help you," he whispered. "Please don't leave."

"I promise, I'll return. When I can. With our son," she answered.

"Wait, Ana," Finn pressed.

He held out the ring he'd given her, not so long ago, in a similar moment, desperate to hold on. His mother's ring. "Please."

Ana started to protest, but then his strong hands were around hers. He gently spread her hand into a palm and pressed it in. "No strings."

Gazing down at the beautiful antique ring that had once

belonged to Claire St. Andrews, Ana's strength continued to fade. "But this was your mother's," she whispered.

"And you," he said, lifting her chin, "are the mother of my child. It will be theirs someday."

Remembering himself, he dropped his hand from her face, and looked away, letting go.

My heart, Ana thought with a twisting sadness, as she tried to draw from his unwavering strength. She clutched the ring in her fist and walked away, while she still could.

47- NICOLAS

$\mathcal{F}$inn was in the study, alone. Nicolas sensed his troubled thoughts through the door, presumably, part of his growing abilities. He ignored the closed door, striding toward where Ana waited in the central hall.

Aidrik's hand was pressed against the small of her back. It was a small gesture, but Nicolas read it clear enough: *She is mine. I am hers.*

Nicolas managed to be happy for her, though he sensed she'd abandon an essential part of herself to leave with him. For the first time in her life, though, she was alive.

"You're leaving," Mercy said, eyes fixed on Aidrik.

"Aye," he replied. "In search of Runeans."

The word still meant little to him, but Mercy jumped all over it. "Runeans? Are you mad, Aidrik?"

Aidrik smiled indulgently. "After your recent experiences, I should not have to explain this to you."

Mercy sighed, shifting toward him. I believe you now. Or, I'm trying to. But nothing can be gained by joining the rebels! You'll be taken, and destroyed!" Mercy nodded at Ana. "As will she, for what you've done to her."

"Anasofiya, and the child she carries, are precisely the reasons why we must seek them out," Aidrik explained. His tone was gentle, but there was impatience running just under the surface.

"Wait," Nicolas said, knowing Mercy shared the question, from her own startled reaction. "What child?"

"Anasofiya's child," Aidrik explained casually, as if it were old news. "By Finn, and I. A child of two fathers."

"You didn't," Mercy accused.

"I did," Aidrik replied. "And I would do it again, if it saved her life."

Nicolas gaped, open-mouth, from Aidrik to Mercy, until Mercy slipped her hand through his and whispered, "I'll explain it all to you later."

"Fuck's sake, Mercy, did you hear what he just said?"

"It's okay Nic," Ana said.

Nicolas stared at Ana as if she were a complete stranger to him. In some ways, she was his old Ana. His introverted, beautiful cousin. But she was not the same, and never would be again. He hadn't yet decided whether this was good or not.

"Aidrik," Mercy pleaded. "You can't throw yourself to the lions."

"Complacency is no longer sufficient," Aidrik said, "or acceptable. I've told you I believe we could live forever, if the Senetat is unseated. If true, we have much to fight for, and much to lose if we don't."

"Equally as much to lose if you don't win," Mercy challenged, but her shift in tone suggested she knew reasoning with Aidrik was a battle she couldn't win.

"Losing is not an option, then," Aidrik replied. Then he did the damnedest thing. He smiled!

"I'm not the only one who's changed, old friend," Mercy said in a reverent wonder. She watched Aidrik, in the same manner Nicolas had assessed Ana. "It suits you."

Aidrik's eyes momentarily diverted to Ana. Just enough for Nicolas to catch it. Just enough for him to feel, finally, a sense of peace about where Ana's future was going. Whoever this strange motherfucker was, he'd protect her, though it didn't seem Ana would ever need protecting, from anyone, ever again.

"We must go," Aidrik urged.

Nicolas' heart started to race. It was real now. And this time, when she left, it might be forever. He stepped forward, determined not to waste this moment.

"The last time we parted, I said some pretty awful things," he acknowledged. Ana slipped her hands into his, and he was struck again how *hot* they were. Like Mercy's.

"You did," she agreed. "Wanna try again?"

He flashed her a goofy grin. His signature. He knew it would draw a smile from her. "I wish you all the luck in the world. You're going to need it with that cantankerous, cosplaying fuck."

Her face spread into a smile to match his own. "And I wish Mercy all the luck in the world. Because *she's* going to need it keeping your crazy head on," she retorted.

Nicolas pulled Ana close, taking her in one last time. He had an awful feeling he'd never see her again. That, wherever her travels with Aidrik took her, there would be no return. "I do love you, Muffins," he whispered against her ear. "Always have, always will."

"I know," she replied. She planted her lips against the corner of his mouth, a whisper of their scandalous moment earlier, which seemed an eternity ago. "But you're wrong, jerkface. You'll see me again."

Mercy and Nicolas, hand in hand, watched them leave. There were still so many unanswered questions, and a lifetime of things to learn, and discover. He didn't mind.

For the first time, Nicolas looked forward to the future.

48- NICOLAS

a week had passed since Ana and Aidrik's departure. Nicolas and Mercy spent their days and nights revealing the wonders of the very different worlds they'd grown up in. Now that secrets were not a critical component of their relationship, they could speak their truths freely.

Finn hadn't yet made any move to return home to Maine. He wore his broken heart like a battle scar, thoughtfully but privately. He disappeared most of the day to sit by the river-bank, returning in the evenings with more fish than they'd ever consume.

Neither asked Finn how long he would stay. It didn't matter, anyway. His blood was mixed with theirs, now. He was part father to the child Nicolas would choose as his heir, one day.

Mercy awoke one morning bleeding, as if miscarrying. He laid hands on her in a panic, making a desperate wish healing was, somehow, one of his mystic gifts. But when nothing happened, Nicolas knew they couldn't ignore it. As the hours ticked on, she grew paler, weaker, and his fears deepened.

"Colleen," she said, finally. "You have to call her." When

Nicolas hesitated, Mercy added, "Nicolas, I'm mortal now, like you. If I bleed out, I'll die."

She was right, and for more reasons than she said. A normal hospital might detect some of Mercy's abnormalities, the extent of which they still had not yet defined themselves. Colleen's skills in both supernatural and natural medicine, mixed with her pragmatism, could be useful as they waded through the reality of what Mercy had become.

As expected, Aunt Colleen was intrigued and enthusiastic to learn about the Empyreans. She was also almost humorously unsurprised about it.

"It certainly explains a lot," she said, thoughtfully. *Yeah, no shit.*

"Can you help her?" Nicolas asked.

"I haven't even examined her yet," Aunt Colleen chided him. "But if you'll give us some privacy, I'll see to it immediately."

Nicolas gritted his teeth, annoyed, but Mercy nodded, dismissing him. Fine. He wasn't interested in gynecological adventures, anyhow.

Grumbling, he closed the door behind him and went downstairs, into the study. He eyed his mahogany bar; Condoleezza had replaced all of the empty bottles of Hennessy, without ceremony.

Worried about what Aunt Colleen would find with Mercy, he filled his crystal glass full. He longed for the fire water coursing down his throat, warming his stomach, numbing the pain. Then he paused, and poured half of it back. He owed her a level-head in this situation. When he'd asked Mercy to stay, he didn't know what it meant, but she deserved his clarity.

He spotted movement outside, and noticed Anne. He hadn't realized Aunt Colleen had brought her. Anne, his other half-sister, wasn't raised with him and the other sisters. She was a secret of his father's for many years, all the while hiding her own, that she was an arborkinetic, able to command the plants and trees to her bidding.

Aunt Colleen "adopted" her a while back, and Anne had been at The Gardens, Colleen's home in the Garden District, ever since.

Nicolas smiled. Of course Anne would be wandering around the grove.

Then his eyes caught someone else, at the far end. Following Anne's gaze, he saw Finn, kneeling down, studying something with intense scrutiny. He was surprised to see him up at the house during the day.

Anne continued watching Finn as she slowly moved his way. Nicolas strained to find out what Finn was fiddling with, but could see nothing. Anne smiled.

Now, Nicolas was curious. He didn't want to scare the guy, because it seemed like progress that Finn wasn't at the river for once. Of course, there was one way of easily finding out, but Aidrik had forbid him from doing it. Said it was against the rules to engage in nested visions without the subject's consent.

Nicolas' face stretched into a slow, sly smile. Well, what Aidrik didn't know wouldn't hurt him!

He closed his eyes and focused intently on Finn. Becoming Finn. And, just like that, he *was* Finn.

This was getting easier and easier.

Finn was troubled over a tiny baby bird that appeared to have fallen from its nest. A robin. The teeny beak sang a song of woe as Finn held it. It wasn't injured, but was afraid. It looked insignificant in his large, strong hands, but Finn's touch was exceedingly gentle.

Finn gazed upward, eyeing the scene of the crime. He could make out hints of the brown twigs forming the nest, but the branch that held it was at least thirty feet up. He'd already ruled out scaling the tree, though not for lack of agility. The problem facing him was the nest sat on the lowest of many branches, and there was nothing he could use for leverage to hoist himself up.

From the corner of Finn's vision, he witnessed a petite blonde girl raising her thin arms skyward. Her hair blew back and away from her, as if a very slight breeze passed through the garden. Finn jumped as the branches groaned and cracked above him, and nearly fell completely to the ground when he saw the branch containing the nest lowering itself *toward him.*

"What on God's green earth," Finn whispered, his head pivoting from the girl to the branch, and back. When, finally, the branch bowed low enough for Finn to reach, it stopped. In hesitant wonder, Finn gently placed the baby robin back into its home. The mother robin clucked in appreciation, giving Finn a brief, but kind look before attending to her offended baby.

The girl's arms slowly lowered back toward the ground, and as they did, the branch began ascending upward, back into place. Finn stepped back, not sure whether to run or to extend his gratitude.

She walked toward him with a slightly less confident gait than he would expect from someone who had just willed the branch to lower.

"Did you—?" Finn asked, though he already knew the answer to his question.

The girl nodded, biting her lip in an extreme shyness contrasting heavily with her show moments ago. "You must be Finn," she guessed.

"I must be," Finn agreed, still dazed, "but I have no idea who you are."

"Anne," she said, extending her long, pale arm. Finn took her hand hesitantly.

"Nicolas' sister?"

Anne nodded. "I'm here with our aunt. She's seeing to Mercy."

"What's wrong with Mercy?" Finn asked quickly. He was ashamed for not knowing; ashamed his emotions had been so overpowering he'd abandoned his duties in the household.

"I don't know," Anne said, "but if anyone can help her, it's Colleen."

Finn looked in the direction of the house. It still reminded him so much of Ana. Of the moment she revealed she was carrying his child. Her insistence on leaving him. Yet, he couldn't return home to Maine, *either. Home reminded him just as much of Ana, and seeing Jon was not something he looked forward to, either. And there was the promise she'd made, to return with their son. Finn would wait forever for a chance to meet him.*

"Are you gonna go in?" Anne asked, leaning forward to follow his gaze.

Finn shook his head. Not just yet. "That's some ability you have, Anne," he said. "Had I seen it a month ago, I might have fainted like a girl. But after spending time with the Deschanels..."

Anne laughed. "You know, Finn, your ability isn't anything to shake a leaf at."

"My ability?"

She blinked. "Yes, that thing with the robin."

Finn laughed. "Oh, that's nothing. I've always had a way with animals. It's not a big deal."

Anne raised one, bushy eyebrow. "To use your words, had I seen it before I spent time with Deschanels, I might believe that. My aunt says you can also predict storms."

Finn sighed, shaking his head. "Oh for—are you serious?" Heat flooded his face unexpectedly, and he hoped he wasn't blushing. "It's not an ability the way... you all have abilities."

"Deschanels aren't the only people in the world who have talent," she countered, knowingly. "But they do know how to help people culti-vate whatever talent lies within them."

Finn chuckled, choosing to shrug it off. He supposed it was true, that the world was filled with people who were good at something. But he didn't need to be phenomenal, or to stand out. He required very little, and though he'd temporarily lost that which gave his life real meaning, he wasn't easily deterred. The baby robin's miraculous return was all the symbolism he needed to believe that which he most wanted: Ana would return. And when she did, she would bring their son with her. Somehow, they would figure things out. Together.

Finn didn't need to know the intricate details of how things would work out. He only needed to believe they would.

. . .

"Nicolas, are you daft or just being willfully rude?"

Aunt Colleen's voice pulled him out of Finn's vision.

"You weren't concerned at the sight of me having a fucking seizure in my chair?" Nicolas countered, shaking off the vision. He recovered more quickly now that he was getting used to them, but the nauseating dizziness seemed a fixed effect.

His aunt gave the slightest of eye rolls, then said, "You are not a special snowflake, dearest nephew. That isn't the first time I've come upon someone in the midst of a vision."

"Then why did you just call me daft?" he protested, but she was already walking back up the stairs, her slight wag of the wrist beckoning him.

He followed her to the room, where Mercy lay on the bed. Her head was turned to the side, but he didn't miss the tears, or her pale, vacant expression.

"Sit down," Aunt Colleen commanded, and he obeyed, taking a chair next to Mercy. She still wouldn't look at him, but she didn't fight when he took her hand.

"There's no point in sugarcoating this," Aunt Colleen said in a firm, no-nonsense tone. Her kind eyes, though, betrayed her. "Mercy's womb is dying. The bleeding is her body's attempt to expel it."

"I don't understand. Can't you stop it?"

Colleen drew in a deep breath, then shook her head. "No. I tried. Something happened when Ana brought Mercy back. I can't define it because, frankly, I've never had exposure to those brought back through shamanistic resurrection. Whatever it was, it left Mercy's Empyrean womb intact, and her mortal body is now rejecting it."

"But, why can't you heal it?" Nicolas pleaded. Mercy continued to stare blankly forward, with silent tears coursing down her cheeks and on to the satin pillow.

"Because her body is treating it like a foreign object. It's no longer a living piece of her, Nicolas. I can't even detect it when I lay hands on her. There's nothing I can do to stop the process. However," she said, putting a gentle hand against Mercy's forehead. This gesture of tenderness nearly broke his heart. "I was able to stop the bleeding. She will recover."

"I still don't understand," he said, though he did.

Mercy spoke then, and her voice was hollow and full of pain. "I will never have children, Nicolas. Not ever."

LATER, AFTER AUNT COLLEEN AND ANNE LEFT, NICOLAS FOUND the courage to return to Mercy's side. She needed his comfort, and while he was aching to give it to her, he feared it would be inadequate. What the hell did he know about comforting a woman in distress? More, a woman who had lived three thousand years, and was just told she would never bear a child?

Nicolas slid in bed next to her, folding her into his arms. She showed her vulnerability by allowing it, and by burying her face against his chest.

"I'll leave tomorrow," Mercy said. Emotionless. Cold.

Nicolas pulled back, nudging her face so he could see her expression. Empty. "Leave? What the hell are you talking about?"

She wrenched her face free and looked down. "I can't bear you children, Nicolas. You have a responsibility, and I'm getting in the way—"

Nicolas took her cheeks in his hand and silenced her with a kiss. "Shut your mouth," he whispered, kissing her again. "Who the fuck wants kids?"

She blinked, startled. "You're the heir of *Ophélie*. Of the Deschanels. You must have children."

"I must not do any shit I do not want to do," Nicolas corrected her. "And besides you and I hardly know each other!"

Thankfully, she took the comment with the teasing intended. "I suppose I was jumping the gun, assuming..."

"Mercy, I don't want kids. Period. I decided a long time ago Ana would be my heir."

"But—"

"But not a damn thing," he said. "Adrienne wants nothing to do with the estate, and Anne is not a legal member of this family. So it has to be Ana. She's a true Deschanel, through and through. She'll never marry, especially now that she's abandoned poor Finn. Never change her name. Her son will be a Deschanel."

"How do you know it's a boy?"

"I'm sure of it," he said with an indignant confidence. "And he will be born not only of Deschanel blood, but also of Empyrean. Seems fitting, given what we know now."

She didn't say anything. Another woman might have debated the matter with him for hours. But not Mercy. When he assured her things were fine, she took his word for it.

Fellas, harness thy jealousy, for I hath found the perfect woman.

"You know, I don't have to read your mind to know what you're thinking," she dared, flashing him her beautiful, brilliant smile. Perfect.

Yes, perfect. He wouldn't change anything about her.

"I'm glad you ended up on my island." Of all the words that popped into his head, these were the only ones that mattered.

EPILOGUE

NICOLAS

Mercy once again attempted to show Nicolas the proposed budget. As with the previous few attempts, he rolled his eyes, using annoyance to cover the fact that he didn't understand a word she was saying.

"This is important," she insisted. Earlier, she'd slipped a hand down his trousers to secure his attention. Now, she was all business.

"Yes, shit, I know," Nicolas replied. He leaned over her laptop, but there was little hope of improving his concentration. Many accountants over the years had attempted to gain his understanding of *Ophélie's* accounts. All had failed miserably.

She was right, though. It was important. Turning *Ophélie* into a sanctuary for the children of Runean rebels was a very big, fucking deal. Lots of risk, and hopefully significant reward. He was beyond excited at the opportunity to usher Empyreans from fearing shadows to a place of safety. To give them refuge while their mothers and fathers prepared to battle the Senetat. He was *overflowing* with purpose. But it didn't make him any more interested in math, sadly.

The idea had been partly his, partly hers. It first took root one night as Mercy told him about her youth with the Scholars, the august group of eunuchs who instructed all Empyreans through to adulthood. Their graduation was sealed with the infusion of the Mark, and thus a lifetime of control was established.

"What if it didn't have to be that way?" he had asked her.

"It does," she said, sadly. "Many factions have tried to oppose the Senetat, and all have lost. And while I have complete and utter faith in your ability to look pretty and compose witty banter, I'm not sure you're up to the task of thwarting an ancient, evil empire."

With narrowed eyes Nicolas replied, "The shortest distance between two points is a straight line, but the best way to get from point A to point B is often by taking the back roads."

"Nicolas, darling—"

"Yeah, I know, that made no fucking sense," he finished for her. "My point is it's not the size of the army, it's how you put it to use."

Mercy pointedly looked at the crotch of his pants and then raised a knowing eyebrow. "Still not following."

Well, he wasn't either. Not exactly, anyway. There was an idea on the back of his thoughts, but his mind wasn't ready to formulate it yet. But he didn't forget it. And though she had teased him, she hadn't forgotten it, either.

Mercy came to him a week later. Her words were simple. "I don't want any more children to go through what I did." She didn't need to elaborate. She'd told him all about how her parents were executed for trying to bestow upon their only daughter the gift of enlightenment. Of knowledge.

After a long, thoughtful pause, she added, "having children is beyond my means now, but that doesn't preclude me from being a mother in other ways."

Over the next hour, she poured out her plan. A school, secretive and cloaked from the eyes of the Senetat. The students, Empyrean children of the Runeans. Teaching them the essentials of life, reinforcing the truth as they knew it. Giving them sanctuary until the battle for control of the Senetat was resolved.

"Fuck it, let's do it," Nicolas said. He had tons of questions, but he didn't need her to answer them now. They'd get there when they got there.

"The last major detail I need to sort out is where to build the school," she said.

"I live in a motherfucking mansion, Mercy," he reminded her. "One that's protected by Aidrik. You've got your school."

When her pale, lovely face broke into a smile, there was nothing he wouldn't have given her.

This discussion had launched three months of meetings, numbers, and planning. The property would need some work; the outbuildings could be fixed up into cabins, apartments. But they had bigger worries. The Senetat presumably still operated under the assumption Mercy had perished, as planned. Aidrik's protection over *Ophélie* held strong... for now. Once they started harboring Runeans, who knew what type of attention that would draw?

They both decided the risk was worth it. Mercy had spent many lifetimes acting under false belief. She'd watched her parents sacrifice their lives to give her a freedom she never achieved, until death. And whether Nicolas wanted to believe it or not, he was part Empyrean too. He had a stake in this.

Not so long ago, he'd been ready to selfishly declare his life forfeit. To toss it away, as if it meant nothing to him, or to anyone else. This decision would help leave that part of himself behind, forever.

Aunt Colleen was pulled into their planning. Then, Anne. Later, Aunt Evangeline was also folded into discussions. The Deschanel Magi Collective slowly took over. Colleen declared she would determine who else could be brought into the know and when. She was bossy, but effective. He was more than happy to let her run the business side of things.

Finn even took on a new excitement as plans moved forward. He wanted to be a part of the school, to teach the children practical survival skills, such as how to catch their own food, which he felt would be of the utmost use for children of refugees. He even took to spending more time with Anne, though when Nicolas teased him about it, he protested.

"I belong to Ana," Finn said, with a simplicity which was sad, and made sense, all at once. "I'll wait forever, if that's what I need to do."

Nicolas worried he might have to. It wasn't safe for Ana to contact them. While he could no longer access her mind, she surprised him by sending a vision of her own. Aidrik was clearly teaching her many things.

She was sitting on a hillside in France, with Aidrik. There was a silent, comfortable intimacy between them. His hand was pressed against her belly, protectively.

Aidrik gestured down into the small town. Where it all started, he said. He told her of how he met and fell in love with Christiane. Of her death.

Will we ever be safe? Ana asked.

I'll never allow any harm to come to you. Either of you.

"Off in one of your fantasy worlds again?" Mercy asked, coming up behind him

"I'm *living* in a fantasy world, baby!"

Mercy kissed him. Nicolas yanked her into his lap, pulling an excited, contented giggle from her. Whatever happened, they had each other. They would figure it out, together.

Nothing had turned out the way any of them had expected. Yet, somehow, it was exactly as it should be.

ANASOFIYA

Aleksandr was growing at a rapid pace. Ana worried her body wouldn't be capable of carrying him to term, but Aidrik insisted all Empyrean women had this doubt. He didn't keep from her that childbirth would be traumatic, and painful. But he did promise to get her through it.

"Typical gestation is six months," he said, as they trekked through the cold, Scottish Highlands. He didn't need to tell her those things. His memories were her memories now. In speaking of it though, she could wrap the rich comfort of his voice around her fears.

Ana was already three months along. She couldn't fathom three more months of this. She felt as if she already had a full-grown child ready to burst forth into the world.

But oh, how she loved him. Her son. Aidrik had explained to Ana that the bonds fused within him would be very strong. From Finn, his First Father, he would inherit a kindness, and a love of nature. From Aidrik and Ana, powers unparalleled. Aleksandr Deschanel, the ultimate heir, uniting the human Deschanels with the Empyrean ones.

The burden of this knowledge was tremendous. A part of

her wished Aleksandr would grow to be a normal boy, and they could live, quietly, away from danger and fear. But this path wasn't possible, not now or ever. Not while the Senetat remained intact, and their son a mortal crime against their laws.

"Within days of birth, he will begin speaking. In weeks, walking. Months, he will rival you in height." Aidrik explained to Ana what she could expect after their child entered the world. She couldn't begin to comprehend any of it.

As for Ana, she was still dizzy with the knowledge of what she'd become. A powerful healer, with the ability to bring back the dead. A swift, instinctive hunter. A remarkably strong telepath, and a mild conjurer of the elements.

Aidrik insisted she practice, but she found his presence too distracting to focus. When he would come up behind her, bracing her with his strong arms, the slight stubble from his chin scratching her neck, she wished instead he'd leave her alone. Their evigbond, something still so confusing to her, was beginning to take hold. His secret smile off into the distance told Ana he knew, and was glad of it, but she feared it.

That, but never him.

Aidrik's matter-of-fact approach was not off-putting to her, as it might have been to others. She appreciated knowing what he showed her was who he was, always knowing where she stood with him.

Though he often preached about the uselessness of the lusts of Men, it didn't stop his own desires from surfacing. His hunger for her flew in direct contradiction to all he had said. Ana enjoyed knowing this seemingly infallible creature wasn't immune from desire; that he was also imperfect, like her. And though the nature of her feelings for him were still deeply confusing, she began to accept they weren't going away. That giving into them, and allowing herself to embrace this new future, would help cultivate the light inside of her needed to be a good mother.

Sometimes Aidrik attempted to be gentle, but it wasn't long before he understood exactly what she needed. Hard. Remorseless. Infused with passion, and pain. Punishment. She needed him to be nothing like Finn, in any way, and for their moments together to drive away thoughts of her only true love. In her darkest moments, she believed he could do it, too. But even at his most aggressive, Aidrik always finished by laying his healing hands over her. He never said a word when he performed these last few, tender gestures, but Ana thought she understood. He would meet her base needs with the fervor she craved, but he would meet her even deeper needs by offering the love she'd never believed she deserved. The love she'd sacrificed, in Finn.

Finn was on her mind, always. He'd always be a part of her, no matter where she went; no matter how far. Time could pass and his role would never be relegated to only the father of her son. He would always, always, hold half her heart. Knowing there would be a part of Finn in her son gave Ana hope for his future. She and Aidrik were ruthless, intense, and passionate. Together, those traits were magnified. Finn's strength and kindness would ensure Aleksandr grew up with a humanity he would need to face whatever lay ahead.

Ana's guilt at being divided between two men lived with her always, but rather than torturing herself over it, as she would've done before, she reminded herself with a keen pragmatism that she'd chosen this path. For her son. She could embrace it, or she could go home, but she couldn't do both. Suffering helped no one.

Through a willpower she didn't possess before her transformation, Ana tucked her love for Finn away in a deep pocket of her heart. If she ever let it take over, all would be lost. Life was no longer about what she wanted. It was about what her son needed.

Everything, all of it, from now on, would be about Aleksandr.

On the night before they left the Highlands, she fell asleep early and was awakened by Aidrik's ardent stirring. He maneuvered her atop him, and the familiar wash of acceptance coursed through her. It was hard to believe, not so long ago, she'd been utterly lost to the world. Broken, with a darkness inside that couldn't help but consume everyone around her. With Aidrik, that darkness was slowly fading to a dull, but hopeful light.

After, he rested a strong, calloused hand on her belly. She smiled, a languid peace stealing over her as she watched the distant flicker of lights in the town below.

"I am content," he said.

Ana nearly laughed. The man was an expert at understatements.

She watched as his beautiful lips widened into a smile, his deep cupid's bow giving off the effect of a bird in flight. "I am guilty of wanting you for myself, *Kjære*," he confessed. Her heart skipped anytime he called her that; *shyaruh*, he pronounced it.

"You don't sound so guilty," she teased, rolling on to her back. The stars were electric, lighting up the entire sky. "Life doesn't always turn out how we expect it, does it?" The question needed no answer.

"We will not be safe here forever," he said, his expression growing dark. His grip on her belly grew worried, possessive.

Yes, it was hard to forget, despite all they had to be thankful for, the threat of the Senetat would always loom over them, casting shadows.

"Will we ever be safe?" she asked, turning to him. She left the other question unasked: *Will I ever be able to return to Finn?*

His angelic, grizzled face was propped up on the hand not caressing her. His eyes cast down on her, and he drew in a breath of the fresh, Scotland air. "You need not ever worry, *Kjære*. Leave that task to me."

"We're partners," Ana reminded him. "I chose to be here. You didn't force me."

His eyes twinkled, and a small, rogue smile played at the corner of his mouth. "Forcing you was not beyond my ability, or desire."

I belong nowhere, she remembered saying to him. It felt an eternity ago.

"You belong with me," Aidrik replied, reading her mind.

Yes, with you.

With Aleksandr.

With Finn.

Ana's decision soon leads her into danger, and it's Finn she needs, not Aidrik. Will Finn find her in time to save her, and their child?

Don't miss a minute. Download *Bound* today.

CAN'T WAIT? READ FURTHER FOR AN EXCERPT.

BOUND EXCERPT

Nicolas Deschanel had never been a fan of these types of meetings. Or meetings at all, for that matter.

Outside the offices of Sullivan & Associates, the sun was setting over New Orleans' Central Business District. Inside, exhaustion had turned to frustration, as the lawyers and Deschanels continued their verbal tug-of-war for nearly six hours.

Nicolas would periodically lose focus, his thoughts wandering to the unimportant artifacts surrounding him. The long, oval mahogany table sparkled with the scent of almond-oil furniture polish. A silver tray in the middle, housing the day's refreshments, testified to the day's mind-numbing nature. The biscotti had grown drier, and the ice in the cut-crystal carafe had long-since melted. Condensation pooled atop the tray.

It had been a tedious afternoon. He'd loosened his ridiculous tie hours ago, ignoring the glares from Aunt Colleen when the buttons on his shirt also eventually came undone. But as primary heir to the Deschanel estate, he had no choice but to continue suffering through the discussions.

On one side of the table, the Sullivan attorneys most familiar with the Deschanel estate: Colin Sullivan and his brother, Rory.

On the other side, the Deschanels who had a vested interest in the matter: Nicolas, his aunts Colleen and Evangeline, and his uncle, Augustus.

Initially, Nicolas had been offended when Aunt Colleen insisted on bringing in the cavalry. Was he not capable of handling this on his own? But after slogging through hours of dry debate, he decided he was grateful for her intervention. They knew far more about the nuances of the estate. If this had been left up to him, he'd have told everyone to go fuck themselves, and named Ana's unborn son as heir, regardless of their objections. Bastard or no.

"The Deschanel will has been inviolate for almost two hundred years," Colin had rebutted at least a dozen times. He kept saying it whenever an objection was made, as if repetition would put a finer point on the mantra.

"I'm the heir, correct?" Nicolas would rhetorically ask. After their nods, "And you're my attorneys?" which earned him additional agreement. "So just change it for me!"

They'd then exchange looks. Nicolas didn't need to employ his newfound telepathy to read their minds. He was, clearly, not getting it.

But Nicolas *did* get it. He was well aware of how his ancestors had set up the Deschanel will, with very specific codicils, and rules, and other outdated legal garbage. The family had always followed those regulations, without quarrel. He understood the estate passed to the eldest son, through each generation. That, in the absence of a son, a daughter could inherit, so long as *her* son bore the name Deschanel.

Nicolas was never going to have children. He had no interest in following his father's piss poor example and, conveniently, his partner, Mercy, was barren. Nicolas' younger sister, Adrienne, wanted nothing to do with the estate. Anne, his other sister, was the product of an undocumented affair and no amount of negotiation would make the legal team comfortable with her descent being considered—and in any case, she didn't want it any more than Adrienne.

So Nicolas had chosen Anasofiya, his first cousin and dearest friend, as his heir. When Ana learned she was having a child, she asked Nicolas to make her son, Aleksandr, the heir immediately, instead of waiting until he reached maturity.

Filing that paperwork had launched the meeting to end all meetings. They'd tediously worked through most of the concerns presented, but the biggest one lingered: Ana wasn't married. Her child, then, would be born illegitimate.

"This is the 21st century! Who the fuck cares?" Nicolas exclaimed, to a crowd of stoic faces. They were acclimated to his unfiltered outbursts now, so it was impossible to draw a reaction from them.

"Nicolas, I realize this seems archaic to you, but abiding by these rules has been the solitary thread holding this family together," Aunt Colleen explained, in soothing tones which he found incredibly condescending despite his affection for the family matriarch. In her tan linen suit, crisp blouse, and manicured nails, she could have sat on either side of the table.

"Yes, because we're all such a happy, tight-knit bunch," Nicolas said, with biting sarcasm. "Thank God for all this ancient paper."

"Family dynamics aside," Colin interjected, "no one has ever contested your right to be the heir. Or your father's. Or his father's."

Nicolas' other aunt, Evangeline, cleared her throat. Evangeline was a stark contrast to her older sister, Colleen: long, loose hair, no makeup. Her eyes, as always, had a wild, exotic look to them. Evangeline, the scientist, looked every bit the eccentric brainiac. "This family has survived for centuries, as strong as it has, because we honor traditions. Without them, we would have no structure, no cohesion. Why, our Broussard cousins have been arguing for *years* the estate should be divided equally, and there should not even be an heir—"

"Fuck the Broussards!"

"Language," Colleen admonished.

"Whose side are you two on, anyway?" Nicolas snapped.

Colleen wrapped her thin fingers around Nicolas' hand. He moved to pull away, but she tightened her grip, and sent him these thoughts: *I'm on your side, nephew. Always. There are some battles you can't win. This is one of them. We will make this work. I promise.*

Nicolas kept his steely glare, but relaxed slightly. "So, what then? I have to choose someone else? Because that's not an option."

"Ana needs to marry the father of her child," Rory Sullivan asserted. He then added, wrinkling his nose, "Or, if she doesn't *know* who the father is—"

"She's not a whore, Rory," Nicolas defended, through gritted teeth. "Finn St. Andrews is the father, and he's ready and eager to play a role in his son's life."

At this, Augustus, Ana's estranged father, raised an eyebrow. He was here on her behalf, as she couldn't be, but the meeting had been full of displeasing revelations for the formidable businessman. A boardroom in a law office was not the best place to learn about things your only daughter had been up to.

"Nicolas, as your lawyers, we're advising you this child-heir needs to be born in wedlock, and there needs to be no dispute over who his parents are. Is there a reason Ana isn't willing to marry Finn?" Colin inquired, with an affected tone of reasonableness.

"Because she shouldn't have to? Because this isn't the fucking Middle Ages?" Nicolas bitterly retorted, followed by one of his favorite obscene hand gestures. The day, though, had worn him down. When even his two aunts—whom he respected a great deal—were defending the attorneys' stance, he knew it was time to stop being difficult, and start preparing.

"I still fail to understand why Ana cannot be here to speak for herself. No one has offered a single adequate explanation on the matter," Augustus complained gruffly. Nicolas almost felt bad for his uncle. The man truly loved his daughter but had never really understood Ana, instead choosing to ignore the unpleasant, or anything which didn't fit his orderly vision of the world.

No one answered his question. The Sullivans didn't know the answer, and Nicolas and his aunts were sworn to secrecy. But there was a very good reason Ana wasn't present to speak for herself. The same reason she was in hiding, and would stay that way, until it was safe to do otherwise.

Anasofiya Deschanel was no longer entirely human. And her unborn son, Aleksandr, would be born full Empyrean. Within weeks of birth, he'd stand as tall as his two fathers.

Despite Ana being in the capable hands of one of the oldest, and most knowledgeable, of all Empyreans, her life, and that of her unborn son, were in grave danger.

Nicolas joined his aunts for a late dinner at Galatoire's, in the Quarter.

"I know today was frustrating for you, Darling," Evangeline empathized, after a long swallow of her sazerac. "I'm sorry if you felt ganged up on."

Nicolas exchanged a glance with Colleen, remembering the calming thought she'd sent him hours ago. "Apology accepted," he said, with unusual restraint.

"You know Colin and Rory are right. Don't you?" Colleen asked.

"No... I mean, yes, I get their point. But it's fucking dumb, and antediluvian. I just need that stated for the record."

"The record hereby denotes your sentiments," Evangeline

acknowledged, raising her glass in the air. "And the record also notes we agree, and find this equally idiotic."

"But necessary," Colleen added firmly. She leaned in and lowered her voice, despite the restaurant being loud with chatter. "It has never been more important to protect the estate. Now that we know... all we know..."

Yes, Nicolas picked up what she was alluding to. The past months had been full of startling revelations about what it really meant to be a Deschanel. While most of the family had special abilities to some degree—telepathy, healing, telekinesis, among other things—no one had ever stopped to ask the ever-important question: *where the hell did it come from?* Last winter, they'd inadvertently come across the answer.

"So what do we do?" Nicolas asked. His rare deference was driven by exhaustion, but also fear. If they didn't solve this to the satisfaction of the family, there could be dire consequences. This wasn't about one of the other cousins getting butt-hurt and trying to steal his inheritance. They were all in very real danger.

"Go home tonight and speak with Finn," Colleen replied. "He may be more amenable to the arrangement than you might think. He is, after all, still very much in love with Ana, despite her leaving without him. And there's always money if sentiment isn't a selling point."

"It isn't Finn we'll need to convince," Nicolas asserted, staring at the glimmering Hennessy behind the bar, calling his name.

It's been a while, Nicolas. Are we gonna dance?

Pick up your copy of *Bound* now, and have it ready to curl up at your next reading session!

1970

1972

1973

1974

1975

1976

1980

∼

Vampires of the Merovingi Series
The Island

∼

Crimson & Clover Lagniappes (Bonus Stories)
Lagniappes are standalone stories that can be read in any order.
St. Charles at Dusk: The Story of Oz and Adrienne
Flourish: The Story of Anne Fontaine
Surrender: The Story of Oz and Ana
Shame: The Story of Jonathan St. Andrews
Fire & Ice: The Story of Remy & Fleur
Dark Blessing: The Landry Triplets
Pandora's Box: The Story of Jasper & Pandora
The Menagerie: Oriana's Den of Iniquities
A Band of Heather: The Story of Colleen and Noah
The Ephemeral: The Story of Autumn & Gabriel
Banshee: The Story of Giselle Deschanel

For more information, and exciting bonus material, visit www.

EMPYREAN ENCYCLOPEDIA

Aidrik (Also: Aidrik the Wise): One of the oldest living Empyreans, at four millennia old. Once a well-respected member of the Eldre Senetat, after Aidrik discovered their true nature, he sliced his Mark of Emyr from his face, freeing him from the Senetat's tethers. He has lived for the past millennia in exile, and if ever discovered, would be executed.

Aleksandr: Empyrean son of Anasofiya, Finn, and Aidrik. Named heir of the Deschanels by Nicolas.

Anders: An Empyrean Mercy co-habitated with for a short period of time. Devout of Emyr, and Ascended fairly young.

Arborkinetic: A form of telekinesis involving flora and fauna. A strong arborkinetic can command plant life to do their bidding, and some can even communicate with plants. Anne Fontaine Deschanel is an arborkinetic.

Blacksmith: Forger of Ulfberht, and creator of Empyrean Steel.

Brother of Emyr (Also: Sister of Emyr): Another way to reference a Halfling (or, someone who has both Human and Empyrean blood).

Brynja: Female Runean warrior claiming to pre-date the

Senetat. Partner of Einar. Part of Runa's rebels who escaped after her execution, they are often called, by Runeans, "Adam and Eve." Aidrik comes across them in his wanderings.

Child of Man/Men: What Empyreans call Humans.

Christiane de Laurent: Aidrik's original evigbond. Human. Lived at the end of the 16th century, as a courtesan of the French court. Wife of Marquise Deschanel, and mother of Claude.

Claude Deschanel (Also: Viscount Deschanel): The first Halfling Deschanel, being both Human and Empyrean. Child of Christiane and Aidrik.

Dagr: 7,000 years old. Born without Senetat knowledge. One of the few Empyreans who has physically seen Brynja and Einar. Aidrik comes across him in his wandering.

Daughter of Emyr (Also: Son of Emyr): Referencing pure-blooded Empyrean men and women.

Deschanel Magi Collective: A secret, ancient society of Deschanels, created with the intention of cataloguing all the Deschanel abilities, as well as protecting and preserving the family. Each generation has a Magistrate, and the current one is Colleen Deschanel.

Duchess Oriana: Beautiful, wayward daughter of Grand Emperor Aeron. Known for having a menagerie of human pets.

Einar: Male Runean warrior claiming to pre-date the Senetat. Partner of Brynja. Part of Runa's rebels who escaped after her execution, they are often called, by Runeans, "Adam and Eve." Aidrik comes across them in his wanderings.

Eldre Senetat, The: The ruling government over the Empyrean race. Established many millennia ago, they claim to be blessed by Emyr, and charged with doing His will through enacting and protecting laws. The Senetat grew corrupt with this power, and unknown to most Empyreans, are controlling the fates of all Empyreans. The creation and installation of Emyr's Mark is the vehicle by which they exact their control.

Empath: The ability to sense feelings, emotions, or sensations in others. There are varying degrees of empaths (i.e. dream empaths). Amelia Deschanel is considered the strongest empath in the family.

Empyrean (Also: Farværdig): Also known as the Farværdig ("Father's Chosen"), Empyreans are as old as Man, and similar genetically, but with several key differences. Where some DNA is dormant in Humans, it is active in Empyreans, giving them special, paranormal abilities, greater strength and speed, and immortality via perfect cell replication. There are only approximately a thousand living Empyreans due to restrictions on breeding placed by the Eldre Senetat. Their home is Farjhem, in the northern expanses of Norway, but most Empyreans live scattered throughout the world, blending in with Men. All Empyreans are born with red hair (which fades to a chromatic silver as they age), and are exceptionally tall. They are also primarily solitary, not subscribing to traditions such as a nuclear family, marriage, or commitment. The exception to this is evigbond.

Empyrean Laws: Mandates set by the Eldre Senetat. Such as regulations around childbirth, mating with humans, and other fundamental rights.

Empyrean Steel (Also: Crucible Steel): A rare steel with high carbon content, smelted in a small furnace, and cooled slowly. In swords, it was both strong, and flexible. The technology was not used anywhere else in the world, and was considered better even than Damascus Steel, which was the closest point of comparison.

Empyrean traits: Born of fire. Elevated body temperature. Red hair (the redder the strands, the more pure the blood) that takes on silver chromatic hues as they age. When emotions are heightened, they are said to emit an orange glow. Most have pale, smooth skin, and are very tall. All have special telepathic/telekinetic abilities, with some stronger than others.

Average lifespan is 2k years, though it is believed without the Mark, an Empyrean could actually live forever. The DNA is similar to Humans, but what is considered "junk DNA" in a Human strand is actually active and powerful in an Empyrean. Their perfect cell replication is what allows for their limited immortality.

Emyr (Also: Our Father): God, to Empyreans. He is represented by a phoenix, rising from the ashes.

Erikr: Runean resistance leader who led one of the only semi-successful rebel revolutions after Runa's. Was executed in a block of ice. Leader of the Second Runean War.

Evigbond: The physical and chemical bonding process that occurs when an Empyrean meets their permanent mate. It is irreversible, and only severed by death. An evigbond between Empyrean and Humans is especially potent. Aidrik's first evigbond was Christiane, and his current is Anasofiya. Mercy experienced evigbond with Nicolas, until her "death." Evigbond can occur in two different ways. The first is an uncontrolled, chemical reaction. The second is through consummation. This second way results in evigbond 100% of the time when one of the partners is human.

Farjhem: The homeland of the Empyreans. Translated to "Father's Home." Located between two glaciers in northern Norway, it is not accessible by anyone except Empyreans, or those with Empyrean blood.

Farskilt: Deep in the bowels of Farjhem, beneath a volcano. "Separated from father." Empyreans are sentenced here for "rehabilitation" when they commit spiritual offenses. Citizens are told that offenders who are sent there are "reunited with Emyr" and the end of their rehabilitation results in guaranteed Ascension. The reality is they are labor mines, and Empyreans work there until their inevitable starvation and death. The Empyrean equivalent of a prison camp.

Farværdig (Also: Empyrean): See "Empyrean."

Feast of Officium Maximus: Once every hundred years, the Scholars graduate their group of Fledgling Empyreans into the world. This ceremony is accompanied by a great celebration, whereby many Empyreans return home to celebrate.

First Father: When an Empyrean child has multiple fathers (via Sveising), the initial father, at conception, is referred to as First Father.

First Runean War: Resistance to the creation of the Eldre Senetat, led by Runa, a warrior who represented the opinions of many Empyreans. Despite her strong supporters, the rebels were destroyed, and Runa executed publicly. Their stunning defeat weakened the resolve of many Empyreans who believed in her cause (henceforth dubbed Runeans), and most went into hiding.

Fledglings: What the Empyrean youth are referred to when they reach the age of spiritual maturity and are released into the wider world.

Galon: A kinsman of Aidrik who was forced into Ascension by the Senetat after he angered them.

Grand Ascension (Also: Ascension): The ultimate death and rebirth all Empyreans are promised. It is tied to Emyr's Mark, which is said to come alive when their time is near. Once active, the Mark is then supposed to usher them through death and rebirth, into the arms of Emyr. The truth is the Mark is simply an infusion of dark magic administered by the Eldre Senetat, by which they control the activation and subsequent death of the Empyreans.

Grand Emperor Aeron: The current ruling Grand Emperor of Farjhem, and the Empyrean race. Has a reputation for being kind, and benign, but shows no interest in meaningful involvement with his people.

Grand Emperor Seti: Ruling emperor of Farjhem at the time the Senetat was created. Supported the Senetat's inception as he was not interested in being the upholder of the laws.

Great Cleansing: Following the creation of the Senetat, Empyreans who refused the Mark were sought out and executed. Those who survived were branded Runeans.

Great Commitment (Also: Officium Maximus): The graduation ceremony, once every hundred years, when Empyreans reach their age of maturity and are released from the Scholars' tutelage, and out into the world. This ceremony includes the installation of Emyr's Mark, a magical brand in the shape of a phoenix that is said to include a part of Emyr Himself. In reality, it is a device of the Eldre Senetat, as a means to control the Empyreans once they leave Farjhem.

Halfling: Humans with some amount of Empyrean blood/ancestry. A human is considered a Halfling even if their Empyrean blood is many generations back.

I am Yours in the Flames: Traditional Empyrean prayer ending.

Inner Voice: Empyreans often believe in the concept of an "Inner Voice" guiding them toward their destiny. For Mercy, the Inner Voice was an illusion crafted by Aidrik, who was guiding her toward safety.

Kjære: Aidrik's term of endearment for Ana. Translates roughly to "my dear" or "my dearest" in Empyrean.

Mark of Emyr (Also: The Mark, Emyr's Mark): A magical infusion, in the shape of a phoenix, given to all Empyreans at their Great Commitment. The Mark is about 2 inches in diameter, and can be placed anywhere on the body, a choice made by the Empyrean receiving the Mark. Empyreans are told the Mark includes a part of Emyr Himself, and that when it is time for their Grand Ascension, the Mark will call them home to Emyr. In reality, the Mark is a sinister plot by the Eldre Senetat, created as a means to control the Empyreans and destroy them.

Marquise Deschanel: Husband of Christiane de Laurent (Aidrik's first human evigbond). He was the First Father of

Claude Deschanel, who was the first Deschanel born with Empyrean blood.

Mercy (Also: Clementyn): A 3,000 year old Empyrean who has believed, her whole life, in the illusion of the Grand Ascension. Piety has driven all of her life decisions, often to the point of folly. In her youth, she spent many years with Aidrik, and they did not part on good terms. Later, she believes him to be dead, when he has in fact been watching over her.

Mystic: Most powerful of all magi, among Empyreans and Halflings. All mystics manifest their abilities in different ways. Some are strong healers, others can engage in nested visions, and dream suggestion. All are strong telepaths.

Nested Vision: A nested vision is an ability only accessible by mystics, wherein the mystic can travel into the mind of another and observe the world through their eyes. The most powerful mystics can not just observe, but also control the host. Nicolas Deschanel has newly discovered he is a mystic who can engage in nested visions.

Old Aita: Believed to be the oldest living Empyrean, she is shamed for not having experienced her Grand Ascension. Scholars use her as an example of how not to end up, and as a means of driving fear amongst the fledglings. She is said to have pure white hair.

Ophélie: A plantation on the west bank of the River Road in Louisiana, about an hour from New Orleans. *Ophélie* has been the family seat of the Deschanels for over 200 years, and is passed down through the oldest male in each generation. Nicolas Deschanel, the current heir, has lived there his whole life.

Our Father (Also: Emyr, Our Father of Light, Our Father of Fire): Additional names for Emyr. Also the way a prayer is most frequently started.

Resurrection Shaman: A healer who is also able to resurrect the recently deceased. Resurrection shamans are incredibly rare, and the ability is often volatile. Rarely do subjects come back exactly as they were before death. Ana Deschanel discovers she is a resurrection shaman after Aidrik infuses her with Sveising.

Runa: Leader of the minority opposition who rose up when the Senetat was created. Her execution is a symbol of strength for her followers, Runeans. She is often deified amongst her most devout followers. Her uprising is known as the First Runean War.

Runeans: Rebels. Those who oppose the Eldre Senetat are generally lumped together as Runeans (followers of Runa). Not all rebels are necessarily Runeans, but the term rebel and Runean are often used interchangeably. Some Runeans are bloodthirsty and feel a call to action. Others are content to live quietly, off the grid of Empyrean society.

Scholar Saxon: The philosophy Scholar who carried out the execution of Mercy's parents after they were accused of heresy.

Scholars: A group of instructors selected by the Eldre Senetat to oversee the education of all Empyrean children. Their teachings often include propaganda-style support of the Senetat, and a fear-based deterrence of breaking rules. The Scholars spend a hundred years with Empyrean children.

Second Runean War: Led by Erikr, the Runeans came together once more, in the spirit of Runa's beliefs, to overthrow the Senetat. As with the first uprising, they were squelched, and Erikr encased in a block of ice. This was the last large uprising of the Runean rebels, who are now scattered and in hiding.

Shaman (Also: Healer): Another word for healer. There are varying degrees of shaman in the Deschanel family. Colleen Deschanel is said to be the strongest shaman.

Sveising: A process of DNA fusion unique to Empyreans. It is the process that allows multiple fathers for offspring, as well as the process by which Aidrik is able to save Anasofiya. Sveising can occur through sexual consummation (in the case of creating multiple fathers), but a mystic can also do it without consummation.

Ulfberht: A Viking sword produced between 800 and 1000 AD, made from Empyrean Steel (known to Man as Crucible Steel), which was known for its unusual combination of strength and flexibility. Though Man believes this sword was crafted for Vikings, it was, in fact, created by Blacksmith, an ancient Empyrean metallurgist. The technology used to make Ulfberht baffles scientists to this day. Aidrik wields one of the last existing originals.

ABOUT THE AUTHOR

~

Sarah is the *USA Today* Bestselling Author of the Paranormal Southern Gothic world, The Saga of Crimson & Clover, born of her combined passion for New Orleans, and the mysterious complexity of human nature. Her work has been described as rich, emotive, and highly dimensional.

An unabashed geek, Sarah enjoys studying obscure subjects like the Plantagenet and Ptolemaic dynasties, and settling debates on provocative Tolkien topics such as why the Great Eagles are not Gandalf's personal taxi service. Passionate about travel, Sarah has visited over twenty countries collecting sparks of inspiration (though New Orleans is where her heart rests). She's a self-professed expert at crafting original songs to sing to her very patient pets, and a seasoned professional at finding ways to humiliate herself (bonus points if it happens in public). When at home in Oregon, her husband and best friend, James, is very kind about indulging her love of fast German cars and expensive lattes.

www.sarahmcradit.com

Made in the USA
Columbia, SC
09 December 2020